THE PET DOCTOR

EMERSON PASS CONTEMPORARIES, BOOK THREE

TESS THOMPSON

"This is one of those books that make you love to be a reader and fan of the author." -*Pamela Lunder, Vine Voice*

Blue Midnight:
"This is a beautiful book with an unexpected twist that takes the story from romance to mystery and back again. I've already started the 2nd book in the series!" - *Mama O*

"This beautiful book captured my attention and never let it go. I did not want it to end and so very much look forward to reading the next book." - *Pris Shartle*

"I enjoyed this new book cover to cover. I read it on my long flight home from Ireland and it helped the time fly by, I wish it had been longer so my whole flight could have been lost to this lovely novel about second chances and finding the truth. Written with wisdom and humor this novel shares the raw emotions a new divorce can leave behind." - *J. Sorenson*

"Tess Thompson is definitely one of my auto-buy authors! I love her writing style. Her characters are so real to life that you just can't put the book down once you start! Blue Midnight makes you believe in second chances. It makes you believe that everyone deserves an HEA. I loved the twists and turns in this book, the mystery and suspense, the family dynamics and the restoration of trust and security." - *Angela MacIntyre*

"Tess writes books with real characters in them, characters with flaws and baggage and gives them a second chance. (Real people, some remind me of myself and my girlfriends.) Then she cleverly and thoroughly develops those characters and makes you feel deeply for them. Characters are complex and multifaceted, and the plot seems to unfold naturally, and never feels contrived." - *K. Lescinsky*

Caramel and Magnolias:
"Nobody writes characters like Tess Thompson. It's like she looks into our lives and creates her characters based on our best friends, our lovers, and our neighbors. Caramel and Magnolias, and the authors debut novel Riversong, have some of the best characters I've ever had a chance to fall in love with. I don't like leaving spoilers in reviews so just trust me, Nicholas Sparks has nothing on Tess Thompson, her writing flows so smoothly you can't help but to want to read on!" - *T. M. Frazier*

"I love Tess Thompson's books because I love good writing. Her prose is clean and tight, which are increasingly rare qualities, and manages to evoke a full range of emotions with both subtlety and power. Her fiction goes well beyond art imitating life. Thompson's characters are alive and fully-realized, the action is believable, and the story unfolds with the right balance of tension and exuberance. CARAMEL AND MAGNOLIAS is a pleasure to read." - *Tsuruoka*

"The author has an incredible way of painting an image with her words. Her storytelling is beautiful, and leaves you wanting more! I love that the story is about friendship (2 best friends) and love. The characters are richly drawn and I found myself rooting for them from the very beginning. I think you will, too!"
- *Fogvision*

"I got swept off my feet, my heartstrings were pulled, I held my breath, and tightened my muscles in suspense. Tess paints stunning scenery with her words and draws you in to the lives of her characters."- *T. Bean*

Duet For Three Hands:

"Tears trickled down the side of my face when I reached the end of this road. Not because the story left me feeling sad or disappointed, no. Rather, because I already missed them. My friends. Though it isn't goodbye, but see you later. And so I will sit impatiently waiting, with desperate eagerness to hear where life has taken you, what burdens have you downtrodden, and what triumphs warm your heart. And in the meantime, I will go out and live, keeping your lessons and friendship and love close, the light to guide me through any darkness. And to the author I say thank you. My heart, my soul -all of me - needed these words, these friends, this love. I am forever changed by the beauty of your talent." - *Lisa M.Gott*

"I am a great fan of Tess Thompson's books and this new one definitely shows her branching out with an engaging enjoyable historical drama/love story. She is a true pro in the way she weaves her storyline, develops true to life characters that you love! The background and setting is so picturesque and visible just from her words. Each book shows her expanding, growing and excelling in her art. Yet another one not to miss. Buy it you won't be disappointed. The ONLY disappointment is when it ends!!!" - *Sparky's Last*

"There are some definite villains in this book. Ohhhh, how I loved to hate them. But I have to give Thompson credit because they never came off as caricatures or one dimensional. They all felt authentic to me and (sadly) I could easily picture them. I loved to love some and loved to hate others." - *The Baking Bookworm*

"I stayed up the entire night reading Duet For Three Hands and unbeknownst to myself, I fell asleep in the middle of reading the book. I literally woke up the next morning with Tyler the Kindle beside me (thankfully, still safe and intact) with no ounce of battery left. I shouldn't have worried about deadlines because, guess what? Duet For Three Hands was the epitome of unputdownable." - *The Bookish Owl*

Miller's Secret

"From the very first page, I was captivated by this wonderful tale. The cast of characters amazing - very fleshed out and multi-dimensional. The descriptions were perfect - just enough to make you feel like you were transported back to the 20's and 40's.... This book was the perfect escape, filled with so many twists and turns I was on the edge of my seat for the entire read." - *Hilary Grossman*

"The sad story of a freezing-cold orphan looking out the window at his rich benefactors on Christmas Eve started me off with Horatio-Alger expectations for this book. But I quickly got pulled into a completely different world--the complex five-character braid that the plot weaves. The three men and two women characters are so alive I felt I could walk up and start talking to any one of them, and I'd love to have lunch with Henry. Then the plot quickly turned sinister enough to keep me turning the pages.
Class is set against class, poor and rich struggle for happiness and security, yet it is love all but one of them are hungry for. ......Where does love come from? What do you do about it? The story kept me going, and gave me hope. For a little bonus, there are Thompson's delightful observations, like: "You'd never know we could make something this good out of the milk from an animal who eats hats." A really good read!" - *Kay in Seattle*

"She paints vivid word pictures such that I could smell the

ocean and hear the doves. Then there are the stories within a story that twist and turn until they all come together in the end. I really had a hard time putting it down. Five stars aren't enough!" - **M.R. Williams**

ALSO BY TESS THOMPSON

CLIFFSIDE BAY

Traded: Brody and Kara

Deleted: Jackson and Maggie

Jaded: Zane and Honor

Marred: Kyle and Violet

Tainted: Lance and Mary

Cliffside Bay Christmas, The Season of Cats and Babies (Cliffside Bay Novella to be read after Tainted)

Missed: Rafael and Lisa

Cliffside Bay Christmas Wedding (Cliffside Bay Novella to be read after Missed)

Healed: Stone and Pepper

Chateau Wedding (Cliffside Bay Novella to be read after Healed)

Scarred: Trey and Autumn

Jilted: Nico and Sophie

Kissed (Cliffside Bay Novella to be read after Jilted)

Departed: David and Sara

Cliffside Bay Bundle , Books 1,2,3

BLUE MOUNTAIN SERIES

Blue Mountain Bundle, Books 1,2,3

Blue Midnight

Blue Moon

Blue Ink

This is for all the pet lovers. Wherever life takes you, I wish for you two things: a good book and a furry friend. Preferably one who enjoys sitting on your lap while you read!

THE PET DOCTOR

1

TIFFANY

2 ⁰¹¹

UNDER THE SHADE OF AN ASPEN, I waited to be summoned. Bees
buzzed from flower to flower feeding on sweet pollen. Free to
fly, those bees. In the quiet of the warm afternoon, I imagined
the sound of their tiny wings. But no, it was more likely the
buzz from the electric fence that surrounded the compound.

I drew my knees to my chest and wrapped my arms around
them. Sweat dribbled down the back of my spine and dampened
the rough material of my skirt. Sweat trailed down the small of
my back, dampening the rough material of my gray dress. I
glanced behind me at the double doors of the elders' building.
When would they come to fetch me? What did the elders do
before the girls were presented on Promise Day? Shine the
floors? Feast on a meal of roast beef and potatoes?

The elders' building was our finest. White paint and pillars,
perched atop the only elevation on the entire compound.

1

Aspens in a line like soldiers protected it from wind, and hedges were perfectly trimmed by the groundskeepers. Small windows like narrowed eyes, seeing everything. It had been built in the Georgian tradition, Martha, my dad's first wife, had mentioned to me once, pride in her voice. She hadn't been born here. She knew of the outside world.

Inside the white building, the elders had their private quarters. I'd never seen one of these residences. I would soon, though. On my wedding night, I would have the privilege of spending my first night with Elder Ryan. I'd only been in the hall where they gathered as a council to make big decisions. And the location of Promise Day.

The crude buildings where the women and children spent most of our time matched the color of the dirt paths that ran between the cafeteria and schoolhouse. Each set of wives had a house. The order of which was kept sacred by the first wife. The lucky one.

I would be the sixth wife to Elder Ryan. If he found nothing wrong with me today, that is. What if he did? What would happen to me then? There had been a few girls in the past few years who had been rejected. They'd been given menial jobs and sent to live in the house at the farthest end of the property. Shamed outcasts instead of beloved wives.

Matthew. The boy I loved but could not have. He was an underling, a stray they'd found on the streets. A runaway, he'd told me, from a bad situation. Here he was fed and clothed and had a bed to sleep in. No one touched him here. He'd accepted the society as it was. Perhaps had even been grateful. Until he fell in love with me. Now we knew what was missing. What we would miss once I married Elder Ryan.

I tightened my arms around my knees, holding myself, trying not to weep from fright. Waiting and waiting. The last month had raced by, days of my innocence waning away one by one until it was today. I could no longer hide. Everything would be bared before them.

I tilted my head back until I could feel the bark on my scalp. Light filtered through the leaves. Such a blue. One I didn't have a name for, because it was the only sky I'd ever seen. My father said it was the kind of sky that only existed in Colorado. I had to take him at his word, on that and everything else. If there were other shades of blue I wouldn't know.

Who knew what horror awaited me? I'd learned in the sixteen years of my life to take in the beauty of my surroundings whenever they presented. Soon enough, invariably, I would witness the opposite of beauty. That was life within the electric fence of the compound.

Out of curiosity, I'd recently looked up the word *beauty* in the thesaurus to find the antonym. It was nothing but the word *ugliness*. Which I found limiting. There were many ways in which the opposite of beauty manifested and thus as many words. All was equal in that way, this balance of beauty and ugly. As far as I knew, anyway. Was it different out there? I'd probably never know.

Still, this was all mine to contemplate. They couldn't take my thoughts from me. My thoughts were as free and vast as the sky itself. Someday, my soul would be free. For now, I must accept my fate, as all the girls here did. As long as they remained inside my mind and not uttered from my mouth, I could think and think and think. My mother had not been as discreet. She'd died rebelling. What good had come of that? A motherless girl? Surely not.

A sheet on the line swayed gently in the breeze. An ant wandered lazily onto my big toe. On a branch, somewhere unseen, a bird sang. These juxtapositions might have fascinated me if I hadn't been terrified. Today marked one month until it was my turn to be married. As much as I wished they wouldn't, these days raced by, folding one after the other, bringing me closer to the time when he would call me to his bed. In a month's time, I would be Elder Ryan's sixth wife.

We all wore the same long skirt and long-sleeved dress. I had been trained specifically to be one of the dressmakers. My fingers were nimble and careful, the perfect combination. I could whip up a dress faster than the other two seamstresses. This should have been a source of pride but made me ashamed instead. If I were brave like my mother, I would throw the material at their faces and let them shoot me trying to climb over the electric fence.

Today, exactly a month before our marriage, I would be presented to Elder Ryan one last time. During this inspection, I would be stripped completely of clothes so that he could inspect me carefully. The elders said it was only fair. They should be able to see if anything amiss had happened in the two years since the first inspection. We couldn't expect them to marry a girl with flaws.

The first presentation to the elders came when we turned fourteen. On that day, we were paraded in front of all the elders in their private room. Women were allowed into this room only twice in our lifetimes. Once at fourteen and the other thirty days before our weddings.

I'd trembled violently as I walked before them. They'd sat at a long table, elevated onto a platform, to judge all of the girls in my age group. There were only three of us, as we were the first of the batch of girls actually born within the compound. They'd had to recruit the early wives from the outside world.

Usually we dressed modestly in our long skirts and sleeves but for judgment day, we were stripped to our underclothes, nothing more than panties and a see-through blouse. It was this way they were able to see if the womanly curves of my body were adequate. Otherwise, we understood from an early age, a woman must never show herself to anyone but her husband. They could see without the production our faces, obviously.

Pretty children didn't always grow up to be lovely women, after all. Could we expect them to make a decision before the age of fourteen? Certainly not. The older women had told us the realities of our situation. The pretty ones were the fortunate. If we had small noses, large eyes, and cheekbones suitably noticeable, we were considered one of the chosen few. Chosen by God to be the bearers of offspring, helping to populate our utopia.

I knew because I'd heard the women whispering that I was considered unusual-looking because of my fair skin paired with dark brown hair and light blue eyes. My figure was not remarkable either way, neither curvy nor straight but nice enough as far as I could discern. At least it had seemed that way, because Elder Ryan had chosen me. As second-in-command, he was allowed first choice after our leader, Elder William. After the announcement, many of the women and girls had all gushed with congratulations and perhaps a little envy. They'd said how lucky I was to be considered a prize. Elder Ryan had only beautiful wives. I should be honored. The only honor greater? To be given to Elder William. But he had not even looked at me during the showing. He'd looked carefully at the other two, I'd noticed. Not that it mattered to me. They were all old men. Disgusting to me with their wrinkles, stained teeth, and nasty beards. Who knew what was under their dark suits?

Around age twelve, I'd been given a book to learn about the male anatomy. Written by Elder Thomas, it included guidance about what would happen on our wedding night. Specific instructions that laid out exactly what we were supposed to do that night and any of the other times we were asked to their bedchambers.

We'd all read it together, having been excused from our usual lessons. Two of the three of us vomited afterward. How could it be as described? Was this really how babies came to be? We'd been sheltered from the boys and divided into separate classrooms. Until that day, I'd had no idea their private parts were different from ours. Or what they did with that body part. The idea sickened me and made me tremble with fear.

One of the wives had taken pity on the three of us and had covertly taken us aside. "It's not as bad as it sounds. You'll close your eyes and think of something else and in no time it will be over. Then, God will award you with a child. If you're particularly blessed, all your children will be boys." She'd added that the rotation of nights made it easier to bear. "The more wives, the less you have to be with him."

We'd clung to her words. I'd wanted to ask more questions, but that was all the counsel she could provide. Wives were notorious for tattling on one another to gain favor. It was too risky to say more.

I hadn't paid much attention to Elder Ryan until he'd picked me. From then on, I watched him eat meals at the big table with the other elders and tried to imagine how it was possible that I'd soon be forced to give him my body and my soul. We would be united by God. Our marriage was forever. Even in heaven, I would be with him.

The idea repulsed me. Elder Ryan had a long beard, as did all the elders. But instead of being meticulous about his appearance as my own father was, he often had food stuck to the coarse hair of his chin. His eyes were beady yet bright, reminding me of the coyotes that waited for an entrance into the compound from behind the electric fences. They were not afraid of the guards at the gates with their long guns that looked like alligators. I couldn't understand those coyotes. Didn't they know what could happen? Shouldn't their instincts take them far away from here?

Trust in your elders. That was taught to us from the time we could understand such things. Elders were close to God, my father often said. *Elders know more than the rest of you. We know,* he was quick to add. He was one of them. Unlike Elder William and Elder Ryan, and although he was third-in-command, there was an uneasiness about my father. He held his shoulders too high, as if he were worried about an attack, and his eyes shifted in their sockets, back and forth like a pendulum, never seeming to focus on one thing.

Perhaps he understood that he could not protect me and was thus ashamed. *No,* I thought, just as quickly as the idea came to me. *He's an elder, not a father.*

Now a shadow came over me, shielding me from the soft glow of sunshine filtering through the blank spaces between the leaves. I looked up into the green eyes of Matthew. Tears pricked my own eyes at the sight of him. His face was made of shapes without sharp corners or edges. No matter the time of year, his cheeks were the color of cherry blossoms. All that magnificence in one face never ceased to astound me. It befuddled me too. How could a man so pure of heart grow from a place such as this?

"Michelle." His long legs bent so that he was crouched beside me, no small feat to fold into a petite package when you were the size of Matthew. The dewy grass played dead under the soles of his feet.

"Hey," I whispered before biting the inside of my lip to keep from crying. I'd come to know him better since my betrothal to Elder Ryan because Matthew was the head secretary to the elders. Keeper of schedules and secrets, he'd told me once.

"They've sent for both of us." He glanced toward the elders' building. "They know."

My heart stopped beating for a split second. I went hot, then cold. "How?"

"Someone must have seen us." Matthew should have been afraid, but he wasn't. His eyes glittered with courage and anger. A dangerous combination. Especially for the girl who loved him. "I have a plan. We'll confess and beg their forgiveness and ask for permission to leave."

"But how will we live?" Banishment from the community

was a popular topic among the youth. We'd had more conversations than I could possibly count about the possibility of excommunication. A fate worse than death, we were told. The ultimate punishment for sinning. God would hate you. Everyone you loved and who had loved you would be ripped from your life.

"They won't let us go," I said. As much as I wanted to believe there was a chance for us, I knew it wasn't to be. I wanted Matthew and to be free. I wanted to run. At the same time, the idea made my limbs heavy and useless.

"We have to try. Otherwise, I'd rather be dead. I can't live this way any longer." He looked around before squeezing my hand.

My mother had tried to escape. Once upon a time. Long ago. Tales of her demise were almost folklore around here. I'd been too young to remember, but she'd taken me from my crib and tried to sneak away in the middle of the darkest night of the year. She'd been electrocuted by the fence. That was the first time, according to legend, that anyone had ever tempted fate. The fence was deadly. That hadn't been a lie. My mother's death was proof. How had she not known it would kill her? Or had she? If so, had she expected that I would die too? Why else would she have taken that kind of risk?

"What if they say no? They *will* say no. Elder Ryan wants me for himself."

"I'll figure out a way." Matthew looked up between the fluttering leaves. "Don't forget, I've been out there. I know what it's like. It's nothing but choices. Opportunities. If we can just get out, I can keep us alive until we find our way."

I searched his face, hoping for something to cling to. Anything that would reassure me.

He looked right back at me, unflinching. "We can't stay here, not like this. If they say no, then we have to escape."

"But how? The fence. The guards."

"I've been digging a hole."

I stared at him. "What?"

"Behind the horse stalls. It's the most sheltered spot on the whole compound. I wanted a few more nights to dig deeper, but we'll have to pass through as best as we can."

What would we do? Would our skills be useful in the real world? Would we be able to find work? In here, we had jobs. I was a seamstress, making most of the dresses for the girls and women in our community. Matthew had one of the best jobs of all. Working for the elders was so much better than manual labor as some of the others had to do.

"Do you really think we can make it through the hole?" I asked. A light of hope expanded my chest. "We could make it. Together, we could." I said it with more assurance than I felt.

"We've talked about it before," Matthew said. "If it came to this, we said we would."

But that had been only talk. Wishes and dreams. Now we had to take action. They'd called for us. One way or the other, we would leave tonight.

Matthew helped me to my feet. Together, we walked toward the elders' offices. My father would be there. Would he help us?

I wanted to slip my hand in Matthew's, but I knew better. Even if our relationship had been outed, it was much too dangerous to seem as if we were flaunting our disobedience. As was always the case here, basic instincts had to be extinguished immediately. Loving a man one's own age, expecting to be able to pick a spouse out of love, these were only romantic notions. This was not the way it was done here.

My feet were made of lead as we climbed the steps of the elders' building. Out of the corner of my eye, I saw a cluster of girls stealing glances our way. One of them had betrayed me. For what favor had my secret been traded? Tattling on a peer was encouraged, especially if it was something as heinous as two young people falling in love. Someone had seen us kissing, I suspected. Perhaps last night when we'd sneaked out of our sleeping cabins.

"Are you sure?" Matthew asked as we walked up the steps.

"I'm sure, but I'm afraid," I whispered. My legs shook so hard now I could barely walk. Still, we continued on, down the long hallway toward Elder William's office. His steps faltered. He looked down at me. "I'm afraid too, but we have to be brave."

"Yes." What neither of us said was that we no longer had a choice.

The first thing I saw when I entered the room was my father.

He was sitting next to Elder William. To my surprise, his face didn't express displeasure with me as I'd thought it would. The stare was more ambivalent, as if here weren't sure what he wanted for lunch. Was it possible we would go unpunished? Could we stay and marry?

I glanced nervously over at Elder Ryan. He wore a black suit and thin yellow tie. His wives and children wore yellow.

Elder William had the typical long beard of all the upper echelon. The longer the beard, the better; I'd heard rumors that he made the other elders trim theirs if they grew longer than his. I didn't know if that was true or if God was actually on his side. Elder William must have the best; this was his right as the founding father of our community.

I stole a glance at Elder Ryan, who sat on the other side of William. His entire face was red. With rage? Of course. What else would it be? I'd dared to shame him just days before our wedding. I trembled under my long skirt. He was such an ugly man. The shape and size of his face made him appear like either a turnip or a beet, depending on his mood. A root vegetable with a beard. At the moment, his uneven patches looked like a scrubbed beet before it was peeled and tossed into a pot of boiling water.

"It's been brought to our attention," Elder William said, "that the two of you have been acting out of accordance with our laws."

"Yes, sir," Matthew said. "We're in love."

I sucked in a breath and waited for the blows that were sure to come.

My father's gaze remained on the papers in front of him. Not on me. Never on me. As his firstborn, I'd have thought I'd be special to him, but I wasn't. Just once, when he told me I was promised to Elder Ryan, had a flicker of pride come to his eyes. Now I'd shamed him. He had every reason to shun me. Still, I ached for his love and attention.

"Michelle has been promised to Elder Ryan," Elder William said. "You both knew that."

"Yes, sir, but that's not what she wants," Matthew said.

"It's not for you to decide. This is God's work, the matching of women to elders." William's voice rose slightly. "Michelle, what do you have to say for yourself?"

"I'm sorry, but I don't want to marry Elder Ryan. I love Matthew. It's not wrong. God wouldn't give me all these feelings if that were true."

"Nonsense." Elder Ryan slammed his gavel on the table. They all had gavels, like judges. Only these men were not qualified in any laws other than the ones of their own making. "We decide."

"Please, sirs, let us leave," Matthew said. "With nothing but the clothes on our backs. Just let us go, and we'll never say a word about this life or any of you."

Silence stretched for a lifetime until finally Elder William spoke.

"If we let you go, it will be without anything. No money, possessions. Two young people with no skills whatsoever out in the world. Is that really what you want, Michelle? To starve in the streets?" Elder William fixed his small dark eyes on me. They were so far back in his head, it was like peering into a tunnel. A dark tunnel.

"We can make our own way." My voice cracked. *Steady*, I told myself. *Don't let them see how terrified you are.*

Elder William bowed his head for a moment. Perhaps praying for guidance. When he looked up, he peered straight at Matthew. "You've broken the covenant you've had with us. We took you in, a bastard child, and this is how you repay us?"

"I'm sorry, sir," Matthew said. The flint in his voice told me otherwise. He wasn't sorry.

The three men looked at one another and then leaned close to confer in whispers. Finally, Elder William looked directly at us. "We've never made anyone stay here that didn't want to. If you feel this is your calling, then go. Go. Pack your things," Elder William said. "We'll see you off with a toast of dandelion wine."

Dandelion wine? That was reserved for wedding toasts only. Was this his way of giving us his blessing? Did he see the love between us? Had God?

"Thank you, sir," I said before looking over at my father. His gaze had not lifted. Regardless of what Elder William thought, Father would not forgive me. Nor would my sisters and brothers or the wives. Like my mother, they would say. Never satisfied with what was.

They dismissed us and told us to be back in thirty minutes at the wedding square.

We ran all the way to the path that led back to the cabins and houses, then stopped and looked at each other. "Do you think they'll really let us go?" I asked. "With their blessing?"

He shook his head. "I don't know about the blessing part and I don't care, as long as we get to go."

No one was in the room I shared with two of my sisters when I went inside to gather my belongings. In fact, the entire residential area to the property seemed deserted. Where was everyone? My father's wives had never had any affection for me. In fact, they resented me. I was never sure why, but one of my half-sisters had said to me once that it was because of my mother. Her betrayal but also her beauty. Beauty that she'd passed on to me. I'd never seen a photograph of her. They were forbidden within the confines of our society. The elders told us that photos took part of our goodness and that we must always shun the idea of vanity. But those who remembered my mother said I looked just like her.

I didn't care, I told myself. Matthew and I would start over somewhere else. Try to blend into a world we knew nothing about. Or, at least, I knew nothing about. He still remembered the life he'd had before coming to the compound. Like my mother, his was dead. She'd died in an accident when he was eight years old. His aunt had already lived here, having come several years earlier as a convert. But she'd died mysteriously in her sleep one night shortly after Matthew joined us. No one ever told him what the cause of death was.

With hands that shook, I packed my three other dresses and underclothes. We wore long cotton skirts and blouses with the same sailor collars. All were in muted shades of gray and brown. Nothing that would bring attention to ourselves or make us different from one another. The only way to tell the difference between us was the family color sewn into the wristbands of our blouses. My father's was a blue satin. If I married Elder Ryan, it would become yellow.

It was as silent as I'd ever heard our grounds when I walked back down the dirt path toward our central meeting place.

During church days, it was quiet like this. I'd have expected it if it hadn't been for the wedding that would no longer take place. They were letting us go. I thought I'd be more scared, but

I was jubilant. Why had I thought we were stuck here? That was only in our minds, I realized. We'd all bought into the elders' ultimate power. We were able to leave whenever we wanted. *Why the electric fence then, dummy?* I asked myself. *Why did they kill your mother?*

It was a long time ago. Things had changed since then. Hadn't they? I couldn't remember anyone ever leaving. People died, but they never left.

People died.

A shiver went through me. Would we get out of here alive?

As I rounded the corner of the path that led to the center of the community, I drew in a short puff of air. Everyone was there. Just as they would have been if I'd married Elder Ryan. Were they all here to say goodbye?

I caught Matthew's eye. He motioned me over. When I was by his side, he whispered in my ear. "It's not a blessing they're giving us. They're cursing us and casting us out. It's a lesson for the others."

The reality of what we were doing hit me then. We were being tossed out to the street with no money. Inside here, we used a different currency. A barter system. For my seamstress skills, I was able to trade for food and shelter. We all did our part to make up a successful community. How would we survive on the outside?

I looked over to where my father stood with Elder Ryan. They both wore a strange expression. One I'd not seen on either of them before. Uncertainty? Or disapproval?

Elder William handed a glass of clear wine to Matthew. One of his wives handed me one as well, served in a glass I'd never seen before. Small, with a slender flute that felt as if it would burst with the slightest pressure in my fingers. This was not the thick glass we had in the cafeteria. Was this what the elders used at night in their private room? I sniffed. A wave of nausea churned my stomach; I swallowed against the gag reflex in my throat. The wine smelled off; my senses were jumbled from nerves. I'd only had it once before, at my fourteenth birthday ritual. The first sip had made my eyes water, and I'd discreetly poured it onto the grass. Now I lifted the glass to my mouth and pretended to take a drink, never actually bringing any into my mouth. I'd had years of practice with milk. "Drink up, boy," Elder William said to Matthew. "It's a big day for you."

Matthew drank from his glass and then screwed up his face as if he'd had something sour. "Thank you, sir."

Everyone gathered closer, forming a semicircle around us. I couldn't look up, afraid of the angry eyes of my father. The matching gray skirts of the women were a blanket before me. I lifted just my eyes to scan the mob for my siblings. What were they holding in front of their chests? My vision widened and sharpened. The women and girls were holding long, skinny candles that we used during religious holidays and baptisms. The wicks were lit, almost imperceptible under the bright sun. How had I not noticed before? Some of the flames shuddered from their holder's breath. Why were they breathing hard? They weren't on display as Matthew and I was. Suddenly, I hated them all. They were like a many-headed monster, all staring at us with malice in their eyes. Why had it been necessary to gather everyone? Wouldn't it have been better to let us slip away unnoticed? They could simply pretend we'd never existed. That would be enough of a warning to the others. The elders did not see it that way, obviously.

"Today, Matthew and Michelle have decided to leave us—to forge out on their own without any support from those who have loved them and cared for them." Elder William looked out to his flock. His words were as calm and soothing as the creek from which we gathered water. Yet the flat nature of his eyes was more like the rocks banished to the creek bed, gray and hard. What was happening? My bones and muscles seemed to have shriveled and left me standing on hollow legs.

"With this betrayal," Elder William said, "a curse will follow them the rest of their days here on earth and follow them into hell. As you know, once this choice is made, there is no returning."

Dead silence met us. I imagined I could hear the wicks burning into ash.

Elder William raised his glass, then paused dramatically, something he did often in his sermons. "This little piece of trash, who we realize is just like her mother, has made the choice to betray the only home and family she's ever known." He changed his voice to more conversational, as if we were all sitting around a table for a meal. "Should we drink to her and Matthew? I suppose we should. We do not need to pass judgment, for the Lord will do that for us."

I'd started shaking even harder than before. The world tipped slightly. Trash. I was trash. Next to me, Matthew took my hand. "Let's get out of here."

I gave my glass to my father's most senior wife, Martha. "Do I say goodbye to Father?" I whispered in her ear.

Martha's mouth thinned out as she shook her head. "Just go while you have the chance," she whispered.

I looked at her in surprise. She'd never given any indication that she'd contemplated leaving? Did she?

"I'm sorry," I said. "I know you've spent a lot of time grooming me for my marriage to Elder Ryan."

"It's all right. There are enough of us." Father had five wives. "We'll be fine."

The crowd parted as Matthew and I, hand in hand, made our way to the front gates. Gravel shifted under our feet. Behind us came the sounds of people following. The entrance comprised two heavy sheets of metal that operated on a track. One of the guards pushed them open. We stepped closer, hesitating at the precipice between the community and the other side. I looked back. Everyone was still there, staring at us with moon faces.

Some wore scornful expressions. Others simply looked confused. A few watched us with open mouths, as if they weren't sure what kind of creatures we were. I made one last search for Father but he must have left, unable to watch his daughter's betrayal.

My eyes were blurred from unshed tears. I could no longer see individual faces. This was my home. These were the only people I'd ever know. But out there? Freedom. A life with Matthew. Escape from the servitude and depravity of an old man.

Matthew and I stepped outside the gates. In my short life, this was the first time I'd been outside the compound. Before us, a long driveway lined with aspens on either side curved and then disappeared behind a cluster of trees. What was beyond that curve? Would it be as Matthew remembered? Or were we headed to a pack of coyotes waiting to be torn apart?

"The highway's at the end of the driveway. If I remember correctly, it's about a mile." Matthew pointed. "We'll walk to the highway and hope we see cars. Perhaps we can get a ride?"

We locked eyes. For the first time, it occurred to me how little we'd planned for this. Neither of us knew what we were doing or how to do it even if we did. I'd relied on Matthew, but now I could see he had no more idea than I of what came next.

The metal gates closed behind us with a bang that made me jump. I drew in a deep breath and turned back to Matthew to give him my support and encouragement. The words *we can do this* fell away at the sight of him. His features were pale and twisted as if he were in pain. "Matthew?" His eyes widened for a split second before he crumpled to the ground. I cried out and fell to my knees beside him. My bag around my shoulders hit me in the face. The gravel of the driveway cut into my bare knees under the thin fabric of my skirt. His complexion, always so rosy, had gone a chalky white. Spittle formed at the corners of his mouth. And he was still. So very still. Only his eyes seemed capable of still moving. His eyelashes fluttered. He gasped for breath.

"Matthew?"

He uttered the words with only a trace of sound, as if his vocal cords no longer worked. "They've poisoned me. It was too good to be true."

"No, no. That can't be it. Just get up. We'll take you to a real doctor. Like you said were out there. We can find help." Like the morning after a snowfall, a hush befell the world around me. No breeze to ruffle leaves. Not a bug or bee buzzing. Even the birds had quieted. They knew death was near, creeping closer and closer.

I was losing him. "Matthew, fight. Please. I'll get help."

With what appeared to be his last bit of energy, he whispered to me, "Run, please. Run as fast as you can away from here. Make a life. Don't go back. For me, promise? Just keep running until you find people. I love you. Don't ever forget how much. It was all worth it for you to have freedom. Please, promise me you'll make a life for yourself. One that will make me proud." A smile played around his mouth. His eyes were no longer blazing with anger or fight. They were placid now, accepting of his fate.

"I'll make a life. I promise."

The life drained from his eyes until I was left with only the husk of him. I curled over him and cradled his head against my chest. Why hadn't I done that when he was leaving me? If not for my denial, I could have comforted him. "Oh, Matthew, I'm sorry." Grief came, consuming me with its darkness, its utter unforgiving permanence. I sobbed, chest shaking. And then I began to howl like an animal caught between the blades of a trap.

Run, he'd said. Run and run and run. I kissed him one last time, his lips already cold, and then I did as he asked. I ran.

2

BRECK

My morning flew by as they usually did while I was at work. A dog with a thorn in his paw, a pregnant cat the owners had thought was a boy gaining weight, Luci Wentworth's lethargic bunny. Stomach growling, I went out to the lobby to see if there were any stragglers. To my relief, the waiting area was empty. My nurse, Scooter, was at the front desk, looking grumpier than usual. Last week, our middle-aged receptionist, Lori, had given her notice, saying she was leaving town with a man she'd met on the ski slopes. Without her, we were running on fumes, as my mother sometimes said. Scooter was doing both jobs and not happily. Not that it mattered. She was one of those people who was never happy, always finding something negative to which to cling as if it were life-giving instead of the opposite.

When I took over the veterinary practice—a veritable institution here in Emerson Pass run by my family since the 1920s—my mother had made sure I understood Scooter came with the building, clients, and even the tools we used on people's beloved pets. I was now the fifth generation Stokes to head up Emerson

Pass's veterinarian clinic. Scooter, however, hadn't seemed to get the memo that told her I was now the boss. She muttered under her breath at least once a day that Dr. Stokes wouldn't have done it that way. Meaning my mother, not yours truly, even though we were both Dr. Stokes.

"Go to lunch," I said to Scooter. "It's half-price pizza slices over at the grill today." I said this in an attempt at humor and camaraderie.

"Pizza is the food of college boys who live in disgusting dorm rooms, not a woman in her fifties." Scooter pulled at the hem of her pink scrubs, loose over her scrawny, angular frame. Her silver hair was cut in the style of a Dutch pageboy, including the straight-across-her-forehead two-inch bangs. She walked five miles every morning to stay in shape, rain, snow, or shine. I, too, was careful about how I fueled my body. In fact, it was the only commonality between us. One I'd often tried to exploit as a way to bond. No such luck. Unlike me, her discipline seemed to be carried out as a way to prove her superiority over her fellow humans, rather than a desire to live a robust existence.

"I brought my lunch. Lentil soup I made myself," Scooter said. "It's a nice day, so I think I'll wander over to the square to see what's going on in town." The words might have seemed innocuous except for her tone, which implied she was a spy about to head out to observe the enemy.

"That sounds like a great idea," I said, trying to be agreeable instead of apologetic for my presence here in the world Scooter seemed to think belonged to her.

"Did you meet any good candidates for the receptionist position?" I asked as I moved out of her way so she could get her purse from under the counter.

"No. They were all idiots. Honestly, I don't know what's wrong with these young people. No one wants to put in a hard day's work."

Nice, I thought. She invariably included me in the group of young people who would rather play than work. Yes, I did a lot of skiing and hanging out with my best friends. And then there was the nap thing. She'd turned a frightening shade of purple when I had a cot installed in my office. Scooter did not approve. The first time she'd seen my napping cot, she'd rolled her eyes and asked, "Do you need milk and cookies too?" A nap might improve her disposition, but I wasn't about to suggest it.

"Are you sure you're not being too picky?" I knew better than to poke the Scooter Bear, but I couldn't help myself.

She gave me one of her looks that told me in no uncertain terms that no, she was not too picky and in fact, I was not picky enough. "It took me five years to train Mermaid. Then she just up and leaves."

"She's getting married. It's romantic and wonderful that she found someone," I said. "And she hated it when you called her that." Mermaid's real name was Lori. Scooter had thought she looked like Daryl Hannah in the eighties movie *Splash* and had continued to call her that despite Lori's protests.

"She said she hated it, but she actually loved it." Scooter let out a long sigh. "I miss the ding-dong, if you want to know the truth."

"I do too. She brightened up the place." Lori had one of those smiles and personalities that made a person feel as if nothing could stay bad for long.

Scooter scowled. "What? Am I not bright enough for you?"

"Do you really want me to answer that?" I smiled, hoping to tease her into a better mood.

"It's a luxury I don't have." Scooter lifted her chin. "I'm the only grown-up left here. Someone has to keep us from flying off the rails."

The sound of tittering came from the break room. Our two vet techs were eating together and had presumably overheard Scooter.

"I'll see you later, then." *You old battle-ax.* "After lunch, I have to go out the Martins' farm. They have a horse that needs a checkup."

She rolled her eyes. "The Martins. More money than brains."

That may have been true, but I didn't comment. My mother had taught me long ago that this was a small town. Making any sort of judgment on our clients or their pets was ill-advised. We were to provide care, not opinions.

"Set your alarm if you're going to nap," Scooter said.

I grinned. "No need. My internal clock wakes me up five minutes to one."

"Of course it does." Scooter headed out, muttering something else under her breath.

Before I could put the Closed for Lunch sign on the door, Tiffany Birt rushed into the lobby. My breath hitched at the sight of her. Those ice-blue eyes did not leave me cold but rather sent waves of longing through me. I'd never seen eyes that color except on a Siberian husky. She had her long brown hair pulled into a bun and wore a pair of loose-fitting jeans and a flannel shirt. Strange. Most of the time she dressed professionally for her work as a wedding planner. She must not have any clients today. Since the forest fire last summer, tourism was down, as were destination weddings.

For almost a year now, I'd been trying to muster the courage to ask her out. I'd had plenty of chances. As pretty and sweet as she was, she was also a bit of a worrier about her white fluff ball of a dog, Muffy. There had been more than a few times Tiffany had brought her in when nothing at all seemed to be wrong with the puffball of a dog.

Something about her stopped me from asking the simple question, Would you like to go to dinner with me sometime? Was it the wariness in her eyes? Or the way she often covered her chest with her arms in a symbol of self-protection? Or the skittishness to her that reminded me of a frightened kitten? One who had been harmed by a man. Who had hurt her? I'd spent a lot of time pondering this question but had not found any answers. As a healer of animals, I knew on an instinctual level that she'd suffered trauma of some kind. Our pasts followed us into the present. Just when we thought we'd moved away from all that had hurt us, they came roaring back, crushing hope with a cruel fist.

"Are you just closing for lunch?" Tiffany asked, slightly breathless. She had Muffy in her arms, who tilted her head at the sight of me and rewarded me with a few tail wags.

"I was about to, yes." But my nap could wait. "Is something wrong with Muffy?"

"I don't know. She won't eat."

"Have you changed her food? Sometimes they can be finicky." Not sometimes for my friend Muffy. She was possibly the most spoiled dog in town, and that was saying a lot.

Tiffany glanced down at her shoes. Adorable feet in cute black sandals. The cuffs on her pants reminded me of beach-combing. A walk on the beach with Tiffany? Now there was an idea. Only the beach was far away from Colorado. If I were to ever ask her for a date, it wouldn't be to the beach. That could wait for the honeymoon. *Very funny,* I told myself. *You can't even ask her out to dinner.* "Well, yes. I had to start buying the cheap kind. Business hasn't exactly been booming."

I reached out to take Muffy from her. The little dog licked my hand and then nestled against my chest. "She's such a doll."

Tiffany gave me the proud mom smile. "Isn't she, though? She's all I have. If anything were to happen to her…" She drifted off without saying what she thought would happen to her if she lost her furry baby. However, I knew. I'd seen this with many of my clients and their pets. There was no love like the one we felt for our pets. They filled even the loneliest of lives with unconditional love. Income or education didn't matter. Not even the size of one's dwelling. As long as they had a spot beside you, they were happy. Which meant their owners were too.

"I know she's spoiled," Tiffany said. "Responsible party right here." She pointed at herself with her thumb. Her nails were short, possibly bitten. No polish. Ragged cuticles. She wore a little makeup, but not much. A pink gloss on her lips had smeared onto the skin next to her mouth. Such a nice mouth, full and kissable.

I stroked Muffy's head and ears to distract myself from thoughts of Tiffany's kisses.

"What kind of food do you normally give her?" I asked.

"The Millford brand. Chicken cutlets is her favorite."

"I have some cans in the back. Let me get them for you. To tide you over." I borrowed a phrase I often heard my mother use.

She protested using her hands like a traffic cop. "I can't take your food. Don't you need it for your dogs?"

"Nah, these are some samples the sales rep dropped off here. We sometimes send new owners off with a few."

She breathed what had to be a sigh of relief. "Thank you. I've been so worried."

I handed Muffy back to her. "Hang on. I'll grab them."

I walked back to my office. Scooter had a whole shelf devoted to samples of food, toys, and whatever else the sales-people were hoping to sell to us. A dozen small cans of Millford Organic dog food were stacked on the top shelf. I scanned the labels: beef and corn, pork and rice, chicken and rice. No chicken cutlets. Would Muffy mind chicken and rice instead? I grabbed two cans of each kind and returned to the lobby.

Muffy was curled up in a circle of sunlight on one of the chairs. My mother had insisted that dogs weren't allowed up on the chairs, but that was a detail I didn't really sweat. It was a vet office, not a museum. What did I care if there were some pet hairs here and there?

Tiffany stood by the door holding our Help Wanted sign, which had been carefully displayed in the front window by Scooter. She stared down at it, as if the words were written in a foreign language. Her brow knit, and she had her bottom lip sucked inside her mouth. The Scotch tape used to hang it in the window had stuck to the sign and flapped in the breeze from the air-conditioner duct up above her head.

"Do you think Muffy is a silly name?" Tiffany looked up from the sign to focus, not on me, but a poster of a basket of kittens.

"I think it's a perfectly fine name. In fact, it suits her."

She turned toward me. "That's what I thought."

"Why do you ask?" I had the feeling it wasn't a question she would welcome, but my curiosity about this lovely, mysterious woman took precedence.

"I heard some children mocking her name. The other day." She gestured toward the window. "At the park." She sat next to Muffy, still holding the sign between her hands. "I don't know why, but it bothered me."

"Kids can be obnoxious. Don't think anything of it. If it makes you feel any better, classmates were always making fun of my name when I was a kid."

"I didn't go to a regular school. Was that a common thing?"

Didn't go to school? That was interesting. "Were you home-schooled?"

"Kind of, yeah." She swiped the tip of her thin nose with the back of one hand. "What kind of help do you need?" Her voice rose higher in tone. She wouldn't look directly at me.

"We need a new receptionist," I said. "Do you know someone?"

"Me. I could use the work. Since the fires, the weddings at

the lodge have decreased. I'm not making enough to stay…" She placed a hand on top of Muffy's head. "Afloat."

My mind raced ahead, trying to decide if this was a good thing or bad. She wanted a job here? My heartbeat seemed to speed up at the idea of her in my reception area every day. However, did she have experience? The position was deceptively easy-seeming: answering phones and scheduling patients. However, it was also dealing with frantic pet owners, both on the phone and in the waiting room. The tasks required a certain calmness and ability to assure even the most distraught pet owner that everything was going to be fine. Then, perhaps harder than anything, she would have to be strong as she ushered loved ones in and out of the clinic after putting a pet down. Sadly, this was essential to my practice. The natural inclination toward empathy and sympathy was necessary. Knowing the right words to say. She ran a wedding planning business, though. Who could be more difficult than a bride-to-be? Or their mothers?

"Do you have any experience in office work?" I asked.

"What kind of experience?" She asked this with a wide-open expression. Did she really not know what I meant?

"Phones. Computers. Managing, you know, office things." I grinned, unsure actually what Scooter expected. She and my mother had decided on the division of duties between the receptionist and the veterinarian assistants before I took over the practice. Until we lost Lori, I'd taken for granted that everything around the office was done well and without any input from me. Besides Scooter, we had two assistants to the vet, plus the receptionist. We were a small-town operation, after all. My work at the shelter was separate from what we did here. We had a volunteer who ran most of that—a wealthy widow with time and money to spare.

"I know how to talk on the phone." She hiccuped and seemed mortified, covering her mouth with her hand. A spot of red showed on each of her cheeks. "Excuse me. I get the hiccups when I'm nervous. I've been getting them a lot lately."

What was she nervous about? Me? Her financial worries? It would be nice if it were me but probably not. "Don't be nervous," I said.

"As far as computer skills go, I've managed a small business. I know how to keep financials, pay invoices, and write project plans. I can't imagine I wouldn't be able to learn whatever you need me to." She cast her eyes downward as a flush crept into her cheeks. Who had those kind of cheekbones, other than movie stars and models?

I blinked. *Pay attention to the task before you*, I reminded myself. Daydreaming about my possible employee could only lead to disaster. Possible misdiagnosis? Fumbling one patient for the other?

"How long would you commit to being here?" I asked. Even as I asked it, I felt like a jerk. What right did I have to ask anyone to commit their life to a job that may or may not be mind-numbingly boring? Especially to someone who had owned their own business for—How long had she been working as a wedding planner? I knew so little about her. Not for lack of trying. But she was as tightly closed as a tomb. "Or, actually, that doesn't matter. I know you have your own business. If you wanted to stay until your business picks up, that would be fine."

I peered at her for a moment, watching her fidget. She shifted her weight from one foot to the other, causing her to sway in the way women did when they rocked a baby.

"I don't know how long it will be before things pick up again," Tiffany said. "But I can give you my best for at least the next six months."

"Sure, yes." I wanted to give her the job right then and there, but I knew Scooter would have to give her approval. "Could you come back later to interview with Scooter?"

Her brow knit, and her eyes dulled. "Scooter?"

"She manages the office for me," I said. "Legacy from my mother's reign."

"I know Scooter," she said, as flat as her eyes. "She doesn't like me."

"Why do you say that?"

"I can tell. I bother her for some reason. It's like I can hear her telling me to straighten my posture and stop being such a mouse. All she has to do is send me one of her looks."

I grimaced, knowing just what she meant. "She does the same to me. And everyone, for that matter. It's just her way. I doubt she has anything against you personally."

Tiffany nodded and took in a deep breath. "I'm willing to try, regardless. Desperation causes a person to be more tolerant of strife."

"I don't like to hear you say desperate. Is it that bad?"

She glanced toward Muffy and then back to me. "I'm about out of my savings. If I can't make rent next month, I don't know what I'll do. If it's not a job here, I'll have to hope to find something else. I don't want to leave Emerson Pass."

"Right. Of course, you wouldn't. I mean, who would?" I was babbling. My mouth went dry at the thought of her leaving. If she were still in town, the hope was alive. The idea that at any moment she might look my direction wasn't that easy to let go of, as long as she still lived here. "Come back at three this afternoon to meet with Scooter."

"Will she want me to wear a dress?"

That question surprised me. We dressed casually here. Most days Scooter wore her scrubs. At our last Christmas celebration, she'd had a few champagnes and confessed she prefers scrubs because then she didn't have to spend her hard-earned money on clothes. "I don't think a dress will be necessary. You look fine the way you are."

She looked down at her feet. "The sandals are no good. I'll

put different shoes on and maybe add a blazer over the blouse." She tapped her knuckles against her chin. "I never know what to wear."

"You always look nice," I said. "Whenever I see you around."

"Nice, but am I appropriately dressed? After all this time, I still don't know." This last part seemed to be a thought conveyed out loud. I had the sensation of trespassing, as if I were reading her secret journal. What did she mean by "after all this time?"

"I'm not sure Scooter is the type to judge you about your clothes," I said. "She wears scrubs like they're the new black."

A burst of laughter erupted from her. "That's funny."

"I'm here all week." I borrowed that from my dad. He'd been gone for almost fifteen years, and I could still hear his voice in my head.

"I make all my own clothes. Other than jeans, that is." She tugged on the fabric that bunched at the outer thigh.

"Really? All of them?"

She flushed bright pink. "Not everything, but most things. Blouses and skirts. Dresses, if they're not too complicated."

"I'd have never known. Not that I'm an expert on fashion." At the moment I had on a pair of my favorite jeans and a nice-looking dark blue T-shirt that my mother had given me. She'd given me the same shirt in seven different colors. She knew my affinity for soft shirts. And she wasn't the most imaginative person when it came to gifts. If she found something she liked, she wasn't afraid to commit.

Muffy raised her head from her nap and whined.

Tiffany startled. A look of guilt crossed her face, followed by a discouraged slump of her shoulders. "I should feed her. Do you mind if I take those and head home?"

"Sure, here you go." I'd completely forgotten about the cans I'd set on the counter.

"Wait, let me get a bag for you." I went behind the front desk, hoping there were sacks of some kind hidden in the drawers.

We gave patients samples all the time. I found nothing but paper and ink cartridges. I straightened. "I've got nothing. I can't find anything here."

"I can take them home in my purse," Tiffany said, tugging the strap from her shoulder. "Thanks for setting up an interview with Scooter. I'll do my best."

"Absolutely, we'll see you at three this afternoon." I fluttered my fingers toward my office. "It's time for my nap now." Why had I said that? Naptime. Like a kid. Scooter was right. Sleeping in the midday was a totally ridiculous thing for a grown man to do.

"I love naps." Tiffany's expression brightened. "I take them whenever I can. Muffy likes them too."

She liked naps too. Interesting. Was it a sign we were meant to be? An image of us curled up together for an afternoon rest floated before me. Was she a woman who would snuggle? She was affectionate toward Muffy. Would that extend to humans?

"Scooter doesn't approve of the cot in my office," I said. "But I find that I'm an unnaturally sleepy person."

A short, unexpected laugh cheeped out of her again, reminding me of bubbles from a fish floating to the surface of a tank. "I've never thought about whether my desire for sleep is normal or not." A trace of bitterness glinted in her eyes. "Where I come from, naps were not allowed. We had very exact guidelines about when to go to sleep and when to wake."

"Did you have a strict family?" I asked. My mother had raised me with a firm hand in regard to morality and respect for others and our environment. However, she'd been less so with curfews, sweets, and school-night rituals. She always said she never had to be overly heavy with me because I was always such an obedient and easygoing child. Her only child. Just the two of us after my dad died of cancer when I was fifteen.

Tiffany's glance flickered to Muffy, her expression flat and stoic. "You could say that."

I didn't dare ask her a follow-up question, even though the words were practically crawling up the back of my throat to get out. If she came to work here, I'd have more chances to ask questions. Maybe she'd grow to like me? I'd made her laugh twice since she walked into the lobby. This was a good sign, I decided. Always the optimist.

3

TIFFANY

Wearing a modest wrap dress in sage green and low-heeled sandals, I walked into the clinic with my head held high, hoping it conveyed more confidence than I currently felt. Scooter sat behind the front desk, her horse-like face set in a scowl. Leathery skin from too many days outside without sunscreen a stark contrast to her silver hair. What skin, though? Layers and layers of epidermis made tough by the Colorado elements. And those big teeth. She was like a farm animal, strong, scary, and ready to kick anyone who came too close. When Dr. Stokes had told me I'd have to interview with her, my stomach had dropped to the bottom of my sandals. There was no way I would get by her; I'd be lucky to make it out without lacerations, let alone with a job. Still, I must try. That was all there was to it. I was a survivor, and that's what survivors did.

Scooter lifted her gaze. Flinty eyes looked me up and down. A flash of irritation hardened that leather face. She didn't like what she saw. Who knew why? I sent a silent note of gratitude to Stormi. Despite the casualness of the office and Dr. Stokes's assurance that I come as I was, Stormi had been certain I should dress nicely for an interview. She'd had a lot of jobs, she'd said. "Trust me, it's important to look professional, especially when they don't expect it."

Without her, I might have gone with Dr. Stokes's advice and actually shown up in the jeans and shirt I had on earlier. When I first entered the world, I'd had absolutely no idea how important clothes were to society at large. At first, obviously, it had been the least of my problems. However, as I grew acclimated enough to find a way to feed myself, I quickly realized that if I wanted to fit in, I needed to ditch the weird dresses.

In the ten years since my escape from captivity, I'd learned a lot about normal people. "Normals," as I thought of them, had codes and nuances they learned by going to school. I'd had to figure it out step by step, educating myself from magazines and television. Breck Stokes wasn't the type who had to worry about fitting in. He'd been born that way. When I thought of him, I thought of apple pie, that new-car smell, and sitting in the shade on a porch on a Sunday afternoon. He might even be the king of the Normals. He'd make another Normal very happy and then have a bunch of little Normals. A twinge of envy pierced me. I'd have liked to marry a man like Dr. Stokes. If I'd been born into this life, he might have been interested in me. But I didn't kid myself. I knew I was a freak. Even if they didn't know why, it was obvious. Even Stormi and Jamie, true friends, looked at me sometimes as if I were a puzzle. As much as I'd learned to blend in, there was a separateness between me and the rest of the world. Even here in Emerson Pass, where people were more accepting of differences.

I'd brought a résumé, which I grasped between damp fingers. Although the weather was a pleasant seventy-two today, a bead of sweat dribbled down the back of my spine. The air smelled sweet on this spring day, apple and cherry trees blossoming and daffodils lifting yellow faces toward the sun.

Birds woke me in the mornings. My herb box I had hanging from my apartment window was starting to sprout with new growth.

"Good afternoon," I said, smiling as best as I could even though my knees were practically knocking against each other.

"Come on back," Scooter said. No smile. A curt nod and an attempt to make her mouth prim by pursing her lips. Unfortunately, those big teeth got in the way, and instead she looked constipated. I'd observed her at church, the bossy way she directed people to their seats even though she wasn't the greeter. Back at Briar Rose, she would have been a first wife. I couldn't imagine her accepting it any other way.

I followed her into a small office with a desk and two chairs. Posters of kittens and puppies were hung on the only free space on the wall.

"How's that dog of yours?" Scooter asked as she took the chair behind the desk. Filing cabinets took up three of the four walls. A small succulent and a computer were the only items on her desk.

"She's fine."

"Why'd you bring her in this time?" Scooter yanked open a drawer and took out a yellow notepad.

"She wouldn't eat." I hated that this woman made me feel so apologetic.

"Let her starve a few days and she'll eat what you put out."

I wasn't so sure about that. Muffy might look small and cute, but she had a stubborn streak. Scooter had never seen Muffy at the park. When she wanted to stay and play longer, she put up quite a fuss. Did Muffy seem ridiculous to Scooter? Too fluffy and white? Spoiled maybe? All of which were true, but my Muffy deserved respect.

"Dr. Stokes tells me you're looking for additional work," Scooter said. She tented two bony hands under her chin. Why would anyone choose to be so skinny when there was food everywhere?" "I suppose the whole tourist industry took a hit with the fires."

"Yes, ma'am," I said. "Until things get better I need something to keep things from falling apart."

She continued to gaze at me. "Interesting way of putting it—things falling apart."

"Pardon me?"

"There's something odd about you. Has anyone ever told you that?" Scooter asked this as if it were a perfectly natural thing to ask in an interview.

"Not to my face," I said.

"I suppose they wouldn't." She looked down at the computer screen and made a heaving sigh. Something in her email or me?

"Where are you from?" Scooter asked. "I mean originally. You're from here, obviously. I know everyone who grew up here. Born and raised myself right here in Emerson Pass. My relatives were some of the first settlers here."

"I'm from Nebraska. Small town." I left it at that. Usually that was enough to deter people.

"What town?" Scooter glanced down at my résumé. "You don't have any work experience listed other than Denver and here."

"That's because I moved to Denver when I was sixteen. I didn't work before that." I hoped that would be enough, but she was like a dog with a bone.

"What town did you say it was?"

"I didn't. You wouldn't have heard of it."

"Try me," Scooter said.

"Murphy." When this happened, I used my backup, but only when necessary. I hated lying to people about my past. There was less sin in omission, I figured. Outright lies were another thing. "Do you know where that is?"

"Sure. Murphy. Blight on the land, that town."

"Yes, ma'am." Poor Murphy. The town didn't have a chance.

Still, she was right. If Murphy were a face, only a mother could love it.

She cocked her head to the right, observing me as if I were a zoo animal. "Your parents still there?"

"No, they're deceased."

I could see a thousand questions behind her glittering eyes. Fortunately for me, she wouldn't ask anything more personal for fear of getting in trouble. As far as I understood it, there were rules around what you could ask a candidate. Too personal and you risked delving into dangerous territory.

"It says here you have a degree." Scooter tapped my résumé with her fingers. "How were you able to do such a thing without family support?"

I drew in a shallow breath. This woman was too curious for her own good. "The old-fashioned way," I said. "Community school while working, some loans, and some luck."

"Hospitality. What made you study that? Seems a little light academically."

"I like hotels." Would that satisfy her?

"And? There must be more to it than a love for clean sheets."

An image of white sheets blowing in the wind flashed before my eyes. I shoved the memory away. "I like taking care of people. Giving them their dream wedding or party gives me a lot of pleasure."

"I suppose it never occurs to any of them what a waste of money it is," Scooter said. Not a question but a statement.

"I work with all size budgets." Hoping to steer her away from my past, I attempted to veer the conversation back to the job. "I believe I'd be good with your clients here at the clinic. With my hospitality and service training, I can soothe almost any frayed nerve."

"I can't imagine anyone could be worse than a bride, huh?" Scooter frowned, but a hint of camaraderie played behind her eyes.

"True. Some get a little worked up on their big day, but for the most part, they're grateful for my help."

"How do you know?"

"I can just tell."

"Interesting." Scooter returned to my résumé for a moment. I fidgeted, hot and sweaty. My dress was sticking to the small of my back.

"We want someone we can train for a long-term commitment," Scooter said. "Breck says you're only interested in a short-term position, which is not ideal for us. But to be honest with you, every other applicant has been a bit lacking in the old brain department or they're obviously lazy."

I wondered what would make a person appear lazy just from an interview. Did they yawn?

"Can you work nine to five?" Scooter asked.

"Yes, no problem." My few clients weren't able to meet during regular office hours anyway. Most of the wedding consultations were over the phone or video calls. Surely I could handle receptionist duties? I shivered as a memory of those first weeks after I left the compound threatened to distract me. That life seemed like a long time ago and as though it happened to someone else. Yet at times an inkling would emerge, reminding me of where I'd come from and how hard it had been to make a life for myself.

I rubbed my left temple and focused on Scooter. If I wanted to remain in this life with an apartment and hot water, I needed to secure this position.

"All right, let me talk to the doctor," Scooter said. "I'll give you a call to let you know what we've decided."

I stood. "Thanks so much," I said as I shook her hand.

Was there something more I could have said or done to convince her to give me the job? Breck seemed to have already made up his mind about me or he wouldn't have asked Scooter to talk with me. That said, I had no earthly idea if Scooter liked me enough to hire me. I'd have to work closely with her. No matter; I could handle her. I'd dealt with a lot of bridezillas and, perhaps worse, some of their mothers. Now that I thought about it, Scooter reminded me of one of the mothers from last spring. A corporate lawyer type in a stern black suit and hair pulled back so tightly into a bun that her face appeared as if it were post-face-lift.

"Sure thing," Scooter said. Did she ever soften? The ring on her finger told me she was married. What was her husband like? Did she treat him the same way as she did everyone else?

Walking across the tiled floor to the lobby, I thought again of what I might have said to improve my odds. It didn't matter now. I'd done my best. If Scooter wanted me, she would let me know. Until then, I would apply at a few other places in town. Beggars couldn't be choosers.

Beggar.

I hadn't been that for a long time. I had no intention of doing so again.

I WAS DOWN to a jar of peanut butter and cheap white bread. After a sandwich and a glass of water for dinner, I settled on the couch to read a novel. This time of year, the sun didn't set until almost eight, and the light was silky gold through the open windows in my front room. I'd secured a popular book from the library and had been looking forward to reading tonight. However, I was having trouble concentrating. Lately, my mind drifted. I'd read entire paragraphs without comprehension and have to start over again. Money problems were not easily escaped, even in the pages of a good novel.

I got up and stretched, then wandered to the windows that provided a revolving art exhibit of white or green, depending on the season. In the cold months, my view was that of a winter wonderland, everything covered in snow or ice, the sparkles as precious to me as jewels were to others. Spring was here now with a color palette of shades of greens, white, and pink fruit tree blossoms, and tightly bound buds waiting for their chance to open. Snow remained at the very top of the mountains, pink now in the moments just before sunset. From this angle, I could not see the ski slopes of the northern mountain, brown this time of year without their blankets of snow.

My apartment, in one of the original brick buildings on Barnes Avenue, consisted of a living room, a small kitchen, and two bedrooms. Decades earlier, the owner had renovated the old office building into six apartments, three on each floor. Brick walls and exposed beams made them seem modern even though they were a century old at least. My unit was on the upper level that overlooked most of our downtown area. Tonight, with the warm weather, people had come out to play. The deck at Puck's was full. Occasionally, I could hear a bark of laughter through my open window. Couples meandered along the sidewalk, popping into the quaint shops or restaurants. Lights from our gourmet and ridiculously priced grocery store were on, giving me a direct view into the flower shop at the front. Beyond that, the setting sun sparkled in the ripples made from ducks and geese as they swam happily in our pond. Young people hung out in the gazebo in our town square while others sat on benches near statues of Emerson Pass heroes and hero-ines of yore.

During these moments when the inhabitants of my insulated world bustled with life, I often felt the pull toward them, wishing I could be as carefree and social. But the dust of my past clung to me, never quite washing clean so that I could fully join the life I'd risked everything for.

I pushed the button to begin heating water and went to the cupboard to get a mug. I'd already had a peanut butter and banana sandwich for dinner. I still had another loaf of bread in the freezer and a full jar of peanut butter. However, that had been my last banana. If I didn't get a job soon I'd have to dip into my meager savings, which I really didn't want to do. I lived frugally so that my fears of homelessness and hunger never came to be. My only splurge was to live in this apartment without a roommate. The peace of living alone was worth the sacrifices in other areas. I was too weird for a roommate. If someone lived with me, they'd see all that old dust I couldn't brush away. I'd have to pretend all the time to feel like a Normal when I wasn't. Just the thought of it exhausted me.

I could still make my own clothes and eat peanut butter instead of going out. No coffees from cafés or any of Brandi's delicious pastries or cookies for me. I envied those who could order from a café or restaurant and never look at the prices. For the first few years in Emerson Pass, the wedding planning business had been booming. But in parallel with the charred land, clients had disappeared. They would come back. Of course, they would. Weddings weren't dead here, just temporarily put on hold. Like the new growth on the mountains, tourists would return.

Holding on. That's all it was. Keeping afloat with another job until the schedule filled up with destination weddings once more. I could do that, I reasoned. No problem. Even as I tried to convince myself, a fissure of doubt wormed its way into my thoughts. No one with a past like mine could run from worry. I was more acutely aware than most that disaster was only a paycheck away.

I was fine, I reminded myself against a panic that crept up the back of my throat and made it hard to breathe. There were other jobs in town. If the one at the vet clinic didn't work out for me, I could apply elsewhere. I'd really like that one, though. It was a good fit. Although it hadn't occurred to me until I saw the Help Wanted sign, the idea made perfect sense. I loved animals. Muffy would be able to get free care. At least I assumed she would. Now that I thought about it, Scooter hadn't actually mentioned that as a perk.

I got up again, restless, and went to the window. To calm my nerves, I breathed in the smells of spring from the open window. Puck's kitchen filled the air with the scent of grilled meat. A waft of freshly cut grass and cherry blossoms came in with the gentle breeze.

At the moment, Muffy was curled up on one end of my eggshell-colored couch. Fortunately, she was a dog with hair, not fur, so shedding was nonexistent. Even if she did shed a hair or two, she was the same color as the sofa, so it didn't matter.

Before I'd eaten myself, I'd fed Muffy an entire can of the food Dr. Stokes sent me home with me. Thank God, she'd eaten with great enthusiasm. If anything happened to my fur baby, I don't know if I could recover. She didn't know it, of course, being a dog, but besides my work, Muffy was my whole world. I'd found her on the steps of my apartment building the first morning I moved in here. There she'd been, a wet, muddy mess of a thing, no bigger than my sneaker. Someone had dropped her there, I'd thought as I picked her up and stroked the top of her head. She'd trembled at first, but after I took her upstairs and gave her some chicken and then a bath, she yawned and curled up in my lap and fell asleep. I was immediately in love.

I hadn't known love at first sight was true until I met Muffy. Some might find it with another person. The love of my life was this dog. That first night, I was plagued with worry. Would someone want her back? Was I setting myself up for heartache? What if I went downstairs and her face was plastered all over town? No, that couldn't happen, I convinced myself. A dog that young and small wouldn't have run away. She'd been abandoned. Sent away. Like me.

Kismet. Meant to be. The only explanation. That was three years ago, and I'd never looked back. Fortunately, my virtue had not been tested. There were no signs about a missing puppy anywhere. If there had been, I'm not sure I would have been able to give her back.

I'd have never thought I'd own a dog. When I'd first escaped, I lived in various shelters for the homeless. Taking care of another creature seemed impossible. But look at me now.

All those years ago, I'd lucked my way into a shelter. After learning about foster care from a few runaways, I decided to lie about my age. I told the women who ran the shelter that I'd grown up in a cult and had run away. They didn't ask any further details. At the time, I was relieved, but looking back I suspect they didn't want to know more, because if they did they'd have to do something about it.

Instead, they focused on helping me. First, I enrolled in a GED course so that I could get a high school diploma. While still staying at the shelter, I found a job at a restaurant washing dishes. After only a few months, I qualified for an apartment in an affordable housing unit in Denver. There, I was able to meet the rent and go to community college.

Those years were filled with the wonderment of the world. A world I'd never met. At first, the traffic noise and that of the people in the restaurant where I worked were jarring and depleted me of energy. At night, I would crawl into my bed of blankets on the floor in my newly rented room and fall into a deep, dreamless sleep, waking to the sound of my alarm. I was grateful for the lack of nightmares. I'd lived through hell; I had no interest in revisiting it during sleep.

But slowly, as I acclimated to my new existence, the noises were no longer noticeable. I began to participate in my classes at night school and at work. I even made some casual friends. As long as they were at a distance, they wouldn't ask about my past. People were not very curious about me, though. I was amazed how few asked questions. Perhaps I seemed ordinary on the outside? I was glad of it. Ironically, blending in was key to being left alone.

Now I went into the kitchen and put the kettle on for some tea. While the water boiled, I washed and dried the knife I'd used in the peanut butter and looked around to see if there was anything else that needed tidying. Everything was in its place. A coffee maker that made four cups of perfectly brewed java. A stainless steel toaster I'd found at the thrift store. Toast! Gosh, I loved it, smeared with butter and jam. We hadn't had toast at Briar Rose. I'd had no idea what I was missing. Toast was just one of many discoveries I made those first years. Hot chocolate. Oranges. Pie. French fries. Hair dryers. Fabric sheets. Showers longer than one minute. Down jackets. Mattresses with crisp sheets. It took getting my own apartment to discover the heavenly experience of sleeping on a real mattress instead of a cot.

Satisfied the kitchen was tidy, I took one of my three cups from the cupboard and waited for the kettle to whistle. When it did, I poured hot water over a tea bag, breathing in the aroma of apples and cinnamon from the steam.

Friday night was a tea night. Usually I had a treat to go with it, but until I had a job, I'd have to settle for this.

Muffy lifted her head when I sat on the other end of the couch with my legs folded under me and the steaming mug between my hands. Although the spring weather had been glorious this afternoon with temperatures in the mid-seventies, after the sun went down, a chill came to the air. My apartment, although not drafty, cooled quickly as well. I didn't use the heat this time of year. Too expensive when I could just bundle up in additional layers.

From my seat on the couch, I could see through the open door to my sewing room I'd set up in my spare bedroom. It had taken me a few months, but I'd managed to save enough for a sewing machine. I also had a table to cut patterns as well as a bookshelf that took up most of the small room. I hadn't had money lately for fabric but once I did, I'd make a new dress from a spring pattern I'd ordered.

I jumped when my phone buzzed from the coffee table. I'd repurposed a table I'd found at a garage sale, stripping it and giving it a rustic paint job in white.

"Hello, this is Tiffany," I said into the phone. *Please let it be a new client*, I prayed silently.

It wasn't. Scooter's crisp, cold voice greeted me from the other end—a combination of a green apple and an onion, I thought, as she began to speak. "I'm calling to let you know we'd like to offer you the position at the front desk."

"Great, thank you." My chest rose and fell as I took in a large breath of relief. At this point, I couldn't worry about what it would be like to work for Scooter. I was only grateful for the steady work.

"The new Dr. Stokes offers all the employees health insurance," Scooter was saying. "I forgot to mention that when we spoke earlier."

"Insurance? Wonderful. Great." I'd been paying for my own insurance since I started my wedding planning business. I had the cheapest plan I could find, which basically meant I never went to the doctor. The coverage only kicked in if I had some kind of catastrophe or serious illness. Fortunately, I hadn't had any of those. By the grace of God.

"Can you start on Monday?" Scooter asked.

Today was Friday. I'd have all weekend to prepare myself mentally. "Yes, that would be fine." More than fine.

"Come in around nine to fill out paperwork. Normally, we won't need you until a little before that to prepare the office for opening at nine-thirty. You'll stay until five, with an hour for lunch and two breaks if you want them. Lori never took breaks, but legally we have to offer them to you."

Lori didn't take breaks. Duly noted. Also, "come in *around* nine" meant a little before. I'd worked for people like this before. Everything was a test.

We exchanged a few more details before hanging up. I

picked up Muffy and gave her a snuggle. "You'll get your good food back now, my little love," I said. "Mama has a new job."

I needed to keep it. Would I have preferred to continue working for myself? Absolutely. But I needed to do what I had to in order to survive. Dealing with Scooter was a small price to pay. Until payday, it would be peanut butter and cheap bread for me.

4

BRECK

Friday evening after work, I went straight home to take a quick shower before heading out to meet the guys at Puck's. I dressed in jeans and a light sweater, then ran a comb through my thick hair. The texture was like the bristles of a brush, so I kept it short. I decided against a shave. It was Friday night. A little stubble never hurt anyone.

Carrying my loafers, I walked down the hall in my stocking feet, past the family photographs that hung on the wall. I paused in front of the last photograph taken of my father before he grew ill. He'd been older than I was now, but not by much. I could see myself in his face more every day. The frame hung slightly crooked; I straightened it. "Hey, Dad," I whispered.

My mother was in the kitchen, leaning over the counter while reading from a book. Her white hair, cut short and swept away from her forehead, glimmered under the pendant lights. A batch of silver bracelets jangled on one tanned, muscular arm. All that gardening and tennis added to her youthful energy. She shopped from catalogs with clothes in gray and black that hung in elegant drapes, but this evening she had on a tennis skirt and tank top from an earlier match at her club.

She looked up as I strolled past the island in the middle of the room. Our kitchen had been remodeled not long ago with light cabinets and white granite counters, all very traditional, like my mother.

Careful not to slip on the hardwood in my socks, I touched her shoulder with my fingertips. "How you doing, Mom?"

"I'm fine, thanks." Mom placed tanned hands palm down on the light countertop. Mom, with her bright blue eyes and high cheekbones, was someone who commanded attention, even in her sixties. Tall and slender, she could have passed for a much younger woman.

"What are you up to tonight?" Mom asked. "You look all clean and shiny." She removed her reading glasses and set them on the counter to give me her full attention. I hadn't appreciated this quality when I was younger. As kids do, I figured everyone's mother did the same. Now I understood how precious it was to have someone fully listen to and see you.

"Meeting the guys for dinner and drinks," I said, chuckling at her description. She'd been calling me "clean and shiny" since I was a child. "The usual."

"Ah yes, Huck texted to tell me he was on his way and not to leave without him."

"Why didn't he just text me?" I asked, befuddled, as I often was, by Huck's actions.

"Because you never look at your phone." Mom said this matter-of-factly. *Decent argument,* I thought. Phones were not my favorite thing. Don't even get me started on social media. I abhorred it. Those apps and sites were nothing but a system to make people miserable, children foremost. With the teen suicide rates at an all-time high, one didn't have to look far to know why.

As if we'd conjured him by merely speaking his name, the door from the mudroom into the garage opened and Huck called out to us as he hung his tweed jacket on a hanger. He'd gotten that thing at a thrift shop years ago and claimed it was his writing jacket. Thus, he wore it to the newspaper office almost every day.

"Evening." He sounded grumpy. Nothing new there.

"Did you have a good day?" I asked.

"Depends on how you look at it," Huck said. "The weekend edition is in the bag. However, it's the usual embarrassment."

"How can that be?" Mom asked. "Didn't you write most of the articles?"

As a small-town newspaper owner, Huck was editor-in-chief as well as primary writer.

"That's just it. First, nothing ever happens here. Other than the fire, obviously. When I graduated from journalism school top of my class, I really didn't picture the disaster my career has become."

"You chose to come back here," Mom said in her usual tough-love voice. The one she used on only three people in the world: me, Huck, and Trapper. "If you don't like it, the roads are open to leave."

"Maybe I will someday," Huck said, then groaned as he went to the refrigerator to help himself to a beer. "You know who I sound like? The sisters in *Three Sisters*."

"The Chekhov play?" I asked, confused. "What does that have to do with your declining career?"

"They were always talking about going back to Moscow but never quite got around to it," Mom said.

"Do you want to go back to New York?" I asked. "I thought you were through with all that."

"I am. That doesn't mean I'm not miserable here running this rag. Do you know what I had to write about today?"

"Murder? Embezzlement? Local politician in a scandal?" Mom asked, sounding hopeful.

"Are you kidding? No, none of those things. The front page is about the spring festival." Huck jerked the cap off his beer with a practiced twist and slammed it down onto the counter. "Why does this town have this many festivals? There's one for every stupid season."

"To answer your question," I said. "Four. One for each season."

"It was a rhetorical question, genius," Huck said.

"I have a story for you," Mom said. "You should use your investigative skills on that Henry Wu."

"Henry?" I asked. "What's Henry done?"

"He's annoying," Mom said. "Way too cheerful. Something's not right about him."

I had to press my thumbs into my eye sockets to keep from rolling them. Henry Wu was the nicest man in town. He was also an extremely talented musician and teacher. "You know he played in Nashville as a studio musician? He's a big deal."

"I don't give a fig where he played," Mom said. "He has a lot of nerve educating me on Emerson Pass history. Which he didn't, by the way. I know everything there is to know."

"What did he tell you?" Huck asked as he settled onto one of the stools and took a slug from his bottle of beer.

"I can't remember," Mom said. "But I already knew it."

"What're you reading?" Huck peeked at Mom's book. "Ah, Dad's newest? I'm surprised you haven't read it before now, like the rest of the town." A sharpness crept into his voice. Huck was disdainful about the commercial success of Garrett's best-selling mystery series. He described his father as a "sellout." As if one couldn't write good books and also sell well. Huck was nothing if not enigmatic. I was probably the person who understood him best. However, he perplexed me more often than I understood him. Especially since he'd come back from Afghanistan.

"This is very good." Mom closed the paperback and showed us the front cover, as if we hadn't seen it before now. "I still marvel that I grew up with him. Such a talent."

Garrett Clifton was the closest thing we had to a local celebrity. He wrote a series of historical mystery novels set in a ski town based on Emerson Pass. They were enormously popular and hit the *NYT* best-seller list with every release. Mom was right. They were terrific. His sleuth was a librarian, based on his great-grandmother Josephine Barnes Baker. The real Josephine had been our town's first librarian, having started it with funding from the Carnegie family. Our library, to this day, remained in the beautiful brick building built during the Great War. Huck's father claimed he could hear the whispers of Josephine and her first patrons if he sat in a certain corner of the library. He was often seen writing in that very spot. Locals were accustomed to him and thought nothing of the eccentric writer pounding on his keyboard while they looked for books. As successful as Garrett was, he and his wife, Sally, lived in one of the original cottages built in the twenties not far from our house.

"I'll go shower and be right down." Huck finished off his beer. "You're driving tonight."

I always drove.

"Put on some aftershave," Mom said. "You want to smell nice for that Stormi."

Huck stopped in the doorway and turned back to look at her. "What did you say?" His dark eyes glittered dangerously.

"You heard me." Mom opened her book and returned her gaze to the page.

"I did hear you, but you've apparently lost your mind," Huck said. "I can't stand that woman."

"So you say." From Mom, without looking up from her book.

"I do not like her," Huck said. "Whatever gave you that idea?"

She lifted only her eyes to meet his gaze. "Don't look like I'm an old lady about to lose her faculties. Breck's father and I used to react the exact same way when we were together. We supposedly hated each other too. I could see the electricity between you two and I was five tables away."

"You're entitled to your opinion," Huck said. "I'll be back in a minute." His voice was even and pleasant, but I could see by the splotches of red under his cheekbones that she'd bothered him.

I went to the wine cabinet and pulled down a decent bottle of red. "You want wine, Mom?"

"Yes, please." She set aside her book and went to the cupboard to fetch glasses. "I'm going to put a frozen pizza in since you two are going out."

"There's leftover vegetarian chili from last night," I said, somewhat offended. It was my best yet. I'd exchanged ham for chard to provide extra vitamins. They hadn't even noticed the difference. Or had they?

"Yes, I'll be having pizza. The chard got in my teeth." She returned to her book.

"Fine. It's your heart."

"It is, yes," Mom said.

"Pizza can be paired with greens for a more nutritious meal," I said.

"It's like I raised a hippie." She turned a page in her book.

A hippie? If she only knew all the ideas I kept to myself.

I opened the bottle and poured her a small glass.

"We hired a new receptionist today," I said.

"What?" My mother slammed her book closed. "Really? Who did Scooter find?"

"I found her, not Scooter."

"You found her?" she asked, as if I'd just confessed to a murder.

"Yep." I set the glass of wine near her book.

"Please tell me you had Scooter interview this person." Mom clutched the spot between two buttons of her shirt. "It's her office, you know."

"It's my practice," I said. "Scooter might do well to remember that."

Mom blinked before fixing them on me like a predator who was about to devour me for dinner. "Scooter was with me for thirty years."

"Maybe it's time she retired."

"Good luck running the place without her." Mom's voice remained steady, but two blotches of red had come to her cheeks.

I smiled to hide my annoyance. "You and Scooter seem to be under the impression that I'm incompetent. Which I'm not." I glanced down at the floor, gathering my emotions before they spilled out all over the island counter. "You underestimate me, Mom. You always have."

"I don't. It's just that you're so...mellow. Running a successful practice is not for nice people."

"I disagree."

"Scooter doesn't."

"What does that mean?" I asked. "Did she say something to you?"

"We had lunch the other day. She expressed her apprehension about whether you're decisive enough."

"By decisive, she means roll over and do whatever she wants?"

"Have some respect. She's given her entire life to our family business," Mom said.

"Well, it's my business now. I'll decide if she remains or not. How's that for decisive?"

She opened her mouth, then shut it just as quickly. "I hope I don't regret turning it over to you." She made a stubborn jut with her jaw that reminded me of a blue jay I'd seen the other day.

"Whether you do or not is irrelevant. I own it now." The loans were in my name. I'd bought my mother out, assuming that meant she'd no longer be in my kitchen, so to speak. How wrong I'd been. Two years later she was still backseat managing.

She was quiet for a moment, leading me to believe the conversation was over, but no. "Who did you hire? Do I know her?"

"Tiffany Birt."

"The wedding planner?"

"That's right." My shoulders tensed as I waited for whatever came next.

"You gave a woman with her own business a permanent position?"

"Sure did."

"Well, it's not what I would have done, but as you say, it's your practice now."

If only she meant those words.

"Mom, maybe you should focus on other things. Cultivate some new friendships. You could get a boyfriend. Look at Jack and Jennie. They've found each other after all these years. Isn't there a high school boyfriend we could scare up somewhere?"

"Have you lost your mind?" She squinted her eyes and shook her head.

"Dad's been gone a long time, Mom. You could meet someone. Go traveling or just spend time doing stuff you like to do."

"How would I know he wasn't after the fortune your father grew for us?"

She had a good argument there. What if some old geezer came along only after her money? What if he hurt her? The thought of it was too much.

"Maybe you're right," I said. "You could get a dog." We'd lost both our dogs last year. So far, Mom hadn't seemed inclined to bring another into the house. I understood. Dogs weren't replaceable. Each was special in its own way. Each made a unique mark on our hearts.

"I'm not ready." She picked up her glass and took a sip of the wine. "What is this? I hope you didn't pay more than ten dollars for it."

Actually, she'd bought the bottle last week when she unexpectedly ventured out to the grocery store. Primarily, I'd thought at the time, to buy frozen pizzas and lasagnas. "I'm not sure what it cost."

"You should know these things. Make a mental note for next time."

"You bought this one," I said.

"Oh, well. I'll make a note myself then."

"But seriously, Mom. You retired for a reason. Maybe spend some time on yourself, though? Isn't there anything you've always wanted to do that you couldn't because of work?"

"Where do you hear this kind of self-help nonsense?" Mom asked. "You sound like one of those armchair therapists on a daytime show. Have you any idea of the trash that plays during the day? It's appalling. No wonder we're getting stupider as a species."

"Are we?" She didn't answer, so I asked a more obvious question. "*You've* been watching television?"

"Ava has it on while she cleans. I've learned a lot since I've been home. Like you, Ava is not open to suggestions for improvement."

Ava was our loyal housekeeper who came twice a week. I'd started leaving her a tip in my room. Cleaning while my mother was home had not been in the job description when she'd started with us ten years ago. *She probably misses those days*, I thought.

Huck came in, freshly shaved and dressed in jeans and a black sweater. No wonder the ladies had always gone berserk over the man. Apparently, those dark, piercing eyes and that jaw as square as Superman's made him irresistible.

"Speaking of cleaning," Mom said. "The other day, I dropped an earring under the dining room table. And guess what I saw?"

She waggled her fingers at Huck. "Someone, I'm assuming you, carved 'Huck Was Here' into the underside of the tabletop."

Why was she so light and playful with Huck and so hard on me? I'd asked myself that question too many times to count. Going all the way back to high school.

Huck flushed. "Yeah, that was me—during my stage where I felt certain I was going to die before I reached age thirteen."

Despite the morbid nature of that thought, I laughed. Mom, too, looked amused.

"Why would you think you were going to die?" I asked. It was *my* father who had died.

"I don't know." Huck tapped his temple. "There's something wrong with my brain. We all know that. I used to lie awake at night and listen to all the sounds, thinking it might be my last night to ever hear them."

"What kinds of sounds?" I asked, curious.

Huck rattled off a list, counting off on his fingers. "The house creaking. Cat scratching on her post. Rain on the roof. A tree branch smacking the window. Or the complete silence that comes after a snow. You can actually hear silence. Little-known fact."

"I don't think that's a fact," I said.

"You've always been intense," Mom said. "Nothing wrong with it. Your father was the same way."

"He was?" Huck asked. "When you guys were in high school?"

"Sure." Mom nodded, a faraway expression in her eyes. "He was different from the other boys in town—more romantic, I guess you'd say. He carried handkerchiefs around in his pocket and gave them to young ladies if they were in tears for whatever inane reason. I never needed one."

"He still does," Huck said. "He's stuck in a different time."

"His romantic nature works for his books," I said. "I'd love to be romantic like that. Or write a book, for that matter."

"I'd love to be an opera singer," Mom said. "That doesn't mean it's going to happen."

"True enough," Huck said. "The sooner we set our expectations low for life, the better."

"That's not true," I said. "What if your dad had done that and never written a book?"

"Then I wouldn't have to hear about how great he is twenty-four-seven in this town." Huck looked around the room, as if he'd lost something, and growled. "When are we going? I'm starving."

Maybe these two needed more vitamin B or whatever supplement helped a person be more optimistic. Whatever was wrong with them was starting to rub off on me, and I didn't like it. For now, I put it aside. It was Friday night, and the weather was beautiful. We were going out with Darby, who was almost always encouraging and fun. Anyway, ultimately, these two and their dark moods were not something I could fix. I'd never been able to. And I'd tried. From now on, I'd stick with animals.

5

TIFFANY

After the conversation with Scooter, I tried to return to my book, but my thoughts tore around my mind, distracting me. I was headed for my bedroom and some cozy pajamas when my phone rang. It was my friend Stormi.

"Hi, Stormi," I said into the phone.

"Why didn't you answer my text?" Stormi asked with her New York accent.

"I didn't see it," I said. "I was reading."

"You need to turn the sound on once in a while. Especially on a Friday night. I have the night off, and I want to go out. If we meet at the grill, we can get my employee discount."

She worked at the bar and grill a few nights a week. Her wedding photography business had taken a hit since the fire.

"I thought you were working tonight?" I asked.

"Change in schedule. I finally told boss man I needed at least one weekend night off. The schedule was making me feel like an old lady. Plus, I'm caught up on my bills now, so I can breathe a little."

"I've already had tea." I had no money to go out.

"What does tea have to do with anything?" Stormi asked.

"I mean, I'm kind of cozy here at home."

"Are you kidding me, Grandma? Even Muffy has a better social life than you."

I looked over at her, already curled up on her side of the bed. "I don't think so."

"Come on, please? I really need to blow off some steam. Jamie's in as well."

My resolve to stay home softened. Jamie was my next-door neighbor. She'd moved in after she lost her newly renovated inn during the fire. Just last week she'd confessed to feeling more than a little discouraged about her life. The dream of owning an inn had literally gone up in a cloud of smoke. She had to start all over again, rebuilding what she'd lost. When did it stop? All this turmoil and resurrection? All this struggle to make a living and build a life?

I would just order a water. Alcohol either made me sleepy or weepy. The night wouldn't cost me much. "All right. Give me a few minutes to put myself together. I'll meet you there."

"Awesome. See you soon. And don't worry about money tonight. My mom sent me a birthday check. The night's on me. Let's get some fries and nachos. Really splurge."

"Wouldn't you rather do something else for your birthday?" She was already at Puck's enough.

"Nah. We can get more for our money at Puck's. Plus, there's a good band playing tonight."

"Who?"

"Off-brand," Stormi said. "You liked them last time."

"True." I *had* liked them. They played acoustic versions of classic rock and roll. One of the first things I fell in love with after my escape had been modern music. With the streaming apps on my phone, I could now devour everything I'd missed. "All right. I'll hurry."

"That lead singer's hot," Stormi said. "I heard he was from New York."

Before hanging up, I promised to meet them in thirty minutes. At the mirror, I inspected my current attire. Jeans and a sweatshirt wouldn't do. Even though Emerson Pass was a casual place, young women dressed up to show off their figures on a Friday night. This concept had taken a while to adjust to. Having worn only clothes that made sure to cover up my body, even jeans had seemed too revealing. Slowly, over the years, I'd loosened up somewhat. Regardless, I found myself staring at other women, amazed at what they would wear in public.

I took off the sweatshirt and hung it in the closet while considering what to wear. We'd probably be outside, which would mean it was chilly. I chose a sweater in a pale blue that Stormi had picked out for me from the thrift store. The tag had still been attached. "Never been worn," she'd said triumphantly. "Thank you, rich lady with a shopping problem."

"It's very pretty," I said. "But will it require hand-washing?" Since leaving Briar Rose, I'd discovered the convenience of washing machines and dryers.

"Maybe, but who cares. This will make you look rich and if you look rich, you'll feel rich, and then the world is yours." Stormi spent a lot of time contemplating the difference between those with money and those without. She'd always been in the *without* category.

If she'd only known about my childhood, she might see that hers could have been worse. I kept these kinds of things to myself. Thus far, I'd managed to avoid telling anyone about my past. Instinctually, I knew it would change how people thought of me. Instead of being Tiffany, I'd be the girl who grew up in a cult. I was weird enough without people knowing that detail.

I reapplied foundation, powder, and blush, along with a light eye shadow and mascara. *No need for eyebrow pencil*, I thought. My thick eyebrows perched over my almond-shaped eyes like two monstrous black caterpillars. I hated them. Stormi assured me thick brows were a thing now. That didn't make me feel better. I'd have happily given them to anyone interested.

Using a brush, I painted my full lips with a pale pink lipstick, then brushed out my long hair. Every other day, I washed it and used a flat iron to smooth out any waves. The changes hair dryers and irons had made to my life were too many to count. If I was tired or sick, it was still my instinct to braid my hair the way we had to when I was at Briar Rose. No more, I would remind myself. I could wear my hair down or up or however I pleased. Even with my money worries, I had a great life. I must always remember how blessed I was. I smiled at myself in the mirror and turned to go.

AT PUCK'S a few minutes later, I searched the dining room and bar for Jamie and Stormi but couldn't find them. They must be on the patio. Sure enough, there they were, sitting at a table by the railing. They each had a glass of red wine in front of them and were looking over the plastic menus as if the offerings were new to them.

When I approached, they both turned to look at me. Their faces lit up. "Hey, Tiff," Jamie said. "Come sit." She patted the chair next to her.

"Hey." I sat; my old enemy, insecurity, shared my chair. "How's everything?"

"Nothing new here," Jamie said. "But you look a little beat up. Everything all right?" She tucked a blond lock behind one ear and peered at me from bright blue eyes. If she were a billboard, she would advertise sunshine, fitness equipment, and coconut tanning lotion.

Stormi waved a hand at the young woman waitressing. I

recognized her but couldn't remember her name. Something with an *M* maybe?

"Hey, Shoe, bring Tiff a soda water and lime, would you?" Stormi asked.

That's right. Her last name was Shoemaker and everyone called her Shoe. Maybe I'd never heard her first name?

"Unless you want something stronger?" Stormi asked.

"No, that's good," I said.

"You got it." Shoe had a husky voice that sounded as if she'd spent the night before cheering loudly during a stadium game. "What do you want to eat?"

Friday nights they didn't have any specials. Usually we ordered whatever the deal of the day was, which they listed on one of those chalkboards near the front. For weekends, though, they didn't need to lure people in with specials.

"I guess happy hour's over?" Jamie asked.

"Yeah, sorry," Shoe said.

"I've got money," Stormi said. "Birthday money or blood money, depending on how you look at it. Let's get some appetizers to share."

"Works for me," Jamie said.

We ordered fries and nachos. Shoe said she'd sneak in an order of wings on the house. "Since it's your birthday."

"It's not *technically* today," Stormi said.

"Doesn't matter," Shoe said, tucking her pen behind an ear. *Blue pen and blue hair*, I thought. Did she match them on purpose? How many piercings did she have in that one poor earlobe? "Birthdays should be celebrated all month." She stuck her pad into the front of her red apron. Tattoos ran up and down her arms like black lace. I inwardly shuddered at the thought of the needle.

After she left, I leaned closer to Stormi. "Will she get fired for stealing wings?"

"Nah, our cook doesn't care and the owner's never here."

Stormi ran a finger around the rim of her wineglass. "Plus, it's a batch of frozen wings. They probably cost fifty cents wholesale."

We all nodded. Those in the tourist business knew about markups and margins when it came to food and beverages.

"I have a little news." I told the girls about my new job. Embarrassed, even in front of these two, my skin flushed with heat. It was humbling to have to find a "day" job because my business wasn't doing well. If anyone could understand, it was these two. We'd all been through a lot since the fire took out so much of our town.

"I think it's great." Stormi reached over and squeezed my arm. "Nothing to be ashamed over. A girl has to take care of herself."

"Amen to that." Jamie took a generous slug of wine. "If it weren't for my job at the kitchen store, I'd be screwed right now."

"Not for long," Stormi said. "I drove by the inn today on my way to take photos of the new bridge for the paper. It looked almost done. To me, anyway."

"The guys said I can open for business at the beginning of May," Jamie said. "I'm excited." Her eyes shone with a brightness I hadn't seen in too long. "To lose my dream in the fire only to have it resurrected again has made me realize how much I still want this."

"I can't imagine a worse job," Stormi said. "Running an inn. Having to talk to all those rude guests."

"Why are they rude?" I asked.

They both gave me a look.

"What?" I asked.

"Not *all* people are rude," Stormi said. "But the ones that are always seem to erase the nice ones."

"I love it," Jamie said. "Getting them to relax and have fun is a welcome challenge." She made jazz hands on the side of her face. "Jamie can do her magic, once I have a place to do so."

"Do you have any bookings yet?" Stormi asked.

"My brother and some of his friends from Cliffside Bay are all bringing their wives out for Memorial Day weekend. It's a pity booking, but I'll take it." Jamie's brother, Trey, was an interior designer from California who had redone the inn for her.

"That's sweet," Stormi said. "Must be nice to have family like that."

"It is," Jamie said. "My brother's super talented, obviously, as are his partners at the firm. But they're also such good people. I've been lucky that way."

"You have," I said, longing creeping into my voice. Ironically, given all my father's children, I had no idea how any of them were doing. Were they all still at Briar Rose? Had any managed to leave as I had? There were times I wished I could see them. Most times, however, I counted my blessings to be free.

"Did you guys see this story? Just broke this afternoon," Jamie asked as she pointed to the television that hung under an awning. Most evenings, the television played sports but at the moment, it was turned to one of the news channels.

It took me a moment to realize what I was seeing.

My stomach dropped. I gasped and brought both hands to my mouth. There, on television, was a photograph of my father. The subtitles were on, flashing these words across the screen: *A cult of bigamists was raided by the FBI today. Two members of a group that calls themselves Briar Rose have been killed. One FBI agent is wounded and in critical condition. Inside the compound, they found enough guns to weaponize a small army. The casualties have not been released, but those close to the story believe at least one of them was an elder in the organization.*

My mouth went dry. I realized I was still pressing my fingers into my bottom lip and brought them to my lap, digging my fingernails into the palm of my hand. The children. What had happened to the children? And the wives. The women. Were they taken into custody as well?

"Are you all right, Tiff?" Stormi asked. "You're as white as this plate." She gestured toward the bread plate.

I looked over at her and lied. "I don't understand the story."

"The FBI went after some cult down in southern Colorado," Stormi said. "Basically, it was a bunch of pigs who marry sixteen-year-old girls to add to their collection of wives. They call the place Briar Rose. I've no idea what that means. Huck's been chasing the story for months now."

"Story?" I asked, numb. Briar Rose was a story. William and the others had been busted. After all this time.

"There were rumors that the FBI was investigating them," Stormi said. "Huck wanted to know what went on behind the locked gates. He's suspected for a while now that they were basically keeping members in a kind of prison there, but trying to find anyone to talk was impossible."

I had returned to staring at the television. Already, I'd recognized Elder William and Elder Ryan being marched out of the compound with their hands cuffed. "When did they invade?" Where was my father? Was he one of the casualties?

Jamie, bless her, seemed to understand my question. "This afternoon. It was a standoff all morning. The stupid news has been playing it on a loop. You know how they do."

I rarely watched the news. "Playing what on a loop?" I asked with a croak.

"What you're seeing there." Jamie pointed to the television.

"How'd you miss it?" Stormi asked as she buttered a roll. "It's been everywhere."

I had no social media accounts or anything that could lead them to me. "I've been busy. Muffy wouldn't eat." This sounded absurd even to my own ears, but it was the truth. No one had to know anything. There were no traces of me there. These were people I once knew. That was all. Briar Rose had nothing to do with me. I didn't need to care. Or even watch.

But somehow, my gaze returned to the television.

"The FBI had to finally go in and start shooting," Jamie sa. "They refused to come out, so they swarmed the place. I'm surprised more people weren't hurt."

"Those poor people." Stormi shuddered. "They had the entire community of women and children under lock and key from the sound of it. What with all the wives and the fact that sperm from these old geezers continues to be viable, there are dozens of babies who were born and raised there. The whole thing makes me want to shoot someone myself."

Surprised by the venom in Stormi's voice, I was temporarily distracted from the television. She had a cocktail napkin in her grasp and was folding and unfolding the corners. *What in her past had triggered this response? She wouldn't want to talk about it,* I thought. Just like me. How many other wounds did the women sitting with me hide from the world? I wasn't alone in this. If only we could speak of the atrocities of our childhoods, perhaps we could heal. Or maybe not.

"Hey, Tiff, are you all right?" Jamie asked.

"Is the story upsetting you?" Stormi asked. "I can go change the channel."

Her kindness brought tears to the surface. I hid my face by cupping my hand over my forehead like a visor. As if that would help. We might not articulate our troubles, but other women knew when something had cut deeply.

Stormi scooted her chair closer to me and asked gently, "Yo, babe, what's going on?"

Shaking like Muffy without her coat on a cold Colorado day, I wiped under my eyes with a napkin. Without raising my gaze, I mumbled, "I can't talk about it. Not here. I need to go home."

"We'll take you," Stormi said.

Jamie reached out to give my forearm a quick squeeze. "I'll go tell Shoe to pack up our food. You two go ahead and I'll bring it over when it's ready." Jamie got up from the table and headed inside to the dining room.

…king but strangely numb, I let Stormi take me down
. stairs of the deck and around to the sidewalk. Across
,eet, I could see the outline of Muffy in the window. Had
, been waiting all this time? Did she sense something was
wrong?

"Come on, babe," Stormi said. "Let's get to your apartment
before someone we know stops us."

We crossed the street together. Stormi held on to my arm, as
if I might break into thousands of pieces right there on the
street and never make it up to my apartment.

Somehow, though, Stormi managed to help me up the stairs.
Muffy jumped from her spot at the window and ran toward us
barking with her tiny voice. I picked her up and held her close
to my neck. She licked my cheek. Muffy was here. She knew I
needed her.

"Sit," Stormi said. "Do you want me to make you some of the
herbal tea?" She said *herbal* with an *h*.

"No, thank you."

"I want wine," Stormi said. "Do you still have bottles left
from Jamie's birthday party?" We'd thrown her a party a few
months back, and my guests had arrived with more bottles than
we could possibly drink. I'd stored them away for Stormi and
Jamie.

"In the cupboard above the refrigerator." People in books
were always having a drink to steady their nerves. Desperate to
stop shaking, I decided to try it out for myself. "Bring three
glasses."

She did a double-take but didn't say anything. A moment
later, she returned with an open bottle of red and three of my
mismatched wineglasses. The front door swung open, and Jamie
entered with several bags of our takeout.

"I'm sorry to ruin our night," I said. My voice wavered as I
tried to control myself. Crying would do no good. But those
years seemed to play before my eyes, brought on by the vivid

footage on the television. My usual tricks to repress those memories seemed temporarily out of order.

Matthew. I never thought of him now. I'd purposely put him away in the recesses of my mind so that his death could not hurt me. The poison meant for both of us had taken only him. Only because my sense of smell had detected something off in the wine. That was the only reason. Otherwise, I'd be buried next to him. Wherever that was.

If someone had asked me, I would not have been able to tell them what he looked like. I remembered nothing of our time together or the decision to leave. But now, an image of Matthew's eyes as they drained of life played before me. Green eyes. The color of a male duck's feathers. His sandy hair plastered to his forehead. His mouth had foamed as the poison took hold. He'd said to run, and I had. I'd never known what happened to his body. Had they paraded it around the camp to show people what happened to rebels? Where was he buried? Did anyone remember him?

"I was there," I said out loud to Jamie and Stormi. "At Briar Rose. Before I escaped at sixteen. Trapped in the compound like the others."

"Holy crap." Stormi, for once, appeared speechless.

Jamie placed both her hands on her forehead and pushed back her hair. "Are you serious? Briar Rose?" She fluttered her fingers toward the blank television screen.

"Yes. My mother was a member. She was my father's first wife."

They both stared at me. The vein in Jamie's forehead pulsed. "First wife?"

"The elders all had as many wives as they wanted. We were basically paraded in front of them when we turned fourteen. They chose which of us they wanted, and then at sixteen we married them."

Now that I'd started, I wanted to tell them every grisly detail.

Instead, I kept it simple, telling them about Matthew and how we tried to leave. "They acted like it was okay, but they poisoned him. The poison was meant for me, too, but I didn't drink the wine."

"No wonder you don't drink wine," Stormi said.

"I don't think that's why," I said. Or was it?

"Some instinct in me knew there was something wrong. It was dandelion wine, if you can believe it. Everything was primitive there. We washed clothes and linens by hand. I sewed all the dresses. The ones you saw on television are the ones we wore ten years ago."

"This is unbelievable," Stormi said. "That this can happen in the modern age."

"I know. The elders kept everyone locked up and scared. Our poisoning was partly to punish us, but also to send a message to the others. Matthew knew what they'd done. He knew it as he was dying." I closed my eyes as spasms of remorse seared through me. "He told me to run, and I did."

Stormi cursed under her breath. "And they didn't come after you?"

"No, if they tried to find me, they weren't successful. I changed my name to Tiffany. I used to be Michelle. But honestly, I don't think they thought I'd talk, which I didn't. All this time, they've continued on and I've been here, living my life." Guilt niggled at me. Should I have done something? "Maybe I should have gone to the FBI."

"You can't blame yourself," Jamie said. "You were a child. I can't believe you got out and actually survived at sixteen. The images on the news make me feel sick. The electric fence and the guards. All those guns."

"I don't even know what to say." Stormi poured wine into all three glasses. "It's so weird to think about you in a place like that."

"I didn't know anything else," I said. "Children accept things the way they are."

"Should we see if they've discovered anything else?" Jamie grabbed the remote and turned on my television.

"I have so many questions," I said. What happened to make the FBI raid now? Briar Rose had been there for decades. I'd always gotten the feeling that law enforcement looked the other way. Why had they decided to look now?

We watched in silence, listening to the same information we'd already heard at the bar. The other girls had opened their food and were eating, but I was too nauseous to eat. I took a gulp of wine and almost coughed, but managed to keep it down. The second sip wasn't as bad.

From the television, the reporter said, "Breaking news. We've just learned that one of the casualties was Lawrence Miller. According to sources, he was one of the founding members of the cult. He was taken to the hospital earlier but died of gunshot wounds on the operating table."

I broke down then, sobbing silently. My father was dead. Why did I care? He'd been dead to me all these years. He was a monster like the rest of them. I pointed at the TV as they flashed a photo of my father on the screen. One I'd never seen before from when he was younger. Perhaps his high school portrait, given his slicked-back hair and formal suit. But it was him. No mistake.

The girls exchanged a glance. "What is it, doll?" Stormi asked. "What's going on?"

"Lawrence Miller was my father."

6

BRECK

By the time we arrived in town, the wait for a table was over forty-five minutes. Darby muttered something under his breath about tourists and then suggested we head back to his apartment. "We can order a pizza and get some beer. I think there's a baseball game on."

"Sounds good to me," I said.

"Me too," Huck said.

We stopped in at the grocery store to buy beer and snacks. While I paid, Huck ordered a pizza to be delivered to Darby's. Then, fully stocked for the night, we walked across the street to his apartment building. It didn't occur to me until we were walking up the steps that Tiffany also lived here. In fact, she rented the apartment across the hallway from Darby. *Don't get excited*, I told myself. She was probably out with friends. It was Friday night. Or worse, maybe she had a date.

Darby's apartment contained only a futon couch, two camp chairs, a coffee table made from plywood, and crude bookshelves filled with tattered paperbacks. A discarded "Best Teacher Ever" mug held remnants of morning coffee. The cream had risen to the top and arranged itself into the shape of a cat. A massive flat-screen television hung on the wall.

"Sorry about the decor," Darby said as he ran a hand through his thick, wavy hair. He had one of those faces that could play Superman on the big screen. Even his hair dipped over his forehead. Although tonight, with the fashionable black glasses, he looked more like Clark Kent. "I can't seem to find money in the old budget for some new furniture."

"What more do you need?" Huck unpacked tortilla chips, salsa, Fig Newtons, and a box of microwave popcorn onto the coffee table. "This place is awesome."

"Should I get bowls?" Darby asked.

"What for?" Huck tore open the bag of tortilla chips. "The salsa's in its own bowl." We'd gotten the fresh variety in one of those plastic containers with a sealed lid.

I went into the kitchen to put the beer in the refrigerator. "I don't know if there's enough space in here," I said, joking when I saw only a greasy takeout box and a carton of milk. After grabbing three bottles for consumption now, I closed the door and turned back to Darby.

"Bachelor life." Darby shrugged and grinned. "Just my books and a giant television to keep me company."

"Have you ever heard of leafy green vegetables?" I straightened, taking in the rest of the small kitchen.

"There's salad in the cafeteria at school," he said. "School lunches are much healthier than they used to be."

"Good to hear." I handed him one of the beers.

"The kids only eat the pizza and burgers, so I'm not sure the new menu's helping much," Darby said.

When we returned to the living room, Huck held a chip midair as he stared at the television with glittering, unblinking eyes.

Wondering what had captured his attention, I turned to the

screen to see the story about Briar Rose. I'd seen a glimpse of it earlier. "Sick old men. It's disgusting," I said.

"Agreed," Darby said. "The girls were sixteen. That's how old my sophomores and juniors are. I hope they throw the book at these freaks."

"I've been following this story for months," Huck said. "There were inklings of the raid earlier this week."

"How did they get to them?" Darby asked.

"They'd been building a case for years but didn't have enough proof to bust them," Huck said flatly. "They had their members locked away in there. No one went in or out. The fence was electric. Like they were animals."

"Did anyone else die in the raid?" Darby asked. "Please tell me no children."

"None of the children were hurt," Huck said. "But one of the women was killed and one of the elders, as they called them. The news just broke that he died in surgery."

"How awful," Darby said, sinking into one of his camping chairs. The screen showed women and children being led out to vans where the Feds were taking them to God knows where. The expressions of shock and grief on their faces brought tears to my eyes. Feeling sick, I turned away.

"We should turn this off," Darby said. "As an overly empathetic person, I can't take it. Especially the kids."

"Same here," I said.

Huck flinched, causing the bag of chips in his lap to crinkle. "I should have gone down there this morning. I had a feeling this was going to break."

"I thought you were done with big stories," I said.

"I am. Or I'm supposed to be," Huck said. "It's just this one is in our own state, and it's going to be a huge story. I could have broken it if I'd had my head in the game." He looked at the chip still clutched between his fingers. "But I'm not *in* the game any longer. I need to remember that before I get myself into trouble again."

The *again* part of that sentence remained a mystery. He hadn't even told me what had been the final incident in Afghanistan that had caused him to give up what he'd thought was his dream job and come home.

Darby grabbed the remote from the coffee table and turned the channel to a baseball game between the Mariners and the Padres. He muted the volume and set aside the remote. "We need some women in our lives, man. This is pathetic. I mean, look at me. I'm thirty and living like a college student."

"You have a lot of books," Huck said. "That's not so pathetic."

"Said one nerd to the other," Darby said, leaning over to clink his beer bottle with Huck's. "How's your house coming along?"

"I move in a few weeks," Huck said. "Until then, I'm living like a king over at Breck's."

"My mom spoils him," I said. "She always had a soft spot for the Huckster."

"She loves me more than you," Huck said.

"No doubt." I kicked his foot with the toe of my shoe.

"She actually told me that." Huck delivered this deadpan before finally scooping his chip into the salsa.

"Speaking of women." I sank into one of the chairs and spread my legs out long. "Tiffany's coming to work for me at the clinic."

Huck sat up, suddenly interested. "Are you kidding me? Way to bury the lead." The guys all knew about my unrequited crush on Tiffany Birt.

"Tricky, man," Darby said. "A workplace romance. Good plot twist."

I sighed as I picked up a Fig Newton. "She's not interested. No spark in her eyes when she looks at me. And she never touches her hair."

"Touches her hair?" Darby asked. "You mean, like flirtatiously?"

"Yep," I said.

"Any giggling?" Huck asked.

"Not even a chuckle," I said. "In fact, she's a very serious person."

"What makes you even think you'd be a good match?" Huck said. "You're not a serious person."

"But isn't there something about opposites attract?" Darby asked. "That's always happening in novels."

"In books," I said. "Maybe not in real life. She probably looks at me and thinks I'm a joke. The napping and all."

"You told her about napping?" Huck asked.

"It might have come up," I said.

"Man, you're living the dream," Darby said. "I wish I could nap at lunch. I totally would if I could get away with it."

"How is it that you need a nap *every* day?" Huck asked. "You're not a toddler."

"Or am I?" I asked, laughing.

A knock on the door stopped us from further discussion of my sleeping gifts. "There's our dinner," I said.

"I'm hungry but I wish it were girls," Darby said, leaping to his feet.

"Yeah, right," I said. "They magically fall out of the sky on Friday nights."

Darby yanked open the door. To my surprise, Stormi stood in the doorway. "Sorry to bug you, Darby, but—" She interrupted herself when she saw me standing there. "Oh, hey, Breck. What're you guys up to?" Her eyes darted behind us to Huck. "Huck."

"Stormi," Huck said, before returning his attention to the muted television.

Darby motioned for her to come in. "Hanging out. You want to join us?"

She stepped into the room and closed the door behind her. "Maybe. I'm over at Tiffany's with Jamie. We're having drinks, too, but we ran out of wine, and I was hoping to convince you to help a girl out with some replacements."

"Why can't you walk to the store?" Huck said from the couch.

Stormi glowered at him, her eyes bright under the fringe of dark bangs. "Because it's late and I don't want to walk alone in the dark. If you were a gentleman, you would know that."

"Don't mind him," I said. "He's grumpy because he didn't report on the big story."

"Briar Rose? I knew you were going to be mad about that. I told you to go."

Huck made a "close your mouth" gesture with his hand before digging back into the chips.

"He hates it when I'm right." Stormi fluffed her bangs that hung just above her eyebrows. *What a pretty girl*, I thought. Those green eyes and black hair, plus a few freckles, gave her an edgy, sexy look. If only I could like her. Tonight, she wore black jeans and a tight white T-shirt that showcased her slender shoulders and flat stomach. Sadly, we were comfortable together like a brother and sister. We'd talked about it at a holiday party a few months back. Both of us were alone in the kitchen at Garth's while the rest of the guests mingled around the Christmas tree. Everyone had their special person but me. Stormi had apparently thought the same thing, because she'd turned to me and flashed a mischievous grin. "You and me? Any chemistry?"

"I don't think so," I'd said. "But I could make you another drink and see if anything changes."

We'd had a good laugh and then I'd confessed to her about my crush on Tiffany. She'd told me to ask her out. I'd told her I'd think about it. That was back in December. It was now April. Late April.

Stormi had followed up with a drunken confession that she'd had a kissing dream about Huck. Her nemesis, as she called him. I'd kept my mouth shut, but I was with my mom on this one. Huck's hostility toward Stormi had more to do with how attracted he was to her than anything else.

"Which apartment are you guys hanging out in?" Darby asked. "Tiffany's or Jamie's?"

"Tiffany's. But Jamie's there too." Stormi fluttered her fingers toward the door. "We've gone through two bottles of wine, and it's not midnight."

Huck and I got the reference to the country song, "Two More Bottles of Wine," from one of our favorite Emmylou Harris albums, but Darby looked blank. He should teach country music as poetry in his classes. Maybe I should suggest that?

"You want to join us?" Darby said. "We have a case of beer, snacks, and a pizza coming."

"Two bottles between the three of you?" I asked. "It's definitely not a good idea for you to be walking around town."

"That's what I thought too," Stormi said, making a face at Huck. "And I'm from New York." She hesitated and shifted her weight to one foot, then raised one leg and hooked it behind the other, reminding me of a flamingo.

"You'll be safe here," Darby said. "We were just saying how we needed some beautiful ladies to liven up the place."

Stormi looked around the room. "Or paintings? Maybe a grown-up couch?"

"I wish," Darby said.

"I'll ask the girls if they'd like to cross the hall," Stormi said. "No promises, though. Tiffany's not really in the mood for lively conversation."

"How come?" I asked.

A look crossed Stormi's face I couldn't quite decipher. Indecision might be the best way to describe it.

"She's had a rough day," Stormi said. "But I'll go ask them. Be right back." She darted from the room, slender and quick like a deer.

"That girl's way too cute," Darby said.

"You into her?" Huck asked.

"Nah, just stating a fact." Darby stretched his legs out in front of him and took another swig from his beer. "Plus, I know you're obsessed with her, so I wouldn't want to get in the way of all that."

"If you mean obsessed with how to get her out of my business, then you're correct." Huck sucked angrily from his beer, then shoved his hand into the chip bag.

"Why don't you fire her, if you dislike her that much?" Darby asked, sounding curious instead of judgmental.

"Because there's no one else as good. She's really talented." Huck lowered her voice. "The way she can capture a moment—the composition and lighting—it's really something. I've worked with some talented people over the years, and I'd put her up there with the best of them. Women that talented shouldn't also be pretty. It makes them insufferable." Huck finished his beer and set the empty bottle on the table.

"So you *do* think she's pretty?" Darby asked.

"I have eyes." Huck reached for another chip.

Just then, there was a soft knock on the door followed by Stormi's voice. "Hey, we're here. Let's get this party started." Tiffany and Jamie followed Stormi.

"Thanks for letting us crash," Jamie said.

"It's our pleasure," Darby said.

I'd forgotten everything else the moment I saw Tiffany's face. She'd obviously been crying, given the puffy eyes. Without thinking, I moved toward her, stopping myself at the last moment from grabbing her in my arms.

"Have a seat," Darby said. "Oh, and sorry about the chairs. Can I get you a beer?"

They all nodded. He sauntered off to the kitchen to fetch a round for all of us. We all stood there awkwardly like middle schoolers at a dance.

"We should put some music on," I said. "Liven things up."

"Not too loud," Jamie said. "Mr. Nelson downstairs is already in bed. He has an early shift at the gas station."

"How do you know that?" I asked.

"Jamie knows everything about everybody in the building," Tiffany said, louder than she normally spoke. Her eyes, although red, seemed feverishly bright. "She looks after Mrs. Roy too."

"Who's Mrs. Roy?" Darby asked as he entered carrying six beers, two in each hand and the other two tucked between his arm and side.

"Your downstairs neighbor, dummy," Huck said. "She and Mr. Nelson have lived there for twenty years."

"How am I supposed to know that?" Darby asked as he handed the ladies their drinks. "I'm not like you two." He pointed at Huck and then me. "Who grew up here and know everything and everyone."

"Sometimes we wish we didn't," I said. "There are a lot of secrets in small towns, and most of them I don't want to know."

"Is that true?" Stormi asked. "I love gossip."

Jamie sat on the other end of the couch and plucked at the knee of her skinny jeans. "Around here, you have to be careful what you believe. Gossip can be damaging." She looked in Darby's direction, as if to signal him about something.

"Yes, but I love it anyway. Do you have any?" Darby asked in Huck and Stormi's direction. "I bet you two learn a lot working at the paper."

"I know nothing." Stormi plopped into one of the camp chairs and crossed one leg over the other. "Huck, do you know any gossip?"

"I'm a reporter, not a gossip columnist," Huck said, all growly.

"Sometimes secrets are necessary," Tiffany said.

Was there a little slur in her voice? I couldn't remember ever seeing her with a drink in her hand.

"Otherwise, people like me couldn't live here." Tiffany appeared to consider sitting in one of the camp chairs but seemed to think better of it, easing herself down on the empty end of the couch instead.

"People like me?" What did she mean by that?

"What kind of secrets could *you* have, Tiffany?" Huck's wide shoulders looked even bigger between the two small women. He was too gruff. Too hard on people. Why would he pick on Tiffany? No wonder Stormi hated him.

I sat on the floor with my back against the wall and shot him a look, but he ignored me. Trapper was the only person who could straighten him out when needed. However, Trapper was busy being a husband and father. He was probably wrapped up in his wife's arms watching a movie about now.

"What did you say?" Tiffany turned slightly to look at Huck. "Why couldn't a person like me have secrets?"

"No offense, but you're vanilla. The most vanilla woman I've ever met. Own it." Huck said this in his matter-of-fact reporter tone. *Life was not like a newspaper article*, I thought, irritated. He couldn't treat people as if they were only facts in a story instead of humans with feelings.

"Vanilla? What does that mean exactly?" Tiffany's eyes snapped with anger. She sat up even straighter. "I know it's an insult, but I don't know what it means."

Huck at least had the decency to flush. "Never mind."

"It means ordinary. Bland. Which you are most certainly not." Stormi's fists clenched at her side and she looked as if she might spring up from her end of the couch and pounce on him. *Go ahead. Hit him. He deserves it.*

"Actually, vanilla has an additional meaning," Darby said from the other camp chair. "It means the original something.

For example, the original ice cream was vanilla. So you're an original, Tiff."

"Huck meant it as an insult, but thank you, Darby." Tiffany gave him a lopsided smile before turning her attention back to Huck. "Is it because I make my own clothes? Maybe my profession? Something as mundane and ordinary as a woman who helps couples plan their weddings is certainly vanilla, right? Is Muffy vanilla, or am I vanilla for owning her?"

For once in his life, Huck didn't open his big mouth in his fat face to make her feel even worse.

"All those things make you special," Jamie said.

"Agree one hundred percent." Stormi tugged on her beer and resumed glaring at Huck.

Tiffany's voice shook. "I don't know anything about pop culture. Have you noticed that, Huck? Probably not. I'm not the kind of woman people notice, isn't that right? Just some mild-tasting vanilla ice cream."

"Vanilla's my favorite," I said. "Pure. Beautiful in its simplicity. The first of all the ice creams. Think about it. Without vanilla as the base, we'd have no other flavors."

Tiffany's mouth curved into a smile. "Why is it some men make everything they say to a woman sound like an insult and others make her feel as if she'd been invented just for him to compliment?" She flushed, then picked at the wrapper on her beer bottle before taking a sip. "I've never had a beer before now. That probably makes me vanilla too."

Never had a beer? Should she be drinking? What had happened to unravel her so? I caught Stormi's eye. She shrugged, as if to say "the woman's a grown person."

Tiffany tossed her hair before narrowing her eyes. "Huck, if you're such a great reporter, you'd know I'm the opposite of vanilla. My past is checkered." She fluttered her fingers dramatically.

❄

"Did you hear the news tonight?" Tiffany asked, with her eyes still on Huck.

"Hey, I was just kidding around," Huck said, sounding desperate to change the subject. "Let's just forget it."

Tiffany was having none of it. "No, you weren't. You have an impression about me because of the way I look. I'm here to tell you that you're wrong. That news about Briar Rose? You've all heard about it by now."

A wary look on his face, Darby nodded. "Sure we have."

"What about it?" Huck's voice was like a wood sliver just under the skin of one's thumb. "What's Briar Rose to do with you?"

The air in the room seemed pregnant. I reached under the collar of my shirt. If Huck said anything else to hurt Tiffany, I would punch his arrogant face.

"I grew up there." Tiffany set her bottle on the table as if it were suddenly hot. "That man they killed today. He was my father. *Is* my father. My mother was killed when she tried to escape. I was only a few weeks old then so I don't remember. Like all the girls there, I was groomed to be married to one of the elders." She giggled followed by a hiccup. "To one of the most important of the bigamists in all of Briar Rose. My father's contemporary. I was sixteen years old. I was supposed to marry Elder Ryan." She shuddered. "But I escaped."

None of us moved. For a moment, it seemed I was outside of my body and looking at myself from up above. The awkward way I had one foot resting on the opposite knee and kept fiddling with the shoelace of my sneaker. Huck leaned forward slightly. A man in search of a story. Darby and Jamie, interestingly enough, looked into their laps and appeared miserable.

Stormi spoke first, jarring us all out of our stupors. "Tiff, you don't need to share any of this just to prove anything to anyone."

"It's right here." Tiffany indicated her throat. "All the time, just waiting to get out, to tell someone the truth about who I really am."

"Tiffany..." I said, trailing off before I could ask the question. Darby asked what I wanted to. "How did you get out?"

"It's a long story," Tiffany said. "I escaped, but the boy I was with didn't make it. They poisoned him."

"Holy crap," Darby said. "How did you make it on your own at sixteen?"

"It was hard. I was completely disoriented—if you can imagine being dropped into the middle of a land completely foreign and having to learn how to live. But I found people willing to help me. I took advantage of every opportunity presented. Shelters and the like. There are so many good people in this world. I know it doesn't seem like it sometimes."

My mind reeled with this new information. So much of Tiffany's behavior was starting to make sense to me. Her other-worldliness. The sense of her being from another time. "How have you been able to keep this a secret?" As soon as I said it, I wanted to take it back. "I mean, it seems like it would be really hard to not share it. I'm sorry. I sound like an idiot."

"No, you don't," Tiffany said softly. "It's easier than you might think. No one asks many questions. People don't seem interested in other people that often."

"Really?" Huck asked.

"Not everyone's as nosy as you," Stormi said.

"Did they come after you?" Darby asked.

"No, they didn't. I've never been sure why. Although I did change my name. Maybe they couldn't find me." Her eye glazed over, as if remembering details she'd put away long ago. "I didn't drink the dandelion wine. That's all it was, the difference between living or dying." She touched the tip of her nose. "My sense of smell saved me."

"Amazing," I said, under my breath.

She turned to Huck, eyes blazing and cheeks pink. "How vanilla am I now?"

"I'm sorry," Huck said. "I had no idea."

"You must not be a very good reporter." Tiffany picked up the beer and took a long swig. Her mouth twisted as she swallowed. "Beer's not so good."

"Listen, Tiffany, I'm sorry I offended you," Huck said. "I was trying to be funny, I guess."

"You're not funny," Stormi said.

"I'm glad you made it out," Jamie said to Tiffany.

"Should you be worried?" I asked. "Are you going to contact the FBI and tell them your story?"

She looked at me for a moment with a blank expression. "I hadn't thought about it. Should I?"

"They'd probably like to know what you know," I said. "About your mother and your friend they killed."

"I couldn't before. I was too afraid they'd find me. But I guess they can't hurt me now that they're in custody." She gulped and clutched the cross at her neck. "I don't want the newspapers to know about me, though." She turned toward Huck. "Are you going to write about this in the paper?"

"Absolutely not." He had the decency to look offended. "I would not do that to a friend. Especially one who doesn't want to be found."

"You're my friend now?" Tiffany's brows raised.

"Again, I'm sorry for what I said," Huck said, sounding sincere. "I don't even know why I said it. Sometimes stupid stuff comes out of my mouth."

Her features softened. "It's all right. Maybe I should be glad I look so boring. No one will suspect my secrets that way."

"You should write a book about what happened to you," Huck said. "The inside story of what it's like to live in that kind of community."

Tiffany didn't answer for several beats. From the street

below, a horn bleated, followed by raucous laughter. Locals having fun on a Friday night? Or had the tourists started to arrive? Tomorrow they'd stumble blearily into Brandi's bakery and soothe their hangovers with lattes and muffins.

Tiffany's fingers plucked at the creased fabric of her jeans just above the knee. "I have no interest in reliving it. That's what I would have to do if I wrote about…that time." She swiped at the corners of her eyes. "I want to forget. That's all I've ever wanted, and now it's all back."

"It doesn't have to be," I said. "You can put it away and forget about it."

"But I can't now," she said. "I have no excuse. I have to tell them what I know."

Stormi knelt next to her. "You have us. We'll be here for you every step of the way."

Tiffany shook her head, as if to rid herself of her thoughts. "For now, I guess I'll have another sip of this beer and see if I like it a little better."

"That's my girl," Stormi said.

7

TIFFANY

Somehow, I ended up on the floor with my back against the couch. Stormi had insisted we all forget reality for a while and turn off the news. Breck turned on music, an unobtrusive accompaniment to our chatter. I drank the rest of my beer, hoping it would taste better eventually. It didn't. Nor did it make me feel better.

Now Stormi was telling a story about the time she met a famous photographer. A woman I'd never heard of but the others seemed to know. The milieu before me had become dim, almost gray, like one of those old grainy photographs. *Air*, I thought. *I need more air to clear my head and vision.*

What were the others saying? Who was talking? Darby. He was a charming person, wasn't he? His voice deeply resonated and was interesting. A teacher's presence. Had he always wanted to teach? What was it like to teach high school? What was it like to go to high school? I wouldn't know, now would I? My father had robbed me of that experience.

He was dead. Good Lord, how much more of this could I take? The raid, the scenes of the women and children filing out wearing their drab dresses. While I'd been out here living a regular life, they'd been inside wasting theirs. I should have done more. If I'd gone to the police or the FBI, perhaps they would all have been freed sooner.

A memory wriggled into my alcohol-soaked brain. The road on the day I left, concrete for miles and miles. I'd run at first but after how many miles, I wasn't sure, I'd had to slow to a walk. Finally, a car had come. I'd turned, sure it was them coming to get me. We had a few cars in the compound. The elders used them sometimes. Where did they go? Down this road?

But it wasn't them. It was an old truck with wire netting around the bed. Chickens. There had been chickens in little wooden houses. The driver had stopped and asked if I needed a lift. I'd gratefully accepted. In hindsight, the man could have been a serial killer. Back then, I was naive. I knew only of the atrocities committed in my own little world. I hadn't yet known of all that lurked in the shadows of the new, shiny one I was about to join. Still, the old farmer was a good man. I couldn't remember much about the ride, other than he'd given me a sandwich to eat. Bacon, lettuce, and tomato, his wife's specialty, he'd said. I'd never in my life tasted anything that good.

"Hey, you okay?" Breck nudged me gently with his elbow. He was sitting next to me on the floor. How long had he been there? His legs were stretched out under the coffee table. I could see the tips of his toes all the way on the other side. He smelled spicy and good. His shoulder rubbed mine. Did he realize he'd touched me? Muscles. Lots of muscles.

I turned my head to look at him. "Yes. A little fuzzy in here." I pointed to my head.

"I've never seen you drink before," Breck said.

"I don't drink. Not usually." Not after wine poisoned Matthew.

"You'll want to have some water before you go to bed tonight," he said. "And a painkiller of some kind."

"Painkiller. What a thing it would be if that were something you could have from a pill."

His eyebrows raised. "The kind I was referring to is only for physical aches and pains. The ones in our hearts are not so easily mended."

What remarkable eyes—a shade of blue that sometimes looked gray. "Are your eyes gray or blue?" I asked.

Whatever color they were, they drew me in, made me forget we were with the others. They were soft and inviting, yet exuded intelligence. Why were some eyes like that when others were bland and forgettable?

"Blue, mostly. I think," Breck said.

"They're nice."

"Thanks. Yours are nice too." Was it pity I saw in his face? A man like Breck Stokes wouldn't understand what it was like to be me. Not with the way his life had been laid out in a neat arrangement from the beginning. His mother loved him. Innate talents he knew exactly what to do with. And there was the nurturing sun shining down on Emerson Pass and growing sweet little boys into strong, good men.

"They told me at Briar Rose that my eyes were unusual. The color." I tapped just under my right eye. Words were not coming easily but I soldiered on, suddenly wanting more than anything to make Breck understand me. "The women told me no one had ever seen eyes like mine. They'd said it with a hint of malice. My father didn't have them. Or my mother. The women told me that too. My mother's name was Mona. I know that much. And she didn't have light blue eyes."

"Do you have a photograph of her?" Breck positioned himself so that one of his arms rested on the couch cushion as his hand cradled one cheek. A line between his eyes crinkled as he studied me.

"No, I don't. I don't know anything about her. Except that they took her from me." Had my mother been nurturing?

Perhaps her motherly instinct is what prompted her to risk it all and make a run for it with me in her arms. How did she carry me? Like a football, maybe, so she would have one arm free to climb the fence. How had she not known it was electric? Not that it mattered in the end.

She'd known. Of course, she'd known. She'd risked dying to get over that fence to freedom.

"I'm sorry," Breck said. He sounded far away. I'd lost him. Lost myself.

I'd told them all too much. After all this time keeping my secret, it had certainly spilled out of my drunken mouth tonight. Alcohol was the devil. An evil master that loosened lips. I would regret all of it when I woke in the morning. However, at the moment, I was too drunk to muster up any real angst. I was tired, bone weary from keeping myself sealed tight. No one could get in, not really. Without spilling my secrets, how could I ever explain who I was or how I'd come to be? Now five others knew the truth. Would they wake tomorrow horrified at what they'd learned? Would I lose the only friends I'd ever had?

It wasn't enough. This shadow of a life. This hiding all the time. The faces around me, although blurred, didn't live in the darkness, afraid to step into the light and become seen. I wanted that too.

I lifted my gaze back to Breck. He was a good person, one with integrity and compassion. Would he realize how selfish I'd been? Perhaps I repulsed him because of it? This was a man who'd opened a dog and cat shelter. He would have done the right thing.

Stop thinking about all of this, I commanded myself.

"I don't want anyone else to know about me," I whispered.

"Don't worry about that," Breck said. "No one here tonight tells stories that aren't theirs to tell."

"How do you know?"

"I just do."

Stormi appeared on the other side of the table. Actually, it was two Stormis, wobbling like bobbleheads. "You okay, babe?"

"I see two of everything," I said, giggling. "Two Stormis. Two Brecks."

"Okay, then," Stormi said. "Time for someone to go home."

"How much did she have?" Breck asked.

I held up my fingers. "Three. Two wines and one beer."

"One beer too many," Stormi said.

I giggled again. "You're funny."

"Do you want to go home?" Stormi asked.

"I probably should." My head was heavy, like a bowling ball. It fell against Breck's thick shoulder. I closed my eyes, but everything started spinning so I opened them again.

"I'm going to walk her next door," Breck said.

"We should go with her," Jamie said from somewhere in the room. So far away.

"Jamie?" I asked. "Where are you?" I lifted my head to look around. There she was, in one of the chairs. Her hair had loosened from its ponytail and left tendrils around her heart-shaped face. "Barbie doll." I turned to Breck. "She looks like a Barbie, don't you think? The prettiest one of all."

"She's pretty," Breck said. "No doubt about that."

"Thanks," Jamie said. "Now, maybe get Chatty over there home and put to bed?"

"Are you sure you don't want me to take her?" Stormi asked not me but Breck. He was in charge, apparently. That's what happened with drunk girls, I supposed. Usually I took people home.

"No, stay," I said to Stormi. "Have fun. Breck and his big muscles can take me home."

"Make sure she doesn't get sick," Stormi said. "She might be."

"I'll stay with her," Breck said. "Until I'm sure she's all right."

Still resting against the sofa cushion, I rolled my head to

look over at him. The fabric of the couch was rough against my cheek. "I'm sorry."

"Don't be. It happens to all of us at one time or the other." He brought his legs out from under the table. As he rose, he bumped a shin against the table. "Come on. Let's get you home and get some water in you."

"Ibuprofen," I said, slurring. It was such a hard word to say. I'd never noticed that before. I giggled thinking about the funny word. It was too long. No one would be able to spell it.

"Up you go." Breck took both my hands and helped me to my feet. "Let's go see Muffy."

Muffy. My best friend. She would be happy to see me, even if I was not in the finest form. "Lead the way."

BRECK UNLOCKED my door and held it open for me to enter. "Home sweet home."

"How do you have my key?" I asked.

"You gave it to me," he said. "Just a minute ago."

"I don't remember that." I didn't remember to say thank you to Darby. Did I say goodbye to anyone? "I forgot to thank Darby for his hospitality." I forgot all about that when Muffy came running from the bedroom, ears flopping.

"Muffy's here," I said.

Breck led me over to my couch. "Sit here. I'm going to get you some water and some ibuprofen."

I giggled. "It's above the toaster. There's bandages, too, but I never need them."

"Be right back." He strode across the living room to the kitchen. I tilted my head and closed one eye. No reason to miss watching that delicious bottom in his jeans. *Tiffany*, I chided myself. *What's the matter with you? A few drinks and you become a connoisseur of derrieres?*

"All right then, enough of that," I said out loud. *Sit up.* My body didn't listen, sliding sideways until I was resting one cheek against the wide arm of my couch. Muffy jumped up and snuggled next to me. She licked my hand. "I love you, Muffy. I probably don't say it enough." I wanted to close my eyes, but the spinning kept happening.

"Here, drink this all down, then I'll help you to bed." Breck was back. All of him. His legs seemed to go on forever. He sat next to me and pulled me upright.

I drank greedily. Nothing had ever tasted sweeter. "Did you put sweetener in it? So sweet and delicious. Very refreshing."

"No, it's from the tap." The corners of his eyes crinkled. Smiling. He smiled a lot. Such a handsome face.

"How come you don't have a girlfriend?" I asked. Why didn't he? Maybe he did. "Do you have a girlfriend?"

"I do not have one, and I don't know why." He wedged a throw pillow between me and the arm of the couch. Muffy crawled onto his lap. His fingers scratched behind her ears.

I was like a piece of toast between the rungs of a metal rack, only it was lovely Breck and a soft pillow I was between. Much nicer than cold metal, I figured. "But you're good-looking and nice and smart. You have the best job in the whole world. You should take out Stormi. Or Jamie. Either one." I took another sip of water. "This is especially delicious." Had I already said that? Maybe.

"Good, drink it all down."

When I finished, Breck took the glass from me and set it on the coffee table. My shabby chic table I'd refinished myself. "Do you like my table?"

"Sure, it's cute."

"I painted it myself. This whole place is like a French country cottage I saw in a magazine. I learned a lot of things from magazines. We didn't have those at Briar Rose. When I became an adult, I used to cut out photographs from magazines

and put them in a box. Dreams into a box, that's what it was." I
hiccupped. "Isn't Muffy a good girl?"

"Absolutely." He stood, holding Muffy to his shoulder like
she was a human baby. Her little tail wagged with joy. She loved
Breck Stokes. *Dr.* Stokes. My boss. I almost groaned at the idea
of seeing him on Monday.

He helped me from the couch and kept me close as we
headed toward the bedroom. Once there, I sank onto the bed.
My glorious bed with its white-quilted comforter and light
yellow pillows. I'd wanted the look of a daisy, and I thought I'd
done a fine job. Slumped over, I looked down at my feet. How
was I supposed to take off my shoes in this state? "Can you help
with my shoes?"

"Sure," he said.

I collapsed onto the bed. My legs dangled from the side.
Above me, the ceiling fan remained motionless. In the summer,
I would turn it on at night. "You're a very pleasant man. Very
very pleasant."

From the floor, he tugged my ankle boots off my feet. "Do
you want socks off too?"

"Yes, please. Socks and sheets don't mix."

He pulled the socks from my feet. "In you go, then."

I jerked upright and pressed my feet into the area rug and
with great effort, rose to my feet. I stumbled and fell against his
hard chest.

One arm wrapped around my waist. "Come here." He
swung me up and into his arms, as if he were a groom about
to walk me over the threshold. If only I could get a proper
look at his face, but everything was too blurry. "Steady as
we go."

He'd somehow pulled back the covers. Gently, he set me
down on the sheet. They weren't cool, though. I liked to feel the
soft sheets next to my skin. These jeans were in the way. I
wanted them off. But how could I tug them off in this state?

"What is it?" Breck pulled the top sheet and quilt over my shoulder.

"I can't sleep with these pants on."

"Are you sure? Just this once?" Breck asked.

"No, I won't be able to sleep."

"All right. Hang on. I'll help."

"Don't look at my skin," I said.

"I'll do my best." Breck used the same voice with me that he did with Muffy when I brought her into the clinic. I was just another one of his furry patients. Only I had no fur. That caused me to giggle again.

"What's so funny?" He pushed back the covers.

"That I have no fur." Muffy whined as she settled on her side of the bed. "See? Muffy thinks that's terrible."

"You don't need fur. You're perfect the way you are." His fingers undid the top button of my jeans and tugged at the zipper. "Darn, it's stuck."

"These jeans are tight, that's why. They wear them tight out here in the world." I sucked in my stomach and took over for him. But my fingers were too clumsy. They were useless bloated sausages. "You'll have to pull them off. My pants, that is." I barked out another laugh. "I've never had a man take off my pants before. Do you find that strange?"

He muttered something I couldn't hear. Seconds later, his fingers reached under the waist of the jeans and tugged. Fingers on my skin. Did he touch a lot of human skin, or just furry pets? Probably just pets. He was the pet doctor. Muffy's doctor. My new boss.

Oh God, my new boss.

His thumbs were inside my jeans as he tugged. How was I aware of that when I couldn't focus on anything for more than a second? "I don't know," I whispered to myself.

"Don't know what?" Breck asked.

"How come your fingers feel so good."

"Oh." A whiff of his breath warmed the bare skin of my belly. He grunted as he tugged my jeans down to my knees. Little by little, he inched them from my hips and then, finally, pulled them all the way off in a dramatic swoop.

Cold air hit my bare legs. What panties did I have on? Could he see them? "I think they're lace."

"What's that?"

"My underwear."

"I'm not looking," Breck said. His face loomed over me. "See here, my eyes are on your face."

Why was that disappointing? Never mind. I wasn't thinking straight.

"I don't know what I don't know." I turned to my side and wrapped my arms together. I was more thankful for the soft pillow than I'd ever been, and that was saying something. We'd had hard pillows, stuffed with old rags, at Briar Rose. *No, don't think of it. Just go to sleep.*

"That makes two of us." Breck knelt on his knees. "What can I do? Anything? Do you feel sick?"

I closed my eyes. It was as if I were on a twirling boat. I opened my eyes, hoping to make it stop. Breck was there, watching me, concern in his eyes. "Everything's spinning. Do you know how to make it stop?"

"Just sleep it off. That's the best way."

"Jamie threw up once when she was like this," I said. "I'm never going to do this ever again. I'm very sorry."

He brushed wisps of my hair away from my face. "You already said that."

"I'm afraid." My vision no longer saw double. Now it was as if I were looking out a window with water dripping down the glass.

"Of what?" Breck tucked a bunch of my hair behind my shoulder.

"Everything. Everybody. Being alone."

"That's not unusual. We all feel that at one time or the other."

"Not you." I shook my head. "You have everything."

"Not everything but a lot. I'm blessed, yes."

"What do you want that you don't have?" I asked.

"Love, I suppose. Romantic love. A partner."

"You'll have that soon. I know you will."

The corners of his mouth twitched into a smile. "I hope you're right. For now, though, I want you to get some sleep. I'm going to be right here in case you need me."

"Why would you do that?"

"Because I like you," he said.

"Thank you." I closed my eyes. "Still spinning."

"I'll get you a bowl."

As his footsteps thudded across the floor I wondered out loud, "A bowl of what?"

Then I passed out.

I JERKED AWAKE. For a second, everything was black and still. Where was I? My fingers felt for the familiar stitching in the quilt. Okay, I was home in bed. All was well. Except for this throbbing in my head and a thirst I'd never before experienced. What had happened? The party. Wine and beer. The room spinning. Breck had been here. He'd tucked me in. I had no pants on. A fuzzy memory returned. He'd helped me undress. We'd had trouble with my jeans. The zipper had stuck. Oh God, he'd taken my jeans off? Had I said something about my panties having lace? Had he seen my legs without clothes, or had it been dark? I don't think it was dark. Oh, no, no, no. What if he'd gotten the wrong idea?

Shame and embarrassment seeped from my pores and soaked my blouse. The underwire of my bra pressed into my flesh. I reached over to feel for Muffy. She was there, soft and asleep.

I groaned and turned onto my back, which caused a whole new level of pain in my head, so I rolled back to my side. That was no good, either. I sat up. The room no longer spun. I had that going for me. But good Lord, my churning stomach and this bitter, acrid taste in my mouth. Obviously, I'd had way too much alcohol. What time was it? Not morning. Not yet. In the spring, it was light in the mornings and birds chirped.

I turned toward the table where I kept my phone in the charger. Thank goodness, my phone was there. I hadn't managed to lose it as well as my mind. I pressed the screen to see that it was half-past three in the morning. I tossed back the covers to cool, waking Muffy, who whined as if complaining. "Sorry, honey," I whispered, as I rubbed her head with my thumb. She sighed, already on her way back to sleep.

If only I could do the same.

A noise from the corner of the bedroom startled me. Heart pounding, I squinted into the dark and made out the form of a man in my chair. Breck. He'd stayed?

"You all right?" Breck asked. "Do you need more water?"

"I think so."

"I'll be right back. I should've put some by your bed. Sorry about that." He disappeared for a moment. Long enough that while I waited I remembered the events of the evening. The news. My father's death. I'd told my friends about my past. I dropped my head into my hands and tried to talk myself out of vomiting.

The shadow of Breck appeared in the doorway. "Do you feel sick? There's a bowl right below you. On the floor."

"I think I'm all right. My head feels like it's in a vise."

"Yeah, that's the hangover." He perched on the side of the bed. "Drink this and take some more Advil."

More? Had he already given me some? After I swallowed the

pills and drank the rest of the water, I gave it back to him. "Thanks for helping me. I'm mortified."

"Don't be. It happens."

"Why are you still here?"

"I didn't want to leave you alone. You should never leave a drunk friend. Not safe."

I'd always left Stormi and Jamie to sleep alone when they'd been inebriated. Was I not supposed to? "There's so much I don't know. About this kind of thing."

"You said that before," Breck said.

"I did?"

"Sort of."

I wanted to rub my eyes but knew I'd gone to bed with my makeup on. Jamie said I'd pull the lashes out that way. "Did I tell you guys all about Briar Rose?" I asked, hoping it was a dream but knowing it wasn't.

"Yeah. But it's not a big deal. We all have stuff, you know, from our past, that's hard."

"Do you?"

"Sure. No one in that room tonight doesn't have some grief or darkness to contend with."

I put my hand over my mouth. My breath must smell terrible. "I should brush my teeth."

"Do you want me to help?"

"I don't think it's possible to help someone brush their teeth."

"Right, that's only animals." He grinned.

"Right." Despite my aching head, I smiled. Gingerly, careful not to make any sudden moves that would worsen my symptoms, I pulled back the covers and got out of bed. Too late, I remembered my pants-less state. There I stood, almost naked, in front of Breck. I didn't even know where my pants were. The cool air against my warm skin made me shiver. The longer I stood here, the more Breck saw. "I'll just go this way." I pointed toward the bathroom before racing across the room and into the bathroom. Did my butt cheeks flap around without pants to cover them? Probably.

Once inside, I closed the door and leaned against it. My blouse clung to my overheated chest and back. Bile rose to the back of my throat. What had I done? My careful secrets spilled all over the floor for all to see? And a man in my apartment? Undressing me?

I looked down at my underwear. Horrors, they were big, cotton, and ragged. Was that a hole by the crotch? At least he wouldn't have seen much, not with these grandma panties. Other than what he could see through that hole.

I used the toilet, then went to the sink. My reflection in the mirror was of a girl I didn't recognize. Mascara smeared into muddy smudges on my cheeks. Tangled hair fell limply around my shoulders. Purple shadows under my eyes made me look like a woman on a bender.

I washed my face, brushed my teeth, and combed my hair. The mint of the toothpaste refreshed me somewhat. I drank more water using my hands as a cup. With deft fingers, I braided my hair. When I returned my gaze to the mirror, I looked a little more like myself.

A nightgown hung on the hook over the door. As I slipped it over my head, the thought occurred to me—why hadn't I suggested Breck leave just now? The poor man probably yearned for his own bed.

Selfish. Inconsiderate. Is this what alcohol did to a person? I would never drink again. It had made me into a different woman. A big-mouthed, secret-telling person.

When I returned to my room, feeling considerably better than I had moments ago, I was surprised to see that Breck had fallen asleep on Muffy's side of the bed. As for her, she was curled up between his chest and arm just as happy as she could be. She didn't even lift her head when I came to stand at the end of the bed.

Watching them sleep filled me with a strange sense of peace. Breck looked young and vulnerable and as pretty as a full moon on an August night. Muffy had made herself into a ball of fur and looked even cuter than usual wrapped against Breck's wide torso. How was Briar Rose possible when there was such beauty as this?

I shook my head. What was it with this Breck Stokes? Was he one of the last true gentlemen left in the world? A man with less moral character might have taken advantage of me, given my drunken state. I wiped more of the shame sweat from my forehead. What should I do now?

I wanted to climb back into bed and be part of the picture before me.

I'd never had a man stay the night. This wasn't the type of staying over that Jamie and Stormi did. Both had gone home with men from the bar on various occasions. I hadn't slept a wink afterward, imagining all kinds of things that could happen to them. They were fine, thankfully. But I couldn't understand why they would take the risk. Or how they would ever feel comfortable going home with a stranger. As much as I'd adjusted to life on the outside, there were still aspects of the modern world I didn't understand. I was like a time traveler in a book. Never quite comfortable in this unfamiliar world.

I glanced through the open door of my bedroom to the living room. The couch was there. My sweating had now made me cold. Going out to the other room would require me to take a blanket with me. I didn't keep the heat on at night, preferring to snuggle under the covers for warmth. If I were to take the comforter from my bed, I'd wake him. He was probably exhausted from looking after me.

I'd just slip between the covers. What harm could come from that? It wasn't like a man like Breck would be interested in me. He was a doctor from a good family. A solid citizen and lover of abandoned animals. A good man. Not a boy in any sense of the word.

I grabbed the extra blanket from the chair and placed it over him. It was cold in here, and he had a short-sleeved shirt on with his jeans. As quietly as possible, I got back in bed, scooting as far as I could onto my side of the mattress.

The bed moved. I felt rather than saw Breck turning over on his side. In the dark, I couldn't tell if his eyes were open or closed. I held my breath.

"You awake?" Breck whispered.

"Yeah. Did I wake you?"

"Yes, but I didn't mean to fall asleep. This bed is very comfortable. Do you have one of those mattress toppers?"

"I do. It's nice, right?"

"I like the stars too."

My eyes had adjusted to the dark, and I could see his hand gesture to my ceiling. I'd fastened glow-in-the-dark stars and a quarter-moon above my bed. It had gotten to the point that I never even noticed them. "It must seem childish to you."

"Not at all," he said. "In fact, my mom did the same with my ceiling when I was a kid."

"When you were a kid."

"Whatever. If more adults remembered what they loved as kids, we might not be in the state we're in. Everyone should remember to play and do things that make them happy for no real reason other than they like it."

"Like my stars," I said softly.

"I should go. Now that you're okay."

"You don't have to. It's late…or early. And dark."

"I should never have lain down on this bed. Rookie mistake."

"What does that mean? Rookie mistake?" I asked.

"You know what a rookie is, right?"

"Yeah, in sports or whatever. Someone new."

"Right. I can sleep anywhere." Breck chuckled. "I knew if I

lay down I might fall asleep, but it just looked so cozy next to Muffy."

"She is pretty cozy." I smiled. "Thanks for taking care of me. I'm very embarrassed."

"You shouldn't be. You're the cutest drunk I've ever met."

"Have you met a lot of them?" I asked.

He laughed softly. "No, not really. I meant that you're cute when you let loose a little—without all the walls you make around yourself."

I thought about that for a moment. People noticed how careful I was? Or, at least, Breck did. "I can't believe I told you guys all that stuff."

"I'm glad you did," he said.

"Why?"

"Because it makes us feel closer to you."

"Oh." I hadn't thought about it from that angle.

"It explains things about you," he said.

"It does?"

"Sure. You're different. Innocent maybe? I don't know how to explain it."

We were quiet for a second or two. "Are you warm enough?" I asked.

"Yeah, I'm fine. Thanks."

"Good." I drew the covers up to my chin but stayed on my side. I could just make out his bulk in the dark room. Apparently, the bed had shrunk with him in it.

"If you ever want to talk about things, I'm here," Breck said.

I stared up at the glowing plastic stars as teardrops gathered at the corners of my eyes. "Thank you. That's very kind."

"And for the record, I hope they nail each and every one of the bastards." He turned on his side. "I'm also grateful you got out."

"Me too."

"I can't imagine what it must have been like," Breck said. "Coming into this whole new world."

"Yes, even after ten years, I'm still surprised by certain things."

"Like what?"

"Television, movie theaters, libraries full of books with no censored on them. Junk food. Grocery stores packed with any kind of food a person could afford. Pets."

"It's funny when you list them that way—how normal stuff is actually so miraculous."

"That's the gift of my past. I notice all the small and large blessings of an ordinary life. I'm grateful for being able to be normal, at least on the outside."

"No one feels normal on the inside, regardless of their upbringing."

"Even you?"

I felt him shift again. "Sure. There are defining moments in every life, ones that shape us into the people we become. My dad died of cancer when I was fifteen. That was the abrupt end of my childhood. I never felt young again."

"I'm sorry," I said.

"Thanks. I miss him every day."

My eyes grew heavy as I lay there. "Good night, Breck."

"Good night. Sweet dreams." Seconds later, he was snoring softly.

I thought I would lie there until the light of dawn crept under the shades, but I was wrong. As if epic sleeping were contagious, I fell fast asleep.

I WOKE to the smell of brewed coffee and bacon. For a moment, I couldn't fathom how those scents were coming from my kitchen. Last night. Drinking. Breck in my bed. I rolled over.

There was a dent in the pillow where his head had lain. No Muffy, though. The little social butterfly was not in her usual spot. She'd followed either him or the smell of those slabs of fatty pork.

Even though I'd brushed my teeth and washed my face, I still felt disgusting. I locked the bathroom door and started the shower. He felt comfortable enough to make breakfast? Was this odd or thoughtful? Or maybe it was another social norm I didn't truly understand. If a friend stayed over that meant they made breakfast? He was a friend. A male buddy. Who was staying over to make breakfast for his hungover friend.

As I stood under the hot water of the shower, I thought more about what I'd learned on the news. It had all been too much. Thus, the alcohol. Sometimes I drank a glass of wine on the nights we went out but never more. I didn't feel the desire. Last night, however, I wanted to make the memories disappear. I wanted to numb out everything. It didn't work.

I scrubbed my long hair and conditioned the ends, all with my eyes closed, wishing I didn't have to face the long day alone. I would not be able to keep from turning on the television. It would be impossible.

Another thought struck me as I reached for my shaver. What if the FBI came to me to ask questions? Now that I thought about it, why hadn't they before now? If they'd been investigating for months, it seemed that they would want to talk to someone from the inside.

Maybe they didn't know about me. How could they, after all? I'd been erased by the community. When I'd gone to the first shelter and told the women there my story, they'd known how to get a Social Security card and ultimately, a driver's license using a new name. We had no record of my birth, since I was born on the compound, but somehow they'd gotten around that. Thank God, or where would I be now?

After I towel-dried my hair and dressed in loose, soft jeans and a sweater, I went into the kitchen. Breck was there, leaning against the sink while chewing on a piece of bacon.

"Good morning." I knelt to pick up Muffy for a snuggle. She wagged her tail and licked my neck before I set her back down.

"I hope you don't mind," Breck said, looking a bit sheepish. "I ran to the store and got a few things for breakfast."

"The smell of bacon is not something I wake up to often." Or ever.

"Do you need another Advil?" Breck asked. He pointed at my small kitchen table where two pink pills sat next to a glass of orange juice. "I'll pour you some hot coffee. How do you like your eggs?"

"Fried? Hard. I hate runny yolk." I sat at the table and drank from the orange juice glass. A burst of sweet, tangy citrus hit my tongue. "This is incredible."

"I squeezed it myself."

"You did?" I glanced around the kitchen. I didn't see proof of oranges or a juicer anywhere. How had he done it?'

"I'm just teasing you. It's the fancy kind, though. Lots of pulp." He set a steaming cup of coffee in front of me. "Cream or sugar?"

"Just black." The pink pills glistened under the lights. I popped them in my mouth, then chased them with juice. "I actually don't feel as bad as I did earlier."

"I'm glad. Some food will help too." He slid a plate with toast and bacon in front of me. "Give me a second for the eggs."

While I nibbled on my toast, he went back to the stove and cracked eggs into a skillet. The sound of eggs sizzling seemed especially loud. "I've never had a hangover. It's not too fun."

He flipped the eggs without a spatula. "Yeah. Every time I think, never again. But then I forget and do it again. Not like I used to when Huck, Trapper, and I were young. We had some wild nights."

"Here? When you were in high school?"

"No, not then. When we were all three at college. We spent most breaks together. Either skiing or someplace tropical."

That must have been nice. Having the money to go on trips instead of paying for peanut butter and cheap bread to stay alive.

"What did I say?" Breck asked. "You went quiet."

"What? Nothing." I bent my head over the steam of the coffee and breathed in the nutty scent. "It must have been nice to have friends like that."

"It was. Still is. Those two would do anything for me." He flipped the eggs, giving me a chance to admire his backside. I didn't know what this was exactly, but it felt good to have him in my kitchen.

I picked up a piece of bacon and waited for what would happen next. So far, this weekend was full of surprises. Some good, some bad. It wasn't a mystery which side the man in my kitchen fell in the scheme of things. Good. Definitely good.

8

BRECK

"May I join you at the table?" I'd taken a huge risk to invite myself to stay at her home on a Saturday morning and make breakfast in her kitchen. If it had been one of the other girls, I wouldn't have hesitated. However, Tiffany was not an ordinary girl. And how I felt about her wasn't how I felt about the others.

"Yes, you made the food, after all." She gestured toward the other chair.

I sat across from her with a plate of eggs. I'd already devoured two slices of toast earlier. My neck was stiff from sleeping on the chair for much of the night. I used a hand to stretch my head from one side to the other.

"Is your neck bothering you?" Tiffany's brow wrinkled.

Could she be any cuter? "A little stiff, that's all." I waved my hand to show her how inconsequential it was.

"Sleeping in a chair will do that to you."

"It's no problem, really."

"This is delicious." She smiled and picked up her fork. "I'm not used to a full breakfast. Thank you."

"I know it was presumptuous to stay this morning." How

could I explain I hadn't wanted to leave without talking to her first? "I hope I haven't overstepped."

"Well, it's unexpected. Last night was too. But I liked having you there." She broke a piece of toast in two and held a piece in each hand. "Facing the day alone is hard. Sometimes, anyway. Days like…this."

"Yeah." Especially when you'd had a bomb like the one she'd had yesterday. "Your life kind of went upside down yesterday." I scooped a teaspoon of sugar into my coffee. The spoon made a clanging sound against the cup as I stirred.

"This is good coffee," she said. "I've been too broke to get anything decent."

"It's my favorite."

"Are you always like this?" She tilted her head, staring at me with eyes the color of a frozen pond under a blue sky.

"Like what?"

"Taking care of everyone."

"Yeah, I guess so. It's my default mode." After my dad had died, I'd stepped in to take care of my mother. Even if she wouldn't admit to it. "My dad was a nurturer type. I got it from him. Is it annoying?"

"Not at all. Why would you ask that?"

"Huck and my mother say I get on their nerves," I said. "Fussing over them."

"They don't think they need you, but they do," Tiffany said. "If you ever stopped, there would be this huge void in their lives."

"You think?" I faced her, vulnerable, wishing for reassurance. This was not typical of me. I didn't need others to validate me. But this woman? I wanted desperately for her to like me.

"Yeah, for sure. Like cats. They don't appreciate you until you're gone."

I laughed. "That too."

"They don't know how lucky they are." She waved a piece of bacon at me. "This isn't what you normally eat, is it?"

"No. How did you know?"

"I've noticed."

She'd noticed what I ate. This was a good sign, wasn't it? We ate in silence for a moment. What could we talk about? My mother was a quiet person, as was Huck. It was often nearly silent in the mornings at my house, all three of us with our nose in a book. This silence felt different, like it needed to be filled.

"Are you looking forward to Monday?" I asked.

"Monday?" She looked at me with a blank expression.

"The clinic. Your new job."

She flushed a lovely shade of pink. "Right. Sure. I'm grateful for the work."

"How come you have so little in your refrigerator?" I asked.

"Same reason I needed a job at your clinic."

"That bad?"

"Yes, that bad." She ate the rest of her toast and then finished off her eggs.

I wanted to ask her questions. What was it like to grow up in that environment? How many wives did her father have? Did she have siblings? Had she ever heard from any of them? What about the boy she'd loved? Did she still mourn him? Was it a love that remained even though so much time had passed?

She sucked in her bottom lip before looking up at me. "I know you have a lot of questions."

"Only because I'm nosy. You don't have to tell me a thing." I put my hands up in the air in a gesture of submission.

"Maybe some other time. Not now." She rubbed her temples. "When I don't have such a headache."

"You'll feel better by the afternoon. Take it easy today." I needed to go before she got really sick of me. "I should get home."

"Finish your coffee, at least?"

"Sure. Will do." I crossed one leg over the opposite knee. *Ask her out, idiot.* Now was the time. "Hey, would you ever want to get dinner sometime?"

She blinked and pushed her long hair behind her shoulders. "A friend dinner or a date?"

"A date. I mean, that's what I'd hope it to be. If you said yes. Which you don't have to. We can stay friends if that's all you want."

"I'll be working for you. Isn't that inappropriate?"

"You're technically working for Scooter. Second, it's only a temporary position."

She smiled and poked her fork into a bit of leftover egg. "I suppose that's true. This is a small town. There's a lot of gossip. Everyone would talk."

"Would that bother you?" I asked.

"No, I don't think so. It's just something to consider."

"Have you dated anyone since you've been here?"

She looked at me blankly, as if I'd asked her something outlandish. "No, I don't really date."

"Why?"

"It's not something I thought would happen. I mean, look at me."

I'm looking at you, I thought. *I love what I see.* "I'm not sure what you mean."

"I'm strange. I've never thought anyone would like me."

"You're not that strange," I said. "And I like you. I've liked you for a while now."

"You have?"

"I've wanted to ask you out but never got the courage up."

"Really?" She grinned.

"Really."

"You don't think I'm weird?"

"Maybe I'm weird too. Most people are, one way or the other. If you dig under the surface, you'll find something they're ashamed of, or regret doing, or yearn for. We're all walking around pretending everything's a peach pie while inside we're more like a garbage disposal."

Her face crinkled right before she laughed. "I've never heard that analogy before."

"I just made it up." I laughed. "I'm a vet, not a poet. Anyway, you get my point. Most everyone has a burden of some kind."

She pointed a finger at me. Her nails were short, filed into half-circles, and painted pink. "You seem light as air."

I jiggled my foot against my knee. "Not really. I have things."

"Like what?"

I looked down at my hand resting on my knee. My knuckles were red and chapped from all the washing I did at work. "Sometimes I imagine I'm walking around with a large chunk of my middle missing. I'm amazed others can't see it."

"You hide it well."

"Is that good?" I asked.

"I don't know."

"Can I ask you something personal?"

"You've already seen me at my worst, so go ahead," she said.

"Why didn't you ask one of your friends for a loan so you could buy some groceries?"

She studied her plate for a moment before answering. "Because people like me don't ask for favors. And don't ask me what that means, because I can't explain it."

"Fair enough."

"My turn to ask a question?" Tiffany asked.

"Ask me anything."

"Why would you let Huck live with you? And does he make you as mad as he seems to make everyone else?"

"He's difficult, I know. But we've been friends all our lives. He's been through some hard stuff. He was always reticent and not exactly an optimist, but he wasn't like he is now. Something in Afghanistan changed him. Made him dark and hopeless."

"You're a good friend to him." She stood to pull Muffy into her arms. "You were a good friend to me last night too. I can't thank you enough. If you have any mending that needs done, please don't hesitate to call."

Mending? "Like shirts?"

"Yes, or pants. I'm not a knitter, though, so no sweaters."

I stared at her for a second, sure she was joking, but the seriousness in her eyes told me otherwise. I hadn't met many women in our age group who mended shirts. Mostly, we just tossed things in the trash if they ripped. Or turned them into rags to wash our cars. "I'll keep that in mind. Thank you."

"And dinner would be nice." She hugged Muffy closer to her chest.

"Excellent. Are you free tonight?" I put up my hands to stop her from answering. "Never mind. That's too soon, isn't it? You might still have a headache."

"We'll see." She walked me to her front door and stood waiting while I slid my feet into my shoes.

"Take care of yourself," I said. "I'll call you or text you about that date."

"Okay." She dipped her chin to gaze at the floor. Muffy's tail wagged from her arms.

"And you call anytime if you need to talk." I reached over to give Muffy a quick pat on the head.

"I'm going to leave the television off," she said. "That should help."

We said our goodbyes, and I headed out to my car, which was parked on the street not far from her building. I glanced up at her window before ducking into my car. She was standing there with Muffy in her arms, watching me. I waved. She waved back at me.

I smiled all the way home.

❄

I DECIDED to head home to shower and change before visiting the shelter. Yawning, I drove home in the brilliant morning light. Days like today made me wonder how heaven could beat this. Wildflowers scattered in the meadows. Snow covered the very tips of the north and south mountains. I rolled the window down a few inches to let the scent of freshly mown grass and flowers into the truck. Spring in Emerson Pass. Full of possibilities. Baby sheep and cows ate grass from the meadows and pastures as I drove down the country road toward my mother's home.

I turned down the driveway, bouncing along in the gravel and holes. I made a mental note to call the guys who'd filled the holes last spring.

Mom and Huck were sitting at the kitchen island when I came in as if waiting for their breakfast at a diner. Both reading from tablets, neither looked up to greet me. Did they have absolutely no interest in where I'd been all night?

"I'm home. Good morning." The aroma of freshly brewed coffee greeted me instead of my loved ones. I breathed in the smell of mornings at our house. Sunshine streamed through the bank of windows that looked out to our yard. Cherry blossoms framed the windows with nature's embroidery. "Beautiful morning."

No comments from either. They continued to gaze intently at their tablets. Huck glowered at his screen. Mom's brows were knit together, obviously concerned with whatever it was she was reading.

"Have you eaten?" Most likely, neither had had breakfast. They would live on coffee and scotch if I let them.

"We had muffins and scones," Huck said without looking at me. "Since you weren't here."

The pink box from Brandi's bakery was nowhere to be seen. "I'm not surprised you hid the evidence," I said.

"We didn't hide the box. It's in the trash because we ate them all." Huck looked up at me long enough to answer but then returned to reading.

Mom glanced up to give me a preoccupied smile. "Oh, hi, sweetheart. I didn't hear you come in. Can you believe this Briar Rose story? When I think about what those bastards have gotten away with it makes me hope they throw the book at them. These girls were sixteen. Children. The whole thing sickens me."

I nodded, distracted. The story was still front and center. Tiffany wouldn't be able to escape from it today. The newspapers and television would cover the story all weekend.

"I was surprised to see your car missing from the driveway this morning," Huck said.

"I stayed with Tiffany, making sure she was all right." I spoke casually, as if it weren't important at all when inside I was dying to tell them everything. "As you know."

"And one thing led to another?" Huck asked.

"Nothing happened." I was about to explain the situation when my mother actually looked up from her reading.

"You were gone all night?" This, apparently, was interesting enough to take her from the story, because she narrowed her eyes to inspect me. "So, you slept over?"

"Not like that," I said.

"Like what?" Mom peered at me from over her reading glasses.

"She had too much to drink, and I didn't want to leave her alone."

"Good boy," Mom said, encouragingly but not hiding her obvious disappointment that there wasn't more to the story. She knew I had a crush on Tiffany and had no patience for my reticence. *Go for what you want. Take what you want.* These were my mother's mottoes for most things, including romance.

"How is she this morning?" Huck asked.

"She's all right. She's tougher than she looks." I wandered

over to the coffeepot and shut down the power. They often left the pot on all day, and I'd come home to the scent of burned coffee.

"What are you talking about?" Mom crossed her arms over her chest. She hated it when she wasn't in the know about everything and everyone.

"Huck didn't tell you?" I asked.

"I just got up," Huck said. "I had a little hangover of my own. Then I got absorbed in the story. It's front page at the *New York Times* today. Darn good reporting, too. I hate them."

"What's Briar Rose have to do with Tiffany?"

I filled her in on what we'd learned last night about Tiffany's childhood. "But, Mom, she doesn't want anyone to know. She's afraid people will judge her."

"Most wouldn't, but I understand," Mom said. "She wants to put it behind her, not be the girl who grew up in the cult."

"If the FBI finds out about her, they'll call her in for questioning," Huck said. "Guaranteed. Unless she goes to them first."

Mom took off her glasses and set them on the counter. "Huck, you should get an exclusive with her. The national papers will pick it up. This could get you back in the game."

Back in the game? Did he want to be back? "I thought you were happy running the newspaper?"

"I'm never happy." Huck closed his tablet and got up from the table to pour another cup of coffee.

"You're happy," Mom said. "You're just too stupid to know it."

This was the way they talked to each other.

"You don't know the inner workings of my mind." Huck scooped two teaspoons of sugar into his coffee, then added a generous pour of half-and-half.

"You've had enough time to be miserable," Mom said. "It's time to start living the life you're meant to live. Posthaste."

Huck went back to his seat at the island, grimacing. "I have a headache."

"For heaven's sake. Is drinking all young people do these days?" Mom asked.

"Not exactly," I said.

"I think it was the scotch in my flask," Huck said. "After you left, we all passed it around while playing poker and finishing the rest of the case of beer."

"With the ladies?" I asked.

He groaned. "Yes. Of course, Stormi cleaned us all out. I should've known she'd be good at poker." Huck swiped a hand through his thick hair, waking his cowlick. "Speaking of Stormi, help me win an argument from last night. Do you think I should bring back the police blotter?"

"To the paper?" Mom asked. "Like in the old days?"

"Yes. My dad always talks about how funny they were back in the day." Huck rolled his eyes. "He's put one in his books."

"They were hilarious," Mom said. "But no, I don't think you should put them back in the paper. They cheapen your vision for the newspaper."

"That's what I thought," Huck said.

When we were kids, there had been a column in the paper with reports of police incidents. Most of the time they were about kids toilet-papering some teacher's tree or some random petty crime. Often, the criminal made a crucial mistake and got caught, which subsequently landed them squarely in the middle of the police blotter. Sometimes, though, the culprit remained a mystery and only the crime was reported. Those were the funny ones.

"How did you get Stormi home?" I asked, irritated that he'd steered the conversation away from last night.

"She stayed with Jamie." Huck opened his laptop. "I slept on Darby's couch until about four this morning."

"Circling back to Tiffany. How about it?" Mom asked Huck.

She wasn't going to let this one go. In her opinion, Huck wasn't working up to his potential. She didn't understand why people didn't just get up and get on with it. Even the horrors of war were no excuse. At least not forever. Apparently, there was an expiration date on trauma.

"Mom, let him be. He doesn't want to write it."

"I might want to." Huck placed both hands on the counter and hung his head, obviously thinking it through for a few seconds before popping back up with his answer. "But I'm the last person Tiffany would tell her story to."

"Were you rude to her last night?" Mom asked matter-of-factly. She knew him well. "You alienated her, didn't you?"

"He was totally rude," I said. "More than usual."

"Tattletale," Huck said to me. "If you must know, I called her vanilla, which then caused her to spill her guts to us about her childhood."

"You used an interview tactic on her?" Mom nodded as if she knew anything about reporting. "Tricky."

"Not purposefully," Huck said. "It was just one of those things that came out of my mouth."

I shot him a look that I wished could hit him like a punch. "One that should have *stayed* in your mouth."

"I know, all right?" Huck's expression darkened. "As usual, I self-sabotaged what could have been a life-changing project. I'd like to write a book with her story," he explained to my mother. "But after last night, there's no chance."

I immediately felt bad. Huck might seem hardened on the outside, but inside he was the sensitive and loving kid I'd grown up with.

"She probably has some issues." Mom pointed at her tablet. "Thanks to those perverts. It would be good revenge for her and probably cathartic to tell you her story."

Sharing trauma helped to heal. Maybe it would also heal Huck from whatever it was that haunted him. "I could bring it

up to her again," I said. "We're supposed to have dinner sometime soon."

"A date?" Mom asked.

"Yes, a date," I said. "Why are you staring at me like that?"

"I'm simply surprised." Mom tugged on one of her diamond
stud earrings. "You don't put yourself out there."

"When are you taking her out?" Huck asked, clearly only
interested in what I could do for him and not my love life. I
wasn't sure who was more annoying in this conversation.

"I'm not sure. I have to call her."

"Well, get on it," Mom said. "We could kill two birds with
one stone."

"What birds are those?" Huck asked.

"You would get your career back and this one might actually
get a girlfriend."

A girlfriend? Were her goals so low for me? I was aiming for
a wife.

9

TIFFANY

Breck hadn't been gone but a few minutes that morning when I noticed he'd forgotten his scarf. Somehow, it had ended up in Muffy's bed. I had a feeling I knew how it got there. Naughty pooch.

I hadn't noticed him wearing the beautiful red wool scarf last night. I brought it to my nose and gave it a sniff worthy of Muffy at the dog park. Indeed, I could smell his spicy cologne within the fiber. I admit, I lingered a little longer than necessary.

A thrill of excitement darted through me at the memory of his long body draped across my bed. Would my pillow smell like him too?

He might need this scarf before I saw him again on Monday. "Should we take it out to him?"

Muffy tilted her head and whined.

"You think I should just call him?"

She barked and wagged her tail.

"No? You think I should drive out to their place and give it to him in person? You're probably right. He might need it tonight, and he wouldn't know where he left it. That could be a total disaster. What's a man to do without his wool scarf?"

Muffy dropped to the floor and showed me her belly.

"All right, fine. You've convinced me."

In addition, I needed something to do to keep my mind off Briar Rose. It had nothing to do with me anymore. I had a life here. A cute boy had asked me out on a date. I had a job that would pay the bills coming due. Briar Rose was my past.

At that moment, we were headed down the country road toward Breck's home. I hadn't been there before but knew the driveway from the mailbox. As I slowed the car and turned into the gravel road, Muffy barked and put her front paws on the dashboard.

"You know where we're going?"

She panted in response.

"You can love him a little," I said. "But you have to love me more. Don't forget that."

I parked next to a big black truck that I was pretty sure belonged to Huck. My stomach clenched at the thought of him. Never mind that. Whatever he thought about me didn't matter. Breck liked me. He'd asked me to dinner. After what I'd told them all last night, I had a feeling Huck would keep his opinions about me to himself.

Still, Huck made me nervous. He was a reporter. Would he be able to resist writing about me? It would be a scoop, I supposed.

Holding Muffy in my arms, I knocked on the front door. This house was so pretty. The kind I'd always admired with its brick and pillars. What had it been like to grow up here? I craned my neck to see around the side of the house. Horses grazed in the meadow. A porch swing swayed gently next to me as I waited.

Huck opened the door. His wavy hair was damp, and he was

dressed in a pair of faded jeans and blue T-shirt. "Tiffany? What are you doing here?"

Typical Huck. Blunt to the point of rudeness.

Muffy whimpered. "It's okay, girl," I said.

"I came by to see Breck." I'd folded the scarf and put it in my tote bag, which I realized now I'd left in the car. "He forgot his scarf. It's in my car." I turned my body slightly to gesture toward the driveway.

Huck scowled as his gaze moved toward the car and then back to me. His chin dipped, and his eyes dropped toward Muffy.

"Is she afraid of me?" Huck asked.

"No, she's just shy." A complete lie. She didn't like him. *Join the club*, I thought.

"Et tú, Muffy?" Huck said this with resignation in his voice.

"No, no." A sliver of sympathy crept into me. This was a lonely man—confused and angry because of whatever had happened to him in the past. I could understand that.

"Breck should be home soon if you want to wait." Huck grimaced as he scratched the back of his neck. "Which would give me a chance to apologize again for my behavior last night."

"It's all right. I don't care about that." Vanilla. Maybe I actually liked being thought of that way. "I'm glad you see that instead of what's truly there."

"Yeah, funny that. People's perceptions are sometimes very off, aren't they?"

"Some might think that's bad, but when you're trying to hide your past, not so much."

We shared a smile.

"Do you want to come in?" Huck asked.

"No, I don't want to intrude." I nodded toward the porch swing. "I'll just wait out here for him."

Huck's eyes narrowed, obviously searching for motives in

my sudden appearance. *A good reporter*, I thought. "Was the scarf an excuse to come by and see him?"

I examined the tips of my toes, painted pink. Brandi had taken me to the nail shop last week as a treat. I'd had them buffed until they shone. Even after ten years of freedom, simple things gave me a spark of pleasure.

"I don't know," I answered honestly. "Today stretched out so long before me that I needed a reason to get out of the house." I smiled and tittered under my breath. "Why did he even have a scarf last night? It was warm, wasn't it?"

"Yeah, that. He hasn't told you?"

"No. Told me what?"

"He's a total hypochondriac. Always thinks he's going to get a cold from a little breeze."

It was my turn to examine him. Was he teasing? "Is that true?"

"Heck yeah. Any little sniffle or bump and he's sure it's cancer. His dad died from it, you know. Quick, too. Diagnosed one day and dead two months later."

Two months. Breck hadn't mentioned it was that fast. "That must have been awful for him."

"It was. His dad was one of those guys the song 'Only the Good Die Young' was written for. He was the greatest."

"I'm nervous about Muffy's health all the time, so I shouldn't judge," I said.

"You have that in common then." Huck stuck his hands into his jeans pockets.

"Why would you say that? You think we don't have anything in common?" My eyes were suddenly dry and itchy as I brought my shoulders back and glowered at him in a way I hoped was menacing. Huck brought out the feistiness in my nature. Made me want to fight. Was that good or bad?

"Hey, no, that's not what I meant." He stepped backward. "I

think you have plenty in common, not that it's any of my business."

"That's right. It's not." But all the bluster had drained out of me as quickly as it had come. "What *do* you think we have in common?"

"You're both quiet, a little reserved. You're kind and smart. You love dogs." He gestured toward Muffy, who was now staring at him with slightly bulging eyes.

"So far that's only one thing. You can share qualities and still not have anything in common. Who does have anything in common with me anyway? Not that many."

"It's true. Your childhood was unique." Huck grimaced and did that same thing where he scratched at the back of his neck. "I was serious last night about writing your story."

"My story." What was he talking about? I had no recollection of this from last night.

"A book about what happened to you."

I stared at him. "A book about Briar Rose? Is that what you mean?"

He nodded and rocked back on his heels. For the first time since I arrived, I realized he didn't have shoes or socks on his feet. I fought the urge to step on his toes as he continued. "It would be interesting to people to hear what it was like to grow up there. Not to mention how you escaped and built a new life for yourself."

"How would you be able to write it if it wasn't your story?" I asked.

"That's what I do. I'm a journalist. The subject is hot right now. I think I could sell it to a publisher pretty easily. It could be lucrative for both of us." He said this as if he'd prepared the speech earlier. Did he truly want this?

"It would?" Lucrative sounded promising. Would anyone really want to hear my story?

"I could talk to my dad's agent and see if they could get us some contacts with some editors and publishing houses. Or we could put it out ourselves. We could decide later." He glanced behind me, possibly because of the rumble of a truck on the long driveway. "That's Breck now. Think about it, okay?"

"Okay, I will."

"And, once more, I'm sorry about last night." He stepped inside and closed the door behind him. I gravitated toward one of the columns and wrapped my arm around it for support. Breck's truck came to a stop next to my car. Muffy's tail started wagging the moment Breck got out and crossed toward us.

A pair of faded jeans hugged his muscular frame a little too well. A T-shirt did the same to his torso.

"Hey, Tiff. Is Muffy all right?" Breck bounded up the stairs and stopped in front of me. He put his long fingers on Muffy's head, scratching her with his thumb.

She shook with happiness and lifted her face to look at him adoringly.

"She's fine," I said. "Since you gave me those samples, she's eating much better."

"Good to hear. Did you come by to see me?" He grinned and gazed at me with twinkling eyes.

My stomach fluttered and my breath caught. Why did he have to be so effortlessly handsome? Despite his casual dress, he seemed carved from another era. The curve of his mouth made it seem that he was always smiling or at the very least, imagining something funny.

"You left your scarf." My mouth had gone dry. He smelled way too good. His biceps flexed as he gave Muffy another pat.

"That was sweet of you. It could have waited until Monday, though," Breck said. "Do you want to come in for some lemonade? Have you met my mom before?"

"Yes, at the clinic before you came home."

"Ah, right, duh." A flicker of pain crossed his face. What had that made him think of?

Muffy wriggled, obviously wanting down. Or she wanted to go to Breck. Is this what happened when a man slept over? Muffy fell in love too easily.

"It's a beautiful day," Breck said. "We could walk out to the stables. Would you want to see the horses?"

"Can Muffy go?"

"Sure she can. Come in first, though, and say hi to Mom. Where did Huck go?"

"I'm not sure," I said. "He disappeared when you arrived."

I followed him into the house and had to hold back my gasp of delight at the interiors. "What a beautiful home." I'd thought perhaps the grandeur of the exterior of the house wouldn't be reflected in the interiors. I was wrong. Dark floors and high ceilings, dramatic white trim and wainscoting matched well with expensive furniture. Or it looked expensive, anyway. We passed through the foyer and down a hallway and entered into a large kitchen. "It's like a magazine," I said, taking in the enormous island with cinnamon-flecked white granite. A pot of red sauce simmered on the six-burner cooktop. "Perfection."

Muffy barked in agreement.

Dr. Stokes sat at the island peering down at a newspaper with a pencil poised in the air. A quick look told me the paper was open to the crossword puzzle. She glanced up at us as we entered.

"Mom, you remember Tiffany and Muffy?"

"Of course. How are you?"

"Fine," I said. Not really, but there was no reason to bring all of that up. "It smells really good in here."

"Breck's making his famous sauce," Dr. Stokes said.

"It's not famous," Breck said, sounding modest. "But I do make it a lot."

"My son does most of the cooking. He thinks I'm incapable of feeding myself." Her eyes sparkled with humor. "What brings you out this way?"

"I forgot my scarf," Breck said. "Tiffany brought it out for me."

Perspiration gathered on the end of my nose. I discreetly brushed the back of my hand over the tip. "I thought he might need it."

"I'm surprised he forgot that thing," Dr. Stokes said. "It was his dad's, and he's always careful with it."

"Oh, I didn't realize that." I shuffled my feet. His dad's scarf? My heart twisted. Could this man be real?

"I was distracted by something beautiful." Breck winked at me. "Otherwise, I wouldn't have forgotten it."

I flushed again, this time with pleasure.

Breck walked around the island and opened the refrigerator. "Who wants lemonade?"

"Thank you, I'd love some." Dr. Stokes set her pen down and folded up the newspaper.

"I'm sorry to interrupt your crossword," I said.

"No worries. It's something I do to make sure I don't lose my marbles until I'm good and ready."

Breck poured us all a glass of lemonade. "I'm going to take Tiffany out to see the horses."

"Great," Dr. Stokes said. "I'll keep Muffy with me. I have a small dog bone in the pantry somewhere."

I thanked her and took the glass of lemonade from Breck. I drank thirstily. The tart and sweet of the lemons were the perfect ratio and a balm to my hangover. "It's really good." I had to forcefully keep myself from smacking my lips with pleasure. "Beats beer any day."

Breck laughed. "I make it from scratch when I have time. It's much better than anything you can get at the store."

"He spends hours on it," Dr. Stokes said. "All because of that evil corn syrup." She smoothed her long cotton skirt with her hands. Tall and thin, Dr. Stokes might have seemed austere if not for her pretty face with all the interesting symmetrical angles. A photograph on the counter drew my attention. It was of a younger Dr. Stokes in a wedding dress next to a man who looked a lot like Breck. His dad. They'd had to forge on without him. A family of two when there had once been three.

We drank the rest of our lemonade, and I left Muffy with Dr. Stokes to follow Breck outside. As we walked down the manicured walkway toward the stables, I thought about the obvious wealth on display here. Was this all from their practice, or had the money come from somewhere else? All questions I'd have to wait to ask. I didn't know how to date, but at least I knew that.

THE STOKESES HAD ONLY two horses. Both were out in the pasture happily grazing when we approached. "That's Jessie there." Breck pointed to a brown-and-white horse. She lifted her head at the sound of her name. "Hey, girl," Breck called out to her. She whinnied in response and then returned to eating. "And the other one is Rocky. They came as a pair after they retired from racing. Now they live the good life, eating grass and being pampered here at Chez Stokes."

"How did you end up with them?" I asked.

"I can't honestly remember. Mom has a lot of contacts. If I recall, she'd heard about them from a friend who said they needed a good home. She can't resist that kind of thing. Especially since my dad died."

I wanted to ask a lot of questions about his father, but I knew better. People didn't want to talk about that kind of thing with a virtual stranger.

We leaned against the fence and watched Rocky gallop across the meadow. "He looks happy," I said.

"He is." Breck turned to get a better look at me. "I'm surprised to see you. Wasn't I supposed to call you?" His eyes twinkled, teasing me.

I returned his flirtatious gaze. "I thought you might need your scarf."

"That was thoughtful of you." He rubbed a hand along the stubble of his chin. "In fact, I need it tonight. I'm going to a party tonight over at Garth and Crystal's place. They're opening up their patio for the first party of the season. But you know the temperatures will drop into the forties or even thirties. I'd hate to be caught unawares." He wriggled his brows at me.

"Huck told me you're a hypochondriac. Is that true?"

He laughed. "I'm overly concerned with health, some might say, including my mother and Huck." He shrugged. "But it's the way I am, and I don't plan to change."

"As long as it doesn't keep you from having experiences," I said.

"I don't think it does that." He turned to get a better look at me. "How are you doing with everything today?"

"I've managed to put it out my mind. Sort of, anyway. I was glad to see your scarf. It gave me a reason to get out of the house." A flush warmed my neck, as if the mere mention of the scarf had the power to spread heat. *It's not the scarf*, a voice whispered to me. *It's the man.*

"You never need an excuse. You're welcome here anytime."

I watched an ant making his way along the bottom rung of the fence. "You might regret saying that."

"Never."

We talked for a bit about the history of the property and house. "So, basically, my family's been here since the early 1900s. All of us veterinarians."

"That's pretty special."

"It is. I take it for granted sometimes until I remember how important it's been to belong somewhere."

"Huck wants to write my story," I blurted out. "What do you think about that idea?"

"It doesn't matter what I think. What do you think?"

"I'm not sure."

"Make a list of the reasons why and why not?" Breck asked. "That always helps me sort through any confusion in my mind."

"I'll do that."

"I'm glad you brought my scarf," Breck said.

"It's the least I could do after last night." How many men would take a drunk girl home and put her to bed without making a pass at her? A girl he liked well enough to ask out, no less. "I don't know how to tell you—what you did…meant a lot to me. All my life I've seen most men as predators, especially ones with power over me. Which has made me distrustful of people. Especially men. The way they organized us, women felt like a commodity, bought or sold. It's hard to believe in true love when a man has six wives, all of them younger than the next."

He covered his eyes as if there were a sight that made him sick. "I'm not a violent man, but that makes me want to…I don't know, actually. I can't think of anything physically punishing enough, but you get my point."

I did. We shared a smile.

"I'm glad you asked me to dinner too," I said. "In case you wondered."

"I've only been trying to get up the courage for a year."

"A year? No way."

"I know, pathetic, right?"

Not pathetic, I thought. *Sweet.* "What stopped you?"

"Just what you said. I could tell you weren't automatically trusting of men. I thought if I was your friend first it might help."

"You were right."

And there we were, smiling at each other like a couple of puppies in love. Wrapped up in Breck's space, sure for that moment that nothing could hurt me and that everything was going to be all right. How was it possible the world held men like Breck and Elder William all in the same breath?

10

BRECK

M onday morning started out the same as all the others, with a workout, then coffee and a shower. By the time I got to the kitchen, Mom and Huck were already there.

"What're you making us for breakfast?" Mom asked. "I'm thinking pancakes."

"How about a couple of poached eggs on wheat toast?" I asked.

"You're impossible," Mom said.

"I want you to live a long time."

"Even if I'm miserable?"

"Wheat toast doesn't make you miserable." I grabbed the carton of eggs out of the refrigerator.

Huck was muttering to himself at the table. He tortured himself by reading his former employer's newspaper every day, complaining all the while about the writing or the reporters' biases being too prevalent. One of his habitual rants was about how journalism had lost its objectivity and that it was rare to find factual reporting these days. During these diatribes, I wanted to mention that the only way to solve a problem was to participate. If he hadn't chosen to leave behind his career, he could be part of the solution. However, it wasn't that simple for Huck. His dream of becoming a war correspondent had come true, only to find it was not at all how he'd thought it would be. Thus, I kept my big trap shut. I was there to support him, not provoke him.

"Anyway, if you had pancakes, the sugar would make you crash an hour later and you'd be very cranky." I lived with two toddlers. "I bought a fresh loaf of the eight-grain bread from Brandi's bakery yesterday. So good."

When I'd moved back to town, I'd found my mother had become alarmingly thin. She was always a slender woman, but living alone had made her neglect her nutrition.

"Why eight grains?" Huck asked, looking up from his reading. "Why not nine? Or seven? And what are these grains you speak of?"

"You'd have to ask Brandi those questions," I said. "But suffice it to say, they're all grains that help you to achieve healthy bowel movements. Fiber, you know."

Huck groaned. "No one our age should talk about bowel movements."

"No one of *any* age." Mom set aside her large-print copy of a novel she'd picked up at the library. "Your father was always talking about the nutritional contents of this or that and bodily functions."

No one spoke for a moment. What she didn't say but we all thought: a lot of good healthy eating did him. He still died at age fifty.

"I'm down for that healthy toast," Huck said after an awkward beat.

I gave him a grateful glance. As difficult as Huck could be, he was loyal and caring. He loved my mother and hated to see her hurting. My dad had been gone thirteen years, and she still grieved him. Huck understood this on some deep level. He understood suffering of all kinds, for that matter. "Will do."

As the morning sun rose higher in the sky and flooded the kitchen, I quickly fixed our breakfast.

"What time are you going into the office?" I asked Huck as I slipped two eggs onto a plate.

"I'm going to run first and then go in," Huck said. He ran five miles every day, rain, snow, or sleet. Albeit during inclement weather months, he used the treadmill down in our recreation room in the basement instead.

Mom said she was going to meet a friend for lunch and then do some shopping. "I have to stop by to see Henry at the museum. He's made a terrible error, and I need to correct it." She said Henry as if it were something bitter in her mouth. She and Henry Wu had been high school chums and now were co-chairs of the Emerson Pass Historical Society. Years ago now, they'd had a falling-out of some kind. Or at least that was my guess. Mom wouldn't talk about whatever it was he'd done that had made her mad. Currently, they were locking horns over the upcoming Emerson Pass historical exhibit featuring remnants, letters, journals, and photographs from the early 1900s. Locals were proud of our heritage, especially those like my mother and Henry Wu, who were descendants of the first citizens of Emerson Pass.

"Actually, honey, would you be able to stop by the museum after work today?" Mom asked me. "I have something I want your opinion on."

"You got it."

"Remember Mrs. Butterworth's and pancakes?" Mom asked as she sat across from Huck. "Those were the good old days."

I cut several slices from the loaf of bread and put them in the toaster with a flourish. "You'll thank me around ten this morning when you're feeling good enough to argue with Mr. Wu."

"You need a kid," Huck said.

"I already have you," I said.

By the time I got to work that morning, Tiffany was already at the front desk. Scooter was beside her, showing her our scheduling system on the computer.

"Morning, ladies," I said. "Chilly today. Sure am glad I have my scarf." I untangled it from my neck and grinned at Tiffany.

She smiled back at me. A smile that rivaled the spring sunshine. We had an inside joke, I thought. Perhaps our first? One of many. *Please make it so*, I prayed silently.

"You and that scarf." Scooter's face morphed into the angry emoji. "It's going to be sixty-five this afternoon. Nothing but sunny skies."

"Yes, but it's forty now, so who's the smart one?" I asked, keeping my voice light as I shrugged out of my peacoat. Scooter would not ruin my mood this morning. She could suck the air out of a room and a man. Not today. Tiffany was here. Even Scooter couldn't ruin my good fortune.

In my office, I hung up my coat and scarf, then donned my white coat.

Scooter had already brought the daily schedule up on my computer screen. Mom hadn't been particularly computer-savvy and had asked Scooter to do anything remotely technical. Thus far, I couldn't convince Scooter that I could open my own calendar. I should change the password just to mess with her. No, not that. She was grumpy enough. I'd learned early on that complying with Scooter's eccentric ideals kept the peace. I liked peace. Especially at work. The animals were usually stressed enough when they came in for help. Even more so than humans, they could feel tension or sickness.

I glanced at the day's appointments. Not bad for a Monday.

The appointments included spaying a kitten, shots for a few others, wellness checkups, and an ancient cat ready to be put down. Mrs. Dunham's cat, Zoro. She was a sweet elderly lady who had given Zoro a great life. Still, she would be devastated to say goodbye. In time, perhaps, she could take home a new kitten. Not yet, though. Pet owners couldn't simply replace their darlings as people often advised, thinking that would ease the pain. It was like suggesting that all dogs and cats were alike and easily replaced. These pets were members of people's families. Letting them go broke a little piece of their owner's hearts. They needed time to mourn.

The morning flew by. I hadn't had time to check on Tiffany and hoped Scooter hadn't been too hard on her. I went to the window of my small office and looked out to the strip of grass between the building and our small parking lot. Should I take her to lunch? Would that be overstepping? *Don't overthink it*, I cautioned myself. I took all new employees to lunch on their first day. Scooter didn't approve, but I didn't care.

I rubbed my thumb along the edges of the window trim. Was it all right, though? I didn't want her to ever feel that she had to go to lunch with me because I was the boss. I'd make sure she knew it was optional. And standard procedure.

I found Tiffany behind the front desk with her head bent over the employee manual. Why we needed an employee manual since we numbered only five eluded me. Scooter loved her manuals.

"Don't put too much worry into learning all that," I said, keeping my voice low. "Scooter loves rules, but I like to break them."

She startled and lifted her gaze to me. "That's a relief. There's so much in here."

"Did she give you a form to sign?"

"It's here." Tiffany lifted a sheet of paper to show me. "She said you're supposed to quiz me and then sign off that I passed."

"Give it to me. I'll sign it now. Would you like to join me for lunch? I usually take new employees out on their first day."

"But aren't I supposed to stay at the desk?"

"No, we close from noon until one. Didn't she tell you that?"

"She didn't." Tiffany pushed the signature page toward me.

What a ridiculous form, I thought, as I signed the bottom of the paper with a flourish.

I marched over to the front window and replaced the Open sign with our standard Closed for Lunch. Back at 1 p.m. "Now, grab your things. Do you have a sweater? Despite the prediction, it's only fifty or so out there."

"I have a sweater. Where's your scarf?"

I'd forgotten all about it in my haste to come see her. "You know what? I'm going to leave it here. Your smile's enough to keep me warm."

She flushed and then flashed me that smile, proving my point. Warmth spread from my heart down to the tips of my fingers and toes. "What about your nap?"

"I don't take one every day," I said, laughing. "Is that what Scooter told you?"

"She might have mentioned it. A few times. More cautionary tale than anything else."

I craned my neck to look down the hallway to Scooter's office. The door was closed, which meant that she'd already gone to lunch. "She might be out to get me. Or I might be paranoid. Regardless, she preferred my mother over me. I'm a disappointment to her on a daily basis. I should care more than I do." I shrugged out of my white coat and hung it over the back of Tiffany's chair. "Scooter still sees me as a little boy tracking in mud instead of a doctor."

"A pet doctor," Tiffany said. "The best kind."

I hurried across the lobby to open the door for her. The scent of cut grass and spring flowers perfumed the air. Above us, a fat, lazy cloud couldn't quite gather the energy to cover the sun.

We walked up Ski Jump Way and turned the corner at Barnes Avenue, chatting about her first morning. "Nothing seemed too hard," she said. "But answering all the lines ringing at once flustered me. It didn't help to have Scooter behind me shouting orders."

"You'll get the hang of the phones. Worst case, people will have to call back."

"Thanks, Breck. I appreciate your belief in me."

"Tiffany Birt, there's nothing you can't do. Today or any day. Don't ever forget that."

We were seated right away at a table by the fireplace. Stormi hustled over to greet us.

"Hey, you two. How's the first day going?" Stormi asked.

"A little rocky but okay," Tiffany said.

"The special is the same as always on Mondays," Stormi said. "Spaghetti and meatballs. Soup of the day is broccoli cheddar."

We ordered waters and asked for a few minutes. "Order whatever you want," I said. "You only get one new employee lunch, so you should make the best of it."

"How come Scooter didn't come?"

"Oh, she has no use for lunch out," I said. "She likes to run home and check on her husband. He's had a little trouble with online gambling in the past."

"Oh dear. That's terrible."

I was distracted by the television over the bar. They'd been showing the same photographs of Briar Rose for days now. The twenty-four-hour news cycle was tedious at best.

"Is it on again?" Tiffany asked me. "Briar Rose?"

"Yeah, sorry." I took my gaze from the television back to her. "It's nothing new."

She seemed to be studying the menu with great intent. I let her be, guessing she probably had a dozen thoughts running through her mind. I could imagine how hard it would be to have to watch it all after having escaped so long ago.

Stormi came with our waters. We ordered lunch. I asked for a grilled chicken sandwich on a wheat roll and a side salad. She got the Cobb salad, not the half but whole.

I flashed upon her empty refrigerator. "Stormi, could you bring a basket of those rolls too?"

"You got it," Stormi said before heading to the bar to enter our order.

"Thanks for that," Tiffany said quietly.

"Pardon?"

"The rolls. You were thinking about my empty refrigerator, weren't you?"

"Nope. Didn't even occur to me. I love bread."

Our gazes locked. She blinked, her curly lashes like a wave. An exquisite ache spread over my chest.

"You're a thoughtful man," she said. "But a liar."

"I'm wounded." I grabbed a sugar packet from the ceramic holder and flicked it across the table at her.

As quick as a soccer goalie, her hand reached out to stop it from sailing off the table. "Not so fast."

"Good reflexes."

"Is that your professional opinion?" Her eyes sparkled, teasing me. If I could have, I'd have leaped across the table and kissed her sweet mouth.

"I specialize more in dogs and cats, so my opinion should be suspect. However, if there were human shows like there are for dogs, you'd be best in show."

She rolled her eyes and God bless her, touched her hair. I was a king just then instead of an ordinary man in the presence of an angel.

Stormi returned with the rolls and a bowl of butter packets. "Fresh from the oven. They're still warm."

We thanked her, but she was already off to the next task.

Scents of the yeasty, buttery goodness lit Tiffany up like a delighted child. "I could eat all of them." She took the largest roll and split it apart with her fingers, then slipped a slab of butter between the halves. "Are you going to have one?"

"I'm having a sandwich," I said. "That's enough bread."

"Is that really a thing? Too much bread?" She bit into one half and chewed, a look of rapture on her face. "Delicious."

How was it that Tiffany could make something as mundane as eating a roll look like a work of art?

OUR ENTRÉES ARRIVED, and we ate without talking for a few minutes. The silence wasn't awkward but comfortable, like old friends. Only she was way prettier than Huck and Trapper.

"What made you choose Emerson Pass?" I asked.

A faint smile lifted the corners of her mouth. "I saw an article about Emerson Pass in a travel magazine featuring the wedding of the actress Lisa Perry. Do you know who she is?"

"Sure." Everyone knew the actress Lisa Perry. She was everywhere lately. "Isn't her husband part of the firm who built Jamie's inn?"

"Yes, that's him. He's good friends with Jamie's brother, Trey. This magazine had a feature with photographs from Lisa Perry's wedding. One of them was of the bride and groom coming out of our church. Red door and all. Lisa said she'd had her heart set on a wedding in Emerson Pass after she saw an article in a magazine featuring the church and lodge as great places for destination weddings twenty years ago. Can you imagine? As if that weren't inspiration enough, I took one look at her wedding photos and decided to move to Emerson Pass and open my wedding planning business. So I did."

"What is it about wedding planning that you love?" Truthfully, the profession sounded hard. "All those brides and their mothers can't be easy."

Her brows knit together, causing an adorable crease just above her nose. "What's not to love? A wedding planner gives every bride the chance to be a princess for the day."

"So, you're a romantic?" I asked. How was it possible after what she'd experienced as a child?

"I guess so. Romance novels were one of the first things I discovered after I left Briar Rose. All these books about people falling in love! I couldn't get enough. I learned a lot from those books." She flushed and dipped her chin, before stabbing a piece of chicken. "I mean about pop culture, not the other."

"Right." I hid a smile behind my hand.

Tiffany poked her fork into the avocado and popped it into her mouth. Goodness, that mouth! Plump and pink like raspberries.

"Do you still love it?" I asked. "When there's enough work?"

She poured dressing from the ramekin over her salad. "I do, yes. But people are meaner than I thought they'd be."

"Service industries can be rough that way."

"Yes, and I'm too sensitive." She tossed her salad with her fork. A droplet of oily dressing popped onto the table.

"What?" I asked softly. "What are you thinking about?"

She studied her salad. "I've been thinking about going to the FBI and telling them what I know. For Matthew and for my mom." Her lips trembled until she pressed them together. "I owe them that much."

"If that's what you want, you should do it."

"I might know something that could help. I'm not sure I can live with myself if I don't at least try." She glanced behind her at the television before returning to her salad. "It scares me to think of going in there."

"I'll take you. I'll go with you."

She lifted her head to stare into my eyes. "Why would you do that?"

"Because you're my friend."

"I'll have to testify at the trials. I don't know if I'm strong enough to face the elders." She closed her eyes and grimaced as if a shock of pain traveled through her body. It reminded me of the way my dad had looked when his medications wore off those last few weeks he was sick.

My mother had sat next to his bed, stroking his hand hour after hour. One day she'd said to me, "I don't know if I'm strong enough to let him go."

I'd been too young to know how to answer her. Her vulnerability had frightened me. I'd floated away into the darkness, screaming silently to my father, "Don't go, don't go, don't go."

But she had been strong enough. We both had been. My mother and I had moved forward, one day at a time. People did survive the darkness to return to love.

"You're stronger than you think you are," I said.

"How do you know?"

"I just do."

We returned our attention back to our meals even though I was no longer hungry. I itched to urge her forward, to convince her that going to the FBI was the right thing. But the truth was —I didn't know what was best for her. I wasn't Tiffany. It was not my place to tell her what to do, but I sure wanted to. Instead, I bit my tongue and offered only support. "Whatever you decide, I'll be here," I said.

11

Tiffany
I spent the evening thinking about my lunch conversation with Breck. I'd managed to avoid seeing the news but that night, I put it on to torture myself, much like pressing against a sore spot. Not much had changed in the last few days, other than more details on my father. A girlfriend from his past had come on to one of the morning shows to share her experiences with a young man she described as "totally normal," other than a little more controlling than some of the other men she'd dated. Following that, a segment speculating about what kinds of people were attracted to religious cults aired.

What had attracted my mother to Briar Rose? To my father? What had happened to him to send him into such a web of evil?

That's the problem with the past. One can never truly escape. Even if one manages to push aside the memories for a decade, they still lurk in the subconscious. Episodes long forgotten or repressed return in nightmares that wake the troubled sleeper at 2:00 a.m., as one did me that morning.

I dreamed I was an egg. Not the inside where I would grow

into a chick, but the entire egg, shell, yolk, and whites. Inside the protected walls of the shell, I crouched, afraid, knowing that at any moment I would crack and spill out upon the counter and be lost forever.

I woke, sweaty and disoriented. My pulse raced, and my cotton pajamas were soaked through. For a moment, I breathed in and out to steady myself. Muffy was asleep, curled on top of her pillow next to me. I reached out to her, burying my fingers in her fur in order to ground myself to reality. Safe and cozy in my bed. That's where I was. Not in the inside of an egg.

I rolled to my side and curled my arms together almost like a yoga pose. The dream wasn't hard to interpret. For a long time, however deluded it was, I'd thought of myself as protected inside my shell. Now, however, it was obvious that I was not. Indeed, I was as vulnerable as an unformed chick, capable of sliding from safety and sloshing all over everything I'd so carefully built around me.

Was Breck correct? Should I go to the FBI and tell them my story? Furthermore, should I tell all the dirty, possibly salacious details to Huck for a book? Would it be better or worse for my mental health to do so?

I had no idea.

My head ached. I turned over to drink from the bottle of water I kept on the nightstand. Then I gathered the covers close to my neck and stared up at the dark ceiling. A nightlight allowed me to make out the shapes of my bedroom furniture. Enough that I would see if someone ever tried to break in through the window.

Or come for me.

That had been my waking and dreaming fear for the first three or four years after my escape. Would they find me and forcibly bring me back into the fold? Over time, my fears had lessened. I'd become acclimated to living what most would think of as a normal existence.

But this latest revelation? This had me without an anchor. I desperately craved something or someone to hold on to. Muffy. I had Muffy. She gave me someone to love and look after and in return provided her unconditional love. Possibly in a way a human never could.

Breck entered my thoughts again. When I was with him, I forgot about my past or present troubles. He made me laugh. He made me feel safe. *Think about him*, I told myself. I closed my eyes and conjured up his face, the way his eyes sparkled when he laughed, his infectious grin. He'd said he'd go with me to the FBI. Yes, we were new friends, but his offer had made me feel courageous. Could I do it? Could I tell my story? If I did, would it do any good in the world or only provide salacious details?

I must have finally drifted back to sleep, because the alarm rang at seven. Groggy, I reached to shut it off and threw off the covers. I found it best to wake that way, without any self-coddling. When I learned to swim after I escaped, I'd approached the water in the same way. Jump right in. No wading in slowly for this girl.

They hadn't taught any of us to swim. They'd given us no lessons even though we collected water from the river. What if one of us had fallen in? We would have drowned. It was all so obvious when I looked back on it. All of their actions were meant to control us.

Another memory came to me. My baptism. I was eight years old, shivering as I stood in the water of the river. Flakes of snow fell from the sky and landed on my eyelashes. Elder William's large hand was around my neck. He plunged me into the frigid black water, once, twice, and again.

Our baptisms came when we were eight years old, an age when we were terrified of water, knowing we couldn't swim. All part of the design, I realized now. Give the girls no tools with which to survive, thus making us powerless and even grateful that we were allowed to stay and marry an elder. A man much wiser than us, obviously. A man to protect us.

Only they hadn't. On the contrary. They'd enslaved us, forcing young girls to have sex with old men. Had they done irreparable damage to us all?

MY JOB at the clinic was surprisingly easy, regardless of how Scooter tried to overcomplicate her instructions. I recognized her desire for control. She wanted the job to be difficult so she might feel important and superior. I wasn't sure what she had against me, but it was obvious she didn't like me. Some might try to win her over. I simply didn't care. I'd do my job and go home at the end of the day.

Bonus? Seeing Breck. Smelling Breck. Taking in his mischievous grin as though it was a delicious meal. I'd been waiting all week for him to ask me to dinner. Had he forgotten that he asked me out? Or had I gotten it mixed up? Maybe he'd changed his mind?

Friday afternoon, I'd finished cleaning up the small employee kitchen and break room before going home when Breck appeared in the doorway. I hadn't seen him much over the last few days. He'd been slammed with patients all week. Scooter watched me like a hawk, so there was never a time for me to seek him out to say hello during work hours.

"Hey there." He filled the doorway to the break room. "Everyone's gone home. You should too."

"I'm done now." I grabbed a towel from a small hook in the wall over the sink to dry my hands. "Are you going too?"

"Yes, in a minute." He put his hands in his khaki pants pockets. "Listen, I was wondering if you wanted to have dinner tonight? I know it's short notice, but I thought I'd ask. Something casual, since you're probably tired. We could even go now."

"I was wondering why you hadn't brought it up again," I said. "I thought you'd decided against it."

"What? No, I was giving you space for your first week. And I didn't want you to feel any pressure, since I'm the boss."

"I don't feel pressured."

He grinned. "Great." Breck leaned against the doorframe. "How was your week? Any troubles?"

"No problems. The job isn't exactly taxing intellectually," I said. "I like keeping everything organized and running smoothly. It's satisfying. Similar to event planning that way, but not nearly as tricky."

"I had a feeling you would find it that way. What about Scooter?" When I didn't answer right away, his face crinkled into a smile. "She's the hardest part, isn't she?"

"I hate to talk about anyone behind their back, but yes."

"For me too." His expression turned sorrowful. "I'm stuck with her."

I wanted to wrap my arms around him, but I stayed where I was, twisting and untwisting the towel in my hands.

"I inherited her from my mother," he said. "You knew that, right?

"I did."

"Where would you like to have dinner?" Breck asked.

"I was wondering if you'd like to go to my place? I've decided. I want to call that tip line and tell them what I know."

"Really?"

"It's taken me all week to decide, but I'm ready. It would be nice if you were there with me," I said. "You said you'd be there with me. Does the offer still stand?"

"Absolutely. Let's get some takeout and make it happen," Breck said. "I'll sit on the couch and be there in case you chicken out. You might decide you're not ready, and that's fine too. Regardless, it's nice to have a friend there."

"That sounds great," I said. "But you get to pick the type of food we order."

"I've been craving Chinese food. There's a new place at the end of town that's really good."

"Lotus?"

He nodded, obviously pleased. "What do you like?"

"Sweet and sour chicken's my favorite."

"That's like a piece of chicken wrapped in a doughnut."

"Is that bad?" I laughed at the look of disgust on his face.

"Just this once I guess it won't kill us," he said. "But I'll get us some green beans too."

A spark like a warning fired in my brain, but it was quickly snuffed out by a feeling of excitement. I wanted to see him. Spend time with him. What that meant, I couldn't yet say. For once, however, I just let myself lean into the uncertainty.

12

BRECK

I sat on the floor with my back up against the armchair in Tiffany's small living room. Cartons of Chinese food were spread over the coffee table. Our empty plates held only leftover traces of grease. Tiffany, sitting on the other end of the table, was typing an email to the hotline.

"All right, I think I'm ready," she said, still staring at the screen. "I told them who I was and that I had information on several deaths and was willing to answer any other questions they might have."

I nodded, hopefully encouragingly. Her hands shook, and she kept bringing her fingers to her mouth as if to chew her nails but then brought them back to the table. "Here goes." She tapped the keys. "Done. Now what?"

"I guess we wait."

"Thanks for this. I appreciate you being here. And for the Chinese food." She took up the sweet and sour pork and scooped a few more pieces onto her plate.

I helped myself to more noodles, and for the next few minutes, we talked about what we wanted to do with the rest of the evening. I suggested a movie. "Or we can just talk."

147

"I do like talking to you." She lowered her head and placed her hands on either side of her face. "I can't believe you're here."

"I'm here. I can't believe you let me in."

"Well, you brought food," Tiffany said.

Her laptop dinged. She sucked in her bottom lip. "There's a new message. Do I open it?"

"Yes, when you're ready."

Her fingers hung over the keyboard for a moment before she clicked. She breathed in and held her breath as she read.

I waited, wondering what they would say and how it was possible they got back to her that quickly on a Friday night.

She looked up. "They want me to come in. To the headquarters in Denver."

"All right, good. They took you seriously."

"I put in a few details that only someone who had lived there would know," Tiffany said. "So they knew I was for real."

"Do they say when?" I stretched my long legs out underneath the table. *Wait*, I thought. *Let her decide what to do next.*

"They want me to come in tomorrow. I'll go, I guess. I mean, I have to now." She nibbled absentmindedly on her thumbnail.

"I'll drive you there and wait in the car so you don't have to deal with traffic and all that."

She blinked, as if she'd been far away and just realized I was still there. "Are you sure you don't mind?"

"I don't mind."

"Yes, then, let's do it tomorrow. Get it over with."

"It takes about three hours to get to Denver," I said, thinking out loud. "Or we can fly. Actually, yeah, we should fly. I can ask Javier to take us. He has his own small plane."

"You have a friend with a plane?" She stared at me, obviously astonished.

"Yeah, he's an old family friend. I'll give him a call. He's always looking for an excuse to use his plane. Totally pretentious." I grinned to let her know I was joking.

"I've never been on an airplane."

"You mean a small one?" The shake of her head told me she'd meant any kind of plane. "I see. Well, it's fun. Especially on a clear day. But if you're scared, I'll drive you."

"No, I'd like to go in that airplane." Her eyes softened. "It must be amazing to see that whole landscape spread out below you."

"Yes." There was nothing like it.

She gave me a tremulous smile that matched her voice. "Why does everything seem easier when you're around?"

I knew the answer but didn't say it out loud. Money. That was the difference. Financial wealth gave one power over their own destiny more so than if you were at the mercy of circumstances. Anyone who said differently was a liar.

"Okay, then. I guess I should write back and tell them I'll be there tomorrow. How long will it take to get there?"

"Tell them we can be there around noon."

"Noon, okay." She nibbled her thumb again before returning her fingers to the laptop. The keys clicked as she typed a message back to them. She typed her answer into the computer and then hit Send with a dramatic flair. "Done."

I excused myself to call Javier from downstairs on the sidewalk. He answered after a few rings. He wasn't the type who needed small talk before asking a favor, so I jumped right to it. "Hey, man, you have room in your plane for two tomorrow? A friend and I need to go to Denver."

"Sure thing. What time?"

"We need to get there around eleven."

"You got it, brother. I'll meet you and your buddy at the airport around nine."

"It's a girl buddy," I said. "Very light weight."

He laughed. "Good to know. Is this a girlfriend type of thing? I asked because you know the wife will want to know the minute I hang up."

I chuckled. Javier and Mandy had been two of my father's best friends from college. My dad had invested in Javier's first business, which made Javier rich and my father richer. There wasn't anything Javier wouldn't do if I asked. "Say hello to Mandy, and I'll see you tomorrow."

"You didn't answer my question."

"Tell Mandy there's potential. If I don't do anything stupid."

"You're a good boy, don't forget that. Your dad's smiling down on you right now."

We hung up, and I sprinted back up the stairs to Tiffany's apartment. I knocked softly on the door, and she called for me to come on in. She'd remained sitting on the floor with Muffy curled up on her lap.

"We're set for tomorrow," I said.

We agreed to watch a movie. "It'll be a good distraction," she said.

I helped her clean up before we settled on the couch together, her on one end and me on the other. Muffy plopped down between us. "This is nice," I said.

"Very nice."

The movie started, and for the next few hours, I was lost in the story. Not too lost to notice when Tiffany got up to use the restroom, returning to sit close to me. I tucked my arm around her shoulders. She fit just right.

It was nearing ten by the time the credits rolled. She yawned, which made me yawn. "I should go. We have a big day tomorrow."

She walked me to the door. Muffy lifted her head from where she'd been napping on the couch to give me a disappointed look.

"Thanks for spending the evening with me," I said.

"Was it okay? You know, sitting next to you like that?"

"Better than okay. But no pressure. We can take this at whatever pace you want."

"Thanks for that. I need it to be like that because, you know, I'm not experienced."

"Oh, right. Not a problem."

"Are you sure? Because I don't know much of anything." She was bright red by this time.

I didn't want to make her embarrassment worse, so I kept my amusement to myself. But she was so darn cute. "There's nothing to know. When and if you're ready for a kiss, you'll know what to do."

She launched herself into my arms. "Thank you."

I stumbled backward from the force of her body but steadied myself before we both landed on the floor.

"What was that for?" I asked.

"Everything. Being you. Has anyone ever told you how special you are?" She lifted her eyes to mine. "I'm pinching myself a little that it's me you want to spend time with. There are so many girls who would jump at the chance to spend a Friday night with you."

"Yes, but none of those girls are you." I wrapped my arms around her and pressed my chin into her glossy hair. "You're beautiful and smart and you make me laugh."

"You make me laugh. I was just thinking that today." She grinned up at me. "What a coincidence."

"It's good to find someone who makes you laugh."

She buried her face in the collar of my peacoat. The material was too rough, I thought. It might scratch her tender skin. "I like you a lot, and it scares me," she said into my chest.

Her warm breath tickled the skin of my neck. I'd forgotten my scarf again. Strange. That was twice now. I put that thought aside and backed up a little so I could look at her face. "What's scary?" Was it something I was doing? Too much pressure?

She spoke without looking at me and twiddling with the oversize buttons on my coat. "All these feelings inside me. I think about you a lot. All the time. When I catch glimpses of you at work, this funny thing happens to my tummy."

My heart soared. I mean, how could it not? "That happens in my stomach too. It's a good thing."

"You're a good thing," she said softly. "The very best thing."

The urge to kiss her was the deepest craving I'd ever had. *Stay cool. Everything happens when it should.* "I'll see you tomorrow, beautiful Tiffany."

"Good night." She let go of me. A chill washed over me without the warmth of her body.

"Night." I opened the door and stepped into the hall before I changed my mind. As I walked back down the hallway, I heard the door close behind me. I hesitated, listening to make sure she locked it. When I heard the bolt latch, I headed down the stairs. I couldn't stop smiling. If a hug did that, I could only imagine what a kiss would do.

TIFFANY HAD her face pressed against the glass of Javier's small plane, as excited as a child. "Look at the lake down there, Breck."

I peered around her shoulder to look down at the scenery below. We flew close to the mountains on our way to Denver. Soon it would be a brown landscape, but for now, a sea of green greeted me. "Spectacular view from up here, isn't it?"

"I thought you might be afraid," Javier said to Tiffany. "When I heard you'd never flown before."

"I thought so too," Tiffany said, a smile plastered on her face. She squeezed my hand. "But I wasn't. I'm pleased with myself.

Javier chuckled. "You should be."

I was glad it seemed to be distracting her from what we were on our way to do. As supportive as I was about the idea, I also worried the meeting would be too hard for her. My mother had given me a stern look as I left this morning and mumbled something about me and my wounded birds. She couldn't possibly understand what I felt for Tiffany. Someday, after an appropriate time, perhaps she would. For now, I operated from my own compass. Instincts told me to give Tiffany all of me, or at least the best of me. The next few months would be a cornerstone in my life. I couldn't explain to anyone, not even myself, how I knew this to be true, yet I knew.

Seeing Tiffany's face lit up like this, she hardly seemed wounded. And God help me, she was ravishing today in a silk blouse, slacks, and black pumps. She had her hair piled on top of her head, bringing attention to her long neck. Dewy and pretty, her skin glowed. No one would know by looking at her what she'd endured. They would see only an attractive young woman with the world at her disposal.

She leaned away from the window to look at me. "I wish we were going somewhere else."

"I know. But it'll be over before you know it. Afterward, I'll take you to a nice dinner."

She leaned her head against my shoulder. "I do enjoy dinner."

I chuckled and took her hand. "I know you do."

A FEW HOURS LATER, I drove a rental car into the parking garage of the FBI building. Neither of us spoke as we took the elevator up to the main lobby. Between the bevy of windows and white marble floors, I was temporarily blinded by the light. When my vision returned, I looked for the reception desk. A few people milled about, wearing suits or other high-powered attire. Security guards stood at the door and in various other locations.

"This way." I pointed to a curved reception desk where two young women in dark blue sat behind computer screens.

Tiffany placed her hand in mine and took a deep breath. "Lead the way. I can barely walk my legs are shaking so badly."

"Hi there," I said to the dark-haired receptionist. "We have an appointment for Tiffany Birt."

"Yes, they're expecting you. I have your badges here." She reached into a neatly ordered stack to pick up temporary ID cards fastened to lanyards and placed them on the counter. "You'll go up to the tenth floor. As long as you're wearing these, you should have no problem."

"Thank you," I said. Our shoes clicked on the tiles as we crossed the lobby to the elevators. An ordinary sound for an extraordinary day.

In the elevator that smelled of strong cologne, I glanced over at Tiffany. She'd paled and had wrapped her arms around her middle. "You all right?"

Her vacant eyes did their obligatory meeting of mine, but I could see she was not truly next to me. Where she'd gone, I couldn't say exactly, but I had a feeling she'd been sucked into the past in preparation for the questions coming her way. "Hmm? Oh, yes. Nervous though." She made a mock gagging sound. "And someone needs to step back from the cologne bottle."

This made us both laugh hysterically. We'd only just gotten ourselves together when the elevator doors opened into a smaller version of the main lobby.

"You've done nothing wrong. Remember that," I said in her ear before stepping into the waiting area.

She nodded and slipped her hand in mine.

The receptionist was an older woman with a cap of gray pin curls. Her hands flew over a keyboard, typing and typing before she finally looked up at us. She narrowed her eyes, taking in our badges and our faces, then clicking a few buttons on the computer. "You're all set. Have a seat, please."

Tiffany sat in the guest chair closest to the door with her

ankles crossed and posture straight, waiting for battle or possibly planning her escape. Too nervous to sit, I busied myself getting her a cup of water from the filtered machine.

She thanked me when I brought it to her. "My mouth's super dry. Sit. You're making me more nervous."

I did as she asked, stretching my legs out in an attempt to relax. It didn't work. I was as hyped-up as a brand-new puppy.

Time dragged like honey dripping from a spoon. The clock on the wall above reception had a second hand. I watched as it ticked away the seconds, imagining I could hear the *click-click-click*. Finally, an agent with a craggy face and dressed in a black suit came for her. I stood, wobbly, and helped her to her feet. She threw her arms around me in a quick hug.

"You can do it," I whispered in her ear. "Just tell your truth."

"And then we go to dinner. I got it."

I kissed her cheek. "I'll be here."

I watched as she walked slowly toward the agent as if she were being taken out to the woodshed for a beating.

Not that I knew anyone who'd ever been beaten behind a woodshed, but my dad had always often used that saying.

The door closed behind them. I remained standing, alone in the lobby except for Pin Curls. What should I do? How long would she be? I should have told her to text me when she was done.

"Do you have any guesses on how long she'll be in there?" I asked Pin Curls.

"None whatsoever." She gave me a coquettish smile. "You're welcome to stay as long as you like right here where I can see you."

"I think I'll get some fresh air. Maybe some coffee."

"We have coffee." She pointed to a pod coffee machine. "Christmas blend's left over from a few months back, but that cinnamon flavor is surprisingly good. I can sneak you some good cream."

"That's all right. I'd like to look around." Warm suddenly, I wanted to take off my sweater but didn't want to give her the wrong impression.

"There's a nice coffee shop across the street," she said, sounding offended. "You can have yourself an overpriced coffee and a mediocre sandwich."

"Good tip, thanks."

She raised one eyebrow before returning to her typing.

When I exited the blue-windowed building, I headed across the street as suggested by Pin Curls. The coffee shop was upscale and indeed did offer overpriced drinks and mediocre sandwiches. *Brandi's bakery had lines out the door for a reason*, I thought, as I took a first sip from a weak latte.

I settled on a tall stool at a counter that overlooked the street. After a few bites of the dry chicken sandwich, I returned to gazing out the window. People watching always entertained me. Huck and I used to make up stories about people whenever we were bored in a public place. He was always a lot better than I was at coming up with details. I'd say things like, "He seems nice. Good hair on that lady." Whereas he'd have them as international spies on a mission to find a missing code.

A man across the street in front of the FBI building caught my eye. Dressed in a cheap-looking gray suit, at first I thought he was an agent but upon further investigation, decided he was too sloppy for an agent. Suit too cheap. Haircut too long.

The hair on the back of my neck stood up. I might not notice all the details or be able to come up with stories for people, but I had instincts like a dog. The man made me nervous. Was he following Tiffany? Where had he come from this morning? How did he know she'd be here?

I'm probably being paranoid, I thought. Regardless, I was going over there to get a better look. Hastily, I stuffed my half-eaten sandwich in the bag next to the one I'd gotten for Tiffany and headed across the street. If only I had a reason for standing outside the main doors. This would be the time to take up smoking. I'd make small talk like I did with my patients. Too bad he didn't have a pet with him. They never failed to provide an entryway into a conversation.

The man continued to study the sidewalk while taking puffs from his cigarette. His cheeks were pocked with acne scars, and his eyebrows could benefit from even the slightest grooming. I guessed him to be around forty, but he could have been closer to my age and have lived hard. His suit didn't quite fit, hanging on his skinny frame.

I took a deep breath and mustered up a bit of courage. "Hey, man," I said. "Could I bum a smoke?"

He looked up at me. A flicker of recognition showed in his eyes before he composed himself. He knew who I was. If only I knew him.

He pulled a pack of Marlboro Lights from an inside pocket in his jacket. "Help yourself."

Awkwardly, I took the pack and tried to remember how smokers pulled a cigarette out of a package. For heaven's sake, they were crammed in there. Must be a new pack. An image of a friend from medical school came to me. He'd done this thing where he smacked the bottom of the package and one poked out, like a groundhog from a hole. I mimicked this but nothing happened.

"New smoker?" he asked.

"Um, no. I've been smoking for like forever." Using my thumb and fingernail, I managed to grip the end of one and tugged it away from its friends.

I handed the package back to him. He brought out a silver lighter, vintage from the fifties if I had my decades right. My grandfather had had one like that. "Great, yeah, a light. Light me up." I stuck the cigarette in my mouth. He raised the flame to the end. I sucked in as if my life depended on it. The end caught and reddened.

I coughed. I'd taken too big a puff. Light-headed, I saw tiny sparks before my eyes. "Good stuff," I said, gasping for air. "Nothing like a smoke."

He stared at me with suspicious eyes. Why had I asked for a cigarette? Now I would have to smoke the whole thing. "Marlboro Lights, the best, am I right?"

"Yeah, sure."

"I'm Breck Stokes. Thanks for the smoke."

He nodded. "Ralph." He didn't make any moves to shake my hand, so I puffed from my cigarette, careful to take in a small amount and blow the smoke out before it reached my lungs. The instinct that this guy was following us was as strong as before; however, I now realized I had no plan. It might have been smarter for me to continue observing him from across the street.

"Ralph. Good name. You have a last name?"

"I do."

Okay then, no plans to share it with me. I'd try something else. "What brings you to the old FBI building?" I asked, as casually and cool as I could muster.

"Business."

"Yeah, me too. Lots of business. So much. Business." I took another drag on the cigarette. Another wave of nausea passed through me. How could I get rid of this thing? The sandwich. I'd have to eat more of the sandwich. I dropped my cigarette and stomped it with the tip of my shoe. "I'm starving. Long day already. You know, what with all my business and all."

"Okay, whatever you say."

"You hungry? I have an extra sandwich in here." I lifted the brown bag to show him. "It's yours. Just say the word. Payback for the cigarette. I'm not one to take without giving back, you know?"

"I could eat."

"Great. It's supposed to be chicken and pesto, but I think they forgot the green stuff."

Ralph's thick eyebrows came together for a second. I obviously baffled and annoyed him in equal measure. However, his desire for the sandwich seemed to outweigh both. "Where did it come from? The sandwich."

"Across the street there." I dug into the bag and came out with the saran-wrapped sandwich. "I had to escape the building because there was this elderly receptionist flirting and offering me cinnamon coffee. I had to get out of there. I'm sure you know what I mean."

"Not really." Ralph dropped his butt onto the cement sidewalk and stomped on it with the heel of his boot. Cowboy boots. Interesting. If I were a real detective, I might be able to do something with that information. However, since I was a veterinarian and not a sleuth, I had nothing. Although, to be honest, they didn't really match his suit. I would have gone with wingtips.

"What brings you to Denver?" I asked.

"I live here." The saran wrap stretched and squeaked as he ripped it open to take a large bite.

Several cars passed and then stopped at the light. I'd have figured there'd be more traffic here in the city, but it was Saturday. Maybe people didn't come this way unless it was to work. *Focus*, I reminded myself. *Figure out what this guy is up to.*

"You work here at the FBI then?" I asked. FBI sounded like a foreign word coming from my mouth, like the first time a boy curses.

Ralph shook his head. "Nope."

Okay, he was good at avoiding answering questions. Duly noted. If only he had a dog, I could get him to talk. People loved to talk about their pets. Rightly so, of course. "I'm here with a friend. She has information on a big case." I tossed that out like a betting man with a pile of poker chips at the end of the night. All in.

Ralph's eyes flickered, but his expression remained bland. "That right? What case?"

"I can't say or they'd have to kill me," I said.

He stared at me for a second before taking another bite of the dry sandwich. Apparently, Ralph didn't have a sense of humor. Or maybe he was a hired killer. A shiver went down my spine. Was Tiffany in danger? Had the cult hired this guy to find out what she knew? What if they hurt her? *Think*, I ordered myself. *Get this guy to talk.*

"You know what? I bet you're a detective." I snapped my fingers, as if I'd just thought of it. "Like a PI. Am I right? I used to dream about that kind of work when I was a kid. I imagined it to be such an adventure. Is it?"

"I wouldn't know." Another big bite and more chewing. He had an unnerving click in his jaw. He should see a dentist about that.

I chuckled in what I hoped sounded like a self-deprecating way. "Guess I had you pegged wrong. Here I had a whole story figured out about you." If only Huck were here. He'd get this jerk to talk. "You have a dangerous vibe, so my mind jumped to romantic conclusions."

He crumbled the empty plastic wrap into a ball. Then, strangely, he put it in his pocket instead of the trash receptacle just feet from us. I hated to think about the crumbs that would invariably get trapped within the seam of the pocket. It was nearly impossible to get breadcrumbs out of there. Or the dust from dog biscuits.

I sneaked a peek at my watch. Tiffany had been in there for an hour. How much longer would she be? She had a lot to tell them. It could take her all day. I hoped they fed her lunch. She would have low blood sugar if they didn't.

I dragged myself away from these thoughts and back to the

mystery man in the bad suit. What to do next? Should I turn the tables on this guy and follow him? If he left, that is, which at the moment, he didn't seem inclined to do. "You like naps?" I asked. Why, why, why had that popped out of my mouth?

"Naps?" More of a growl than a word, but at least I got him to ask a question.

"Yeah, I take them every day. Love them."

"Depends on if I have a gig. But yeah, I guess I like naps as much as the next guy."

"There's a stigma around grown men napping, you know. As if it were a crime or something."

"Is that true?" Ralph's forehead creased. "I don't think it is."

"Take it from me. I get a lot of judgment. Tons." He'd said the word *gig*, implying freelance jobs. Like private detectives had. "Are you a musician?"

"What? No. I mean, I play the piano but just at family get-togethers. That kind of thing."

I'm getting somewhere, I thought, triumphantly. His voice had sounded less guarded, perhaps softened by the thought of playing piano at family gatherings. "I'd love to be able to play for fun. I'm hopeless at music, though. Except for listening. Man, let me tell you, I'm an expert at listening."

"You're a weird dude."

I gave him my best world-weary laugh. "I've heard that before." Pot calling the kettle if there ever was one. But I bet this guy had been called that a million times. I mean, look at him. Not to mention that clicking jaw. "You too, right?"

"Me? No way." He scowled. So it was all right for him to call me weird but when I sent it back to him, he acted like it was an insult?

What could I say next? "You waiting for someone?"

"You ask a lot of questions."

"Sorry about that. Just naturally curious, I guess. Plus, with both of us waiting around, what else is there to do?"

He shook another cigarette from the package. Great, more smoke. Didn't he know each one of those brought him closer to death? He lit it and took in a drag before blowing it out in a remarkably long stream of smoke. He gazed down at his feet before looking back up at the street.

"Listen, Dr. Stokes, I know who you are. I know why you're here, why you're asking all these questions." Ralph, if that was really his name, took another drag.

I swallowed, hoping my sandwich wouldn't come back up. "Okay. Why am I here?"

"You're with the Briar Rose girl. I saw you walk into the lobby with her."

"How do you know who she is?" This was bad. Was he waiting around to harm her? Threaten her? But it was too late. She was in there right now telling the FBI all the secrets of Briar Rose.

"I just do."

"Did they hire you?" I asked. "Briar Rose?"

He blinked and then took another drag of his cigarette. "No. I have nothing to do with those degenerates."

I don't know what I'd expected, but this adamant answer was not it. What I lacked in interview skills, I made up for with my intuition. This was the truth. He was not working for them. I could feel it in my gut. "Time to get real then," I said. "Who are you and why are you here?"

"Why should I tell you?"

"Because my job is to protect Tiffany, and right now you're seeming like a threat."

"Why you? Did she ask that of you? As in, did she hire you?"

It was my turn to feel offended. Who was this guy to ask questions of my legitimacy? I was the one who asked the questions. Furthermore, how dare he imply that I was a hired thug? "I'm not a professional bodyguard, if that's what you're asking. I'm her friend."

"That makes more sense." His bloodshot eyes studied me and seemed to find me lacking.

"I could be her bodyguard," I said.

"You'd have more of a muscular build, I'd think."

"You shouldn't smoke." I sounded slightly like a petulant child but I didn't care.

"I know. *Everyone* knows that," Ralph said. "You and Tiffany doing the nasty?"

My mouth dropped open. "Don't use that kind of language in reference to Tiffany. Nothing about her is nasty."

"All right, fancy college boy. Are you romantically involved with Tiffany?"

"What does that have to do with anything?"

"I'm nosy, that's all." He shrugged. Were those shoulder pads in that jacket?

"Fine. I'm not her boyfriend, but I wish I was. Does that count? Right now, I'm just her friend. Thanks to Briar Rose messing her up royally she's not in a good headspace for a serious boyfriend."

"You think that's the only reason she won't go out with you?"

"Listen, Ralph—if that's actually your name—why should I tell you?"

"The same reason you want me to answer your questions."

"Is that true? I don't think that's true." I repeated his words from earlier back to him. "Anyway, we are dating. I've taken her on a date before. We're taking it slow."

"Slow? Or is it lack of interest on her part? It could be your annoying personality, for example," Ralph said.

"I'm not annoying. I'm a well-liked veterinarian. Actually, people love me. Animals too."

"Or it could be all the napping," Ralph said. "She might find that off-putting in a grown man."

"Napping keeps you young. Unlike smoking."

"Ouch." He placed a hand over his chest.

"Are you going to threaten her? Hurt her?" I asked. "Because I know people."

"You do *not* know people."

"My best friend is an international correspondent for one of the biggest newspapers in the world. He could do a story on you and ruin your bullying business or whatever it is you call it."

"I'm not a bully. I'm a private investigator."

I did a little two-step with my feet, which in hindsight looked juvenile. "I knew it. You *are* working for Briar Rose."

He let out a sigh, rather long-suffering in my opinion, considering the amount of time I'd been "annoying" him. "I'm not working for the devil. I wouldn't work for them, no matter how broke I was. Tiffany's father hired me. Her real father."

I gaped at him. "What? Her father's dead. We saw it on the news. Did he hire you before he was killed?"

His eyes glittered with what I could only translate as superiority combined with a sense of the dramatic. "Lawrence Miller wasn't her real father. My employer, Mason Davies, has been looking for her. It took some clever machinations on my part to find her. He's her biological father."

"Mason Davies." The name sounded familiar. "How is that possible? Her mother was in the cult when she gave birth."

"Mr. Davies had a love affair with Tiffany's mother before she joined the cult. He didn't know until recently about Tiffany. Those DNA kits are good for business."

"What do you want with her?"

"Mr. Davies asked me to locate her and ask if she'd be interested in a meeting. That's all. Nothing to get your panties in a knot over."

"My panties are not in a knot, nor is the rest of me. What's the Davies character like? Is he a good man?"

"I don't make judgments about my clients."

"Maybe you should," I said. "It would keep you from taking on the wrong kind."

"I can tell you this—his intentions for meeting Tiffany are pure. There are no skeletons with this guy. Nothing he's trying to hide. He wants to meet the daughter he never knew he had. That's all."

My mind couldn't quite catch up with all this new information. Tiffany had a father she never knew. A father very much alive.

"Can you help me?" Ralph asked. "Let her know I have a message for her from her father?"

"I'll do what I can."

13

TIFFANY

I didn't find the questioning as difficult as I'd anticipated. The agents, a man named Elliot Hacket and his partner, Meg English, were kind and patient as I shared my story while shedding many tears. Throughout the questioning period, I must have gone through half a box of tissues.

Elliot was in his forties, whether on the lower or upper end, I couldn't say. He looked how I'd imagined an FBI agent to look: clean-shaven, carefully combed hair slicked back with gel, and sharp green eyes. He might have been born and raised in the very conference room in which they questioned me. His partner, Meg, younger and edgier, had a tattoo of a dragonfly on her wrist, which occasionally showed when she moved her arm a certain way. Her dark hair was pulled back into a painful-looking bun on top of her head, and she wore almost no makeup. A thick Southern accent—Tennessee maybe—disarmed me. I could easily see her out at a bar with friends.

"Is there anything else you can remember?" Agent Hacket asked.

"I'm sure there will be as soon as I walk out of here." I'd told them about the rituals, my relationship with Matthew, and how they'd poisoned him. I shared what I knew about my mother and her death.

"Do you have any questions for us?" Agent English asked. "Anything we can do to help you?"

My stomach turned, but I had to ask the question that had been on my mind all morning. "Do you know what's happening with my siblings? Where are they? And what has happened to my dad's wives? What will happen to them all?"

"Right now, they're staying in place," English said. "They have no place else to go."

"Most don't want to leave," Hacket said. "Brainwashing has a way of doing that."

His partner shot him a look that I interpreted as a warning. *Don't step over the line.*

"This case is personal to you, isn't it?" I asked.

"We've been working on it for a long time," English said. "So yeah. It matters to us what happens to the victims."

"And we do believe they were victims." Agent Hacket shifted in his chair and glanced over at his partner. "There's one more thing. Would you be willing to give us a sample of your DNA?"

"Sure, but why?" I asked.

"One of your father's children, a boy of fourteen, told us in an interview that he believes his real father was not Lawrence Miller."

"Who else would it be?"

"William Fellows," English said gently. "He claims that all the pregnancies from his various wives were not from Lawrence Miller but rather William Fellows."

I was trying to follow what was he saying, but the meaning behind the words would not penetrate my consciousness. "I don't understand. Are you saying my father—I mean, Lawrence Miller—wasn't the father of any of us? How could that be? He had five wives when I left." I could see all the children in my mind, blond stairsteps. Their faces were a blur to me, as were those of the mothers. I remembered shapes and colors, heights and figures, but not real people.

"We're uncertain why he would not have fathered the children, other than the obvious," English said.

"The obvious?" I asked.

"Sterile or impotent," English said.

"Oh, yes, right." I flushed, embarrassed, wishing I could fall through the floor to the lobby and run away with Breck.

"There's something else," Hacket said. "We've done DNA testing, and it's conclusive. William Fellows is the father of all of the children born from Lawrence Miller's wives, except for you."

It was as if a bucket of cold water had been dumped on my head. "Everyone but me? But how do you know?"

"From the interviews with wives, we learned your mother was pregnant before she came to Briar Rose," English said. "Your father was not part of the cult. He'd never been, according to the women we talked with."

"Why would my mother go there?" If I'd only had a photograph of her, at least I could look at it and try to understand. Look for something in her eyes that would explain why she would leave the world and walk through the gates of Briar Rose. "And who is this man? My real father?"

"We interviewed him," English said. "He came to us after the story broke. By then, he knew about you."

"But how?" I asked. "I've been secretive about my past."

"He hired a private detective," Hacket said. "It took some doing, apparently, but the P.I. figured out your mother went to Briar Rose and that she had a child. Given the timing, he figured you were his. He contacted us when the story broke, hoping to gain information about you. He assumed you were still there. We had to tell him there was no one on the list of rescued victims that matched your age. This was before you contacted us. We felt certain you were the daughter he'd been hoping to find."

A father. My real father. Out in the world, living a normal life. All this time I'd had no idea. How was it possible I didn't sense him? "What's his name? What's he like?"

The agents exchanged a look but didn't answer.

"Let me guess," I said. "He doesn't want to see me? He has a wife and children and doesn't want anything to mess up his perfect life?"

"No, not at all," English said.

"Like we said, he hired a detective to learn the truth," Hacket said.

"Oh, okay." What was the catch? There would be one. "How come he hasn't called me, then?"

A flash of guilt showed in English's eyes. "We asked him to wait until we had a chance to speak to you. He agreed that it might be easier for you to hear the news from us. That way, you could decide if you wanted to see him. He didn't want you to feel pressure."

"That was thoughtful," I mumbled.

"Yes. And selfishly, we weren't sure you'd come in if you knew you had no genetic tie to Briar Rose," English said. "We knew you'd be more clear on your memories without this momentous news flooding your thoughts."

I sat with that for a moment, thinking through their reasoning. "That's not what would have kept me away. I've been afraid to face all this. For ten years, I've tried to forget."

"What convinced you to come in?" English asked.

"My friend Breck," I said quietly. "Will what I told you be helpful?"

"Enormously so," English said. "We wish we'd known about you sooner."

"They erased me," I said. "Just as I tried to erase them."

"You're brave to come," Hacket said. "Thank you."

"You both made it easier. It feels like my fault, even though I know it's not."

"None of the children born into the disturbing legacy of Briar Rose are at fault." English had sharpened back into an agent. "Your interview and testimony will help put some bad men away."

Testify. Would I have to testify? Face the elders? "Will there be a trial?"

"At some point." English's sharp features softened. "Not for a while. And the prosecutor will help prepare you."

That promise didn't make me feel better, but I kept it to myself. At the moment, I just wanted to get out of there and see Breck. There was a lot to tell him.

"We have your father's contact information," English said. "Would you like it?"

"Yes, I would. I very much would. Thank you."

She handed me a sheet of paper. "There are some details of his life he sent along to us. In case you wanted them."

Without reading it, I took it from her and folded it into a square, then tucked it in my purse. I needed a moment before I learned more. A moment and a sandwich. And Breck.

BRECK WAS SITTING in the main lobby when I came out of the elevator. He sat in an armchair by the window with one leg crossed over the other, reading something on his phone. Whatever it was interested him a great deal, because he didn't hear me say his name the first time.

I stood in front of him. "Breck?"

He jerked and looked up at me. "Well, hey there."

"Why do you look guilty?" I asked, teasing. "Are you reading a forbidden book?"

He stood, shaking his head. "No, nothing like that. I have about a thousand things to tell you."

"Me too."

He looked toward the bank of glass windows. "Do you want to have a meal? You must be starving."

"They gave me a dry muffin but yes, I'm hungry."

"I had two bites of a dry sandwich and got one for you, but then I gave it away."

"To a homeless person?" What a dear thing to do. Breck truly was the kindest man.

"Not exactly." He scratched his chin. "I'll explain it later, okay?"

"Sure." Now he had me curious about what he'd been doing all morning.

"Javier doesn't want to come get us since it's gotten so late. Would you want to stay in Denver overnight? I know a great hotel not far from here. Or, I could rent a car and drive us home."

"There's Muffy. She'll need to go out and be fed." A hotel room? What kind of room would it be? One with two beds?

"I texted Jamie," Breck said. "She's going to pop over to your place and keep her until we get back."

"That's nice." He'd arranged all this while I'd been in with the agents. "You're sweet. Thank you."

"We can't have Muffy all alone." He grinned. "She wouldn't know what to do with herself."

"About the room," I said.

"We'll get two rooms," he said. "Don't worry."

"How did you know?" I asked.

"I could see it on your face. But, you know, we've already slept together."

I shoved his chest. "Very funny."

"Anyway, I thought we could have a nice dinner and you

could tell me all about your day and I can tell you about mine. You won't believe it."

"You won't believe mine," I said. "So that makes two of us."

"Two of us. I like the sound of that."

I dove into his chest and let him put his arm around me. "So do I."

THERE WERE no rooms for us at the hotel. "What's going on? Why is everything sold out?" Breck asked.

The girl behind the desk had purple hair and a nose ring. Her name tag identified her as Larissa. "A medical convention. Downtown is crawling with doctors. Good luck finding anything."

Breck looked at me, apologetic, as if it were his fault. I was the one who had dragged him here in the first place. Me and my dramatic life.

"We can drive home," I said. The idea of driving all that way made me want to start crying again. All I wanted was a good meal and a chance to think through the day's events.

Larissa, perhaps sensing my despair, looked at Breck and then me. "I do have one room left." She lowered her voice. "It's the penthouse suite, but I'll give it to you for the price of the king room. This is my last day, so I can really stick it to them, right?"

Stick it to whom?

"Does it have two beds?" Breck asked.

Larissa seemed confused by this question. Apparently, this hotel didn't do a very good job educating their staff. "I think so. It's like enormous. There's a sick wet bar too. But be careful. That stuff is not free in the little refrigerator."

"You okay with that?" Breck asked me.

I nodded, suddenly too tired to speak.

While he dealt with payment and details, I wandered over to the large fish tank built into a wall. All kinds of tropical fish were swimming, peaceful and without cares.

I placed a fingertip against the cold glass. A blue-finned fish swam up and pressed his mouth against the glass. I tapped my finger to say hello but apparently, he couldn't sense me because he remained, fluttering his fins like silk on a clothesline.

"You ready to go up?" Breck asked from behind me.

His presence made me shiver. I turned around to look at him. "She had some toiletries for us." He held up a plastic bag to show me.

"Toothbrushes?" What if I decided tonight was the night to kiss him? I wanted to have fresh breath.

"Got those too."

"Good," I said, following him into the elevator. I nibbled on my thumbnail the entire way up to the penthouse. How strange life could be. Here I was reeling from a mind-bending development, and yet I could still contemplate kissing. Was this the power Breck Stokes had over me?

When the elevator stopped, the doors opened directly into the suite.

I gasped, delighted and surprised at the beauty of the room. As a student, I'd toured rooms like this during our hospitality training. I never thought I'd stay in one. Furnished in muted shades of brown with splashes of teal and a view that looked over the entire city, it was first-class in every way. There was indeed a bar as well as the largest television I'd ever seen anyplace but the store. A half-circle couch in the mid-century modern aesthetic and a glass coffee table faced the television. Luxurious armchairs and a smaller table were set near the window.

I turned in a full circle to take in the entire place. That's when it hit me. There was only one door, leading into the bedroom. A quick glance informed me that there was only one bed. A large one. But still, only one. Not two as the poorly trained receptionist had told us.

Breck seemed to come to the same realization. "I can sleep on the couch."

I only nodded, figuring we could talk about it later. If the bed was a king then maybe we could just both sleep on it.

"I'm sorry," Breck said. "Maybe this was a bad idea."

"Don't be silly. I love this." I put my hand on his arm. "It's an adventure. I'm glad to be here with you."

"I'm glad to be here with *you*."

My stomach growled. Loudly.

"Yes, let's get some food in you. Do you want to go out for dinner or order room service? My mother loves room service. All those silver tops and white napkins get her every time."

"I vote room service." Black slacks and a sleeveless silk blouse were fine for business or a meeting as I'd had that morning, but not great for a dinner out on the town. Plus, my feet in these pumps were killing me.

"Are you sure? I'll take you anywhere you want to go."

"I'm exhausted, honestly. My feet hurt. Do you mind staying in?" I asked.

"Absolutely not. Whatever suits you, suits me."

"I'm going to wash my face and brush my hair before we eat."

He shook his head. "You know what you need? A bubble bath. This is the perfect place for one."

The idea of a bath sounded heavenly. "Are you sure?"

"I'll miss you, of course. However, I can catch up on sports while you're in there." He handed me the menu. "But first, pick out what you want to eat. I'll order while you're in the bath."

"Just pick something for me," I said. "But not a salad. I want something warm."

"You got it."

He handed me the toiletry bag. I slipped out of my pumps and headed into the bedroom. There might be only one bed but it was a California king, the size of the bedroom in my apartment. Another fireplace and television were positioned perfectly to enjoy from the bed. A room for sweethearts. I could practically see the rose petals and champagne on ice.

The tub in the bathroom was twice the size of a normal one. While it filled, I dumped the entire bottle of flower-scented bath bubbles into the water. I sat on the edge, watching the bubbles puff into clouds before undressing. As I slipped under the bubbles, my skin pricked for a second. I rested my head against the back of the tub and closed my eyes. Did I want to think through what had happened? Not particularly. I'd have preferred my mind to empty of thoughts and memories and leave me as peaceful as the tropical fish, but it was not to be. My thoughts bounced around noisily and disjointed like one of those balls in a pinball machine.

The revelations of the last few hours were too big to fully understand. That was all. I must let it all sink in before deciding one way or the other what to do next. Everything I thought I knew and understood, regardless of how horrific, had been my reality for as long as I could remember. I'd been born in a cult to a father who most likely had ordered my mother's death. He'd wanted me dead as well. But now? I had to wrap my head around a whole new reality. I had a father. Perhaps he was a relatively normal man with a wife and a family. A father who wanted to meet me. One who had gone to considerable trouble to find me.

I opened my eyes to stare at the ceiling above the tub. Moisture from the steam dampened the paint. What did I want? Did I even know?

Yes. I knew. Of course, I knew. I wanted to meet him. Perhaps it would be a disaster, but I had to see him for myself. He was my family.

It would take a while to adjust to this new reality, but what other choice did I have but to embrace it? I'd wanted a community and family, hadn't I? Being alone wasn't the way humans were meant to live.

Anyway, Breck was here. Waiting for me. Willing to take me just as I was. A warmth that had nothing to do with the luxurious water came over me. Was it possible that I'd finally found the right person to share my life with?

Sufficiently pruned, I got out of the tub and wrapped myself in a towel. A robe, folded into a square, waited on a shelf. I grabbed it and pulled it over my toasty, damp skin.

I went to the mirror. My mascara had run, and any trace of lipstick was long gone. I loosened the knot on my head and let my hair cascade down around my shoulders. I'd packed a pouch with my makeup and a comb, which I used now to repair the damage.

Justice, I thought, as I stared back at my reflection. I'd been right to come here and do my part to get justice for my mother and Matthew. I hadn't thought I would ever see the day when they would have to atone for what they did. Everything I thought I knew just a week ago was no longer true. Everything in my life was about to change. For the better. Right?

14

BRECK

While Tiffany was in the bath, I prowled around the room as jumpy as a cat. How could I tell her what I'd learned earlier? There was no easy way to tell her that the man she'd thought of as her father was not actually any blood relation to her.

She came out of the bathroom rosy-cheeked. Her makeup had been smeared when she came down from the interview. I ached at the thought of what she'd had to live through again while telling her story. If I could have saved her from further heartache, I would have. But she had to be told the truth.

"Hey there," I said. "How's the robe?"

"It and the bath were just what I needed." She dazzled me with a smile that made the very soles of my feet tingle. "Don't look like that. I'm fine."

"I know you are." My expression must have betrayed my concern. "But it's been a long day. Is there anything I can get you?"

"No, I'm fine," she said. "Grab yourself something to drink and let's sit. I have lots to tell you."

"Do you want anything? I'm going to have a glass of wine."

"No, I'll wait until my ginger ale comes with my dinner." She plopped onto one end of the circular couch and stared at the unlit fireplace.

"You want me to turn this on?" I asked, referring to the gas fireplace.

"I'd like that, thank you."

I flipped the switch, and the fake logs immediately lit up with gas flames.

"There's something so cozy about a fireplace, isn't there?" Tiffany tucked her legs under her. "We had woodstoves in the cabins where we lived."

I hovered near the couch, hoping for more.

"It was my job to start the fire in the mornings," she said. "Each wife had her own cabin where she lived with her children. I was taken in by my father's first wife even though she wasn't my mother. In reparation, I was to start all the fires in the mornings. I'd dress in the cold, shivering, and then get them going one after the other." She pulled a throw pillow into her lap. "I haven't thought about that in a long time. My hands wouldn't work properly because they were cold, but I somehow managed to get them all lit. I'd huddle there in my flannel nightgown waiting for the stove to start giving out heat. By the end of the routine, I'd smell of woodsmoke."

I waited, expecting her to continue, but she appeared to be finished.

"Get your drink," she said. "You're making me nervous."

"Will do." The minibar had half bottles of wine. I opened a red blend and poured a glass. When I returned, Tiffany seemed lost in thought. I took the other end of the couch. The cushions were surprisingly hard, making it impossible to slouch. What good was a hard sofa, I wondered absently. And how would a man nap on here?

I stretched my feet out under the coffee table. "How are you doing?" When should I tell her what I'd learned? After dinner?

My dad had always said it was best to have a full stomach when facing an ordeal.

"Thanks for coming with me," Tiffany said. "I want to start there." She'd made up her eyes in the restroom and reapplied blush, erasing all remnants of her grief.

"I'm glad to be here," I said.

"This will make me sound weak, but the thought of you being there at the end of the day got me through all that."

Her words warmed me as nothing else could. "That's what I'm here for."

"I learned a lot today." Her voice shook. She pressed her fingers against her windpipe. "You won't believe it."

I might, I thought, given what I'd learned today myself. "Tell me," I said gently before drinking from my glass of wine.

"Lawrence Miller is not my father."

"How did you find out?"

"My real father reached out to the FBI." She narrowed her eyes, observing me. "How come you're not surprised?"

I rubbed my temples. "There was a man hanging around the building, and I got a weird feeling about him. Turns out, he's a private detective. Hired by your real father."

"Oh my God." She breathed out the words more than spoke them. "My mother got pregnant when they were just out of high school, but they broke up and he never knew about the baby. Me. I was that baby. Obviously." Tears glistened in her eyes. "They gave me his contact information as well as details about him." She unfolded her legs and padded over to her purse, pulling out a sheet of paper. "It's all here." She placed it between us on the couch. "I haven't had the courage to look yet."

"Do you want me to read it?"

"Would you?" The corners of her mouth twitched into a sad smile. "It seems easier to hear it all from you."

I picked up the paper and unfolded it, reminded of those paper fortune-tellers Huck used to make when we were in middle school. The information was laid out succinctly, with all the details of this man's life in black and white. Wife named Lennox, a pediatrician. Two young sons. He held the position of CEO at a computer software company. Residence in Denver, Colorado. "He lives here with his wife and two sons."

"Two brothers." She drew in a breath. "That's all I have. After all these years of thinking I had dozens of half-siblings."

"What do you mean?"

"None of the children supposedly fathered by Lawrence Miller are his. The FBI did DNA samples on all the children. They were all traced to Elder William."

"What the—" I stopped myself before the expletive came out of my mouth.

"I know. They've concluded that Elder William impregnated the wives so that no one knew he was either infertile or...you know, the other thing." She flushed and played with the ends of the bathrobe's tie.

"Why would they do that?"

"If you knew them, it might make more sense. They wanted all of us to think they were all just one degree of separation from God himself. Being unable to impregnate the girls would be embarrassing to him and would poke holes in the theory that they'd been chosen to procreate directly by God. That's how they sold it to the women—we were lucky and special to be able to give a near-God offspring, especially boys."

"Good God, that's sick." My stomach churned, thinking about these men selling themselves as God to the poor, deluded flock.

"I want to know why my mother joined and then died trying to escape."

"What do you know about her? I mean, before she joined the cult."

"Nothing. I don't even have a photo of her. I've never seen what she looks like."

"Your real father might have pictures. Regardless, he'll be able to tell you what he knows about her. What made her vulnerable to men like William and Ryan, for example."

"Yes, he will. Unless they were just a little fling or something and he didn't really know her that well. But I want to meet him. I have to meet him."

"Are you ready now, or do you need some time?"

"I have no idea."

"You could call him," I said. "Feel it out. See if he's someone you want to meet in person."

She gazed over at me as if that thought had never occurred to her. "Yes, I suppose I could do that. Tonight rather than later." She returned her gaze to the fire. Insecurity and doubt played out on the profile of her face. A muscle flexed in her cheek as she contemplated the idea. "He has a whole life, though. A family. Probably all perfect and everything. Would he really want me to come along and blow it all up?"

"He hired a detective to make sure you were all right. I think he wants to see you."

"That's what he told the agents." She reached over to pick up the unfolded sheet of paper. "I could call him after we eat maybe? If he wanted to meet me, we could go before we headed home tomorrow."

"I'm here. Whatever you want to do."

She smoothed the paper into the couch cushion with both hands, as if trying to iron out the creases. "I'll eat first and then call." She glanced up at me, a spark in her eyes.

"My dad said it was best to have a full stomach before an ordeal."

"Right. Eat, then call my real dad...the one I never knew I had." She giggled.

"Best practice, that one."

15

TIFFANY

After dinner, with a shaking hand, I typed Mason Davies's number into my phone. Listed on the sheet was his cell phone number. I fully expected the call to go to voice mail. No one answered an unknown number these days. This was nice and safe. I'd leave a message and be done with it. So I almost dropped the phone when a man's deep voice said, "This is Mason."

"Oh, um, hi. This is…this is Tiffany Birt."

Silence greeted me for a few seconds before he said my name. "Tiffany?"

"Yes, I'm your…daughter." I almost choked on the word. "The agents gave me your number." He would know that, obviously. How else would I have gotten his number? I wasn't completely in my body and definitely not my right mind.

"Yes, well, this is…something."

I giggled nervously. "I know."

"How are you?"

Had there ever been more questions encompassed in three little words? "I'm all right. I hope it's okay to call."

"I'm glad you did."

"Good. Here we are, I guess." I bit the inside of my mouth, waiting. What happened now?

"I've thought about this moment many times, but I never actually thought through what I'd say. Isn't that funny?"

"There's not really a script for this kind of thing," I said.

"No, not really. I've been obsessed with my phone since I found out about you. Hoping you'd call. My boys have been giving me a hard time."

"What are their names? The boys."

"Benji and Josh. They're six and eight."

"Does your wife know about me?" I asked.

"She knows everything about me. We don't do things any other way."

"What does she think?" I held my breath. My heart seemed to pound against my rib cage.

"She knows this all happened long before I met her. In fact, she's been hoping you'd call. She understands how important this is to me."

"I don't want to disrupt your life."

"Well, it's a little late for that, isn't?" Mason said, then chuckled. "This is disruptive to both of us. But that doesn't mean it's a bad kind of disruption." He paused, but not long enough for me to figure out what I wanted to say next. "I'd like the chance to meet you, but it's up to you. You're in charge here."

"I'd like to meet you too," I said, feeling about five years old.

"I have a lot of questions," Mason said. "Like where do you live?"

"I'm in Emerson Pass. Do you know where that is?"

"Oh my God. We go there every Christmas break to ski. How long have you been there?"

"About three years. I'm a wedding planner at the lodge."

"That's where we stay. Room 202. Every year since the boys were old enough to ski."

A pregnant pause hung between us. We'd probably been in

the same building at least once or twice. Had I seen him at some point? An overwhelming sadness enveloped me. All those years wasted.

"I thought one of the elders was my father," I said, finally.

"That's what they told me. The elder who was killed in the raid: Lawrence Miller."

I swear I could hear him internally debating about what to say next. "I knew Lawrence Miller. He lived next door to your mother when we were kids." His voice sounded raspy, as if he couldn't get enough air into his lungs. "He was friends with Mona's parents before they…"

"Before what?"

"They were killed in a car accident the summer after we graduated. Listen, how would you feel about coming to see me? I could fly you to Denver. These things should be talked about in person."

"Actually, I'm in Denver. Downtown. I came here to talk to the agents. I'm staying overnight with a friend."

"Do you like breakfast? My wife makes a mean blueberry pancake."

I looked out to the sitting area where Breck watched a cooking show. He wouldn't mind staying longer; I knew that without having to ask. But how much more could I ask of him?

"Is it too much?" Mason asked, sounding so apologetic it hurt my heart. "My wife told me not to push. That you weren't one of my employees."

"I like breakfast." I smiled. "Blueberry pancakes are my favorite."

"Mine too," he said softly. "What hotel are you in? I'll send a car."

The name of the hotel? I didn't even know. I reached for the notepad on the bedside table and read the name on the top.

"I'll have him come around eight-thirty, if that works?"

Again, the hesitancy in his voice told me he was trying as hard as I not to offend or push.

"Can I bring my friend? He came with me to meet with the agents."

"Of course. Is this a boyfriend?" Mason sounded suddenly very fatherly. I warmed from head to toe. Would he be like Brandi and Crystal's dad? Would he be someone I could count on the way they did Jack?

"A friend," I said quietly. "One I like a lot."

"I'll look forward to meeting him."

After agreeing on a few details, we hung up. I tossed the phone into the middle of the bed and sat there staring at it until Breck called out to me from the other room.

"Tiff, you good?"

I nodded, exhausted. Somehow, I managed to get up from the bed and go into the other room.

"Hey." Breck stood while simultaneously turning off the television. "How was it?"

"Strange but nice. He wants me to come to breakfast tomorrow."

"Great. I'll drive you there."

"He's sending a car. For both of us."

His eyebrows rose as he tilted his head to the side. "You sure? This is a big deal. I don't want to be in your way."

"You won't be in the way." I sank into the couch and let out a breath that it felt like I'd been holding in for hours. "Lawrence Miller lived next door to my mother's family. Her parents died in a car accident right after she graduated from high school. Given my birth date, she must have found out right after that she was pregnant. Mason said he'd tell me everything when we see him in person. Every time I think this is it, there's more."

"You're doing great," Breck said.

"I don't have anything to wear. I can't meet him in dirty clothes. I sweated through them today."

He looked at his watch. "The shops are still open. You want to run out and get a new dress?"

"I don't have the money for a new dress." Of everything today, this was the least of my worries, but for some reason, it broke me. I started to cry, and once I started it seemed impossible to stop.

He took me into his arms and let me cry. When I was all done, I lifted my messy face toward him. "I'm sorry."

"I have an idea." His eyes twinkled at me. "I have a friend from college. She's a personal shopper and stylist to the stars. She always has an inventory of clothes she keeps on hand to dress her clients."

"Who has a personal dresser?" I asked, unable to fathom such a thing.

"There's a lot of rich ladies here. Parties and such. Anyway, I could call her and ask her to bring some options over. She owes me a favor. I saved her cat a few years back."

I wanted to ask what had been wrong with the cat but didn't have the energy to veer the subject away from the stylist. "I guess so. I mean, if it's not too much trouble for her."

"I'll order a bottle of wine and some fudge, and Daphne will be happy as a piglet in mud."

Soon, he was on the phone with Daphne explaining that he had a friend in desperate need of a last-minute outfit. He covered his phone with his hand. "She wants to know the occasion."

"Meeting the father you never knew you had for breakfast." I hiccupped and giggled at the same time.

He went back to the phone. "She's meeting a long-lost relative for breakfast." He nodded, obviously in response to whatever Daphne was saying. "Yeah, a dress sounds good. Skinny jeans and tops, sure." He chuckled. "I don't know. But yeah, just bring a couple options. She's not high-maintenance like your clients." He winked at me. I smiled back at him. God, he was cute. "Do you need shoes?"

I looked down at my bare feet, no long wrinkled from the tub. "Maybe. It depends on the outfit."

He relayed that back to her. "She had black pumps on earlier, but you should bring some options."

"Does she need my sizes?" I asked.

"Yes, she does. Hang on, Daph, I'm getting them now."

"Size four or small for clothes. Size eight for shoes."

He repeated this back to Daphne. "Okay, cool. We'll see you in thirty minutes. And hey, red or white wine?" He laughed at her answer. "You got it. See you in a few." He hung up and looked over at me with a triumphant expression. "I'm feeling super smart right now."

"You are smart," I said. "And kind."

He reached for the room phone. "She wants vodka. Apparently, red wine stains your teeth. She's totally vain but also the best."

"I wouldn't mind a drink too," I said, surprising myself. "Like a fruity something or other."

"Strawberry daiquiri?" he asked. "That's what my mom always orders on vacation. Or a piña colada? They're kind of like smoothies with booze."

I'd never had one but if it was like a smoothie, then I was in. "Yes, please. But could I have it without alcohol?

Breck smiled, as if we shared an inside joke. "Virgin, you got it."

He ordered a few brownies in addition to the wine and my drink before thanking them and hanging up. "Should be here soon."

"Did you date this Daphne?" I asked. What was that weird feeling in my belly? Jealousy? Yes, that was it. Daphne was probably stylish and worldly. He might be reminded how much he liked her, especially next to me and my giant baggage.

"No way. She's been with my buddy Joe since college. They're one of those couples that just works." A twinge of envy in his voice surprised me. I'd never heard him envious of anything.

"You want that, don't you?" I asked.

"A relationship that works? Doesn't everyone?"

"I guess so." Did I? I hadn't thought it possible for me until I met Breck.

"You guess so or you know?" His gaze was unusually serious.

"I know so."

His face broke out into a joyful smile. "Good to hear."

DAPHNE SWEPT in like a summer storm, full of blustering wind that brought a sense of change. Tiny and a little too thin, she wore a black sheath dress and heeled boots that came up past her knees. Her platinum hair was cut into a blunt, straight bob that touched her collarbones. The bleached hair might have looked tacky on others, but not Daphne.

She hugged Breck the moment he opened the door. "Well, look at you," Daphne said to him. "You look amazing, even in that."

He looked down at his T-shirt and jeans. "What's wrong with what I'm wearing?"

"Oh, darling, you're the cutest." She turned her elfish face toward me. "This must be Tiffany."

I held out my hand, but she ignored it and pulled me into an embrace.

"You're gorgeous," Daphne said. "Where have you been keeping this one?"

"I don't keep her anywhere," Breck said. "She keeps herself."

"Of course she does," Daphne said. "It's a turn of phrase."

Another knock on the door interrupted whatever Breck was going to say next.

"That's Romero," Daphne said. "With my rack."

Romero, her assistant, entered with a dramatic flourish. He was also dressed in black, but that's where the similarities to Daphne ended. Romero was rotund with dark hair and skin and large brown eyes framed with thick lashes. His full mouth always seemed on the verge of a grin.

"This is our project." Daphne pointed to me.

A trickle of sweat dribbled down the back of my spine. I didn't like being looked at as if I were something to be remade. "I don't want anything too wild," I said with a worried glance over at Breck. But he didn't notice; he was too busy looking through the garments that hung on the mobile clothes rack.

"Do you bring this thing with you everywhere?" Breck asked.

"Most of the time, but not always. I have a dozen or so clients on retainer who stop by the studio." Daphne turned to me. "I'm also a clothes designer with my own shop. People come by for styling, but also if they want something custom-made."

"I won't need any of those things," I said. "Just a dress for tomorrow."

"Right. I have a few things in mind for you to try on," Daphne said. "Tell me a little more about the event, though."

I told her what I knew. "He lives in a wealthy neighborhood. Breck and I just looked it up, and the houses are enormous. There's a swimming pool and maybe we'll eat outside." Embarrassed by the juvenile hopefulness in my voice, I stopped, adding only, "I might need a cardigan depending on the weather."

"A cardigan?" Daphne's perfectly shaped eyebrows wriggled as if she were trying to keep them from raising.

"Yes, a sweater," I said, as if she didn't know what a cardigan was. Apparently, a cardigan was not something Daphne would *ever* recommend.

"All right, well, let's get you into the bedroom. I'll pull a few ideas for you to try on."

Daphne started plucking garments off the rack and handing them to Romero, who dutifully draped them over his arm.

I followed Romero into the bedroom, leaving Daphne and Breck in the other room. Fascinated, I watched Romero lay out the various outfits on the bed as if they were in a display window. There was a spaghetti-strap dress with a pattern of large orange poppies against light blue. In addition, a pair of skinny jeans that probably cost more than a week's salary was paired with a sleeveless yellow silk blouse. Black cropped leggings and a cotton tunic in light blue were the third choice. *They looked comfortable*, I thought, about the time Daphne sailed into the room. She had a halter-style dress made of white cotton fabric sprinkled with tiny pink flowers in her arms.

Daphne shooed Romero out, but not before she instructed him to find suitable shoes for each outfit. The moment he was gone, she shut the door and leaned against it, gazing at me with a look of determination in her eyes. "You're absolutely breathtaking," Daphne said. "And with your height and figure, you could wear anything. So if you don't like these, we can pull others. I want you to be happy."

"I really appreciate it," I said. "I tend toward simple, classic pieces because I'm on a budget. This is a treat."

"You're adorable." She pointed at me. "Now strip down and put the first one on." She plopped onto one of the armchairs and crossed one skinny leg over the other and hooked her foot behind the ankle. How did she wear those spiky heels? I hoped Romero wouldn't pull any of those.

Self-conscious to undress in front of someone, I contemplated escaping into the bathroom but thought better of it. Daphne wouldn't run to the bathroom to change. She would just tear off her clothes with no worries whatsoever. Maybe she'd gone to acting school. Stormi had once told me about an old boyfriend of hers in New York City who'd told her tales of the backstage mayhem during a play. People changed costumes in front of everyone else, regardless of gender. I'd like to be that free, but it wasn't happening today.

I sucked in my tummy and undressed. Standing in my bra and panties, I'd never felt more vulnerable. Daphne, however, didn't seem to notice my insecurities. She stared at me with the eye of an artist looking at a piece of clay.

"What a figure," Daphne said. "Do you intermittent fast?"

"What? No, I'm not sure what that is."

She explained the concept of eating only during certain hours in order to...? I got lost at that point. But it was something good.

"I'm on the broke diet," I said.

She sat up straighter, obviously interested to learn more. "What's that? I've never heard of it. Is it new?"

I smiled, embarrassed. "No, I mean, I'm poor and don't have much money to spend on food."

"Oh God, I must sound like a vapid idiot to you." She covered her mouth with both hands.

"No, you don't." She simply sounded as if she lived in a different world from me. Which she did.

By this time, I'd slipped the dress over my head and tugged it down over my hips. The fabric was incredible, structured yet soft. I'd thought the poppies might be too much, but I liked them.

"That's nice on you." Daphne rose up from the chair and brought me over to the full-length mirror that hung on one wall. She smoothed her hands over my hips as she stood behind me. "It fits well. You're tall enough for it. So jealous."

I looked at my exposed legs. Could I sit in this without showing everyone my underwear? "I don't know. It's kind of short to meet my father." Father? Mason. His name was Mason. I shouldn't get ahead of myself.

"Will you feel worried or self-conscious?" Daphne asked.

"I think so."

"Okay, then, it's out for tomorrow. However, you must keep this one and wear it on a date. Breck will lose it when he sees your legs in that, especially with some high-heeled sandals."

Was she suggesting I keep it? How was I going to pay for all of this? "Um, how much does this one cost?"

She seemed not to hear me, already focused on the next outfit. "Here, try these jeans." She held them up. They looked small enough for a child.

"They're tiny," I said. "Like made for you."

"They stretch, darling. Don't worry. I know what I'm doing when it comes to sizes."

I didn't really want to take off the dress, as it made me feel like a rich person, but I did so and dressed in the jeans and sleeveless blouse. The jeans did miraculously stretch and were much softer than I'd expected. "These feel nice," I said.

"They look great." She once again came to stand behind me. Even with her heels and me in bare feet, I felt like a giant next to her.

Daphne lifted the collar of the blouse and then flattened it against my skin. "I like this color on you. Your eyes are such a remarkable blue. The yellow contrasts nicely with your dark hair too. With your black pumps, this could be a winner."

Pumps? To breakfast? This wasn't a television show. Still, the idea pleased me. This was fun, I realized. Who knew being dressed as if I were a doll could be such a treat?

"Okay, try on the next one."

I did so and was soon standing in front of the mirror again. The tunic hung just past my hips and had wide, puffy sleeves that were in style. The fabric felt light and airy against my skin. "I like this one."

"It's nice, but not as spectacular as the other two. Might be all right for the morning, though. Especially with heels."

Next came the halter dress. The moment I put it on, I fell in love. The fabric was soft and flowing, and surprisingly, the tight bodice and V-neck collar were flattering to my small chest. The A-line skirt hovered just above my knees. "This is the one," I said.

"Agreed. The perfect one for a family gathering. Modest yet elegant, but not too fancy."

We smiled at each other in the mirror. "That's what I thought."

"See? You're getting the hang of this already," Daphne said.

"Could I wear sandals without too much of a heel?" I asked. "I'm afraid I'll fall into the swimming pool with anything too high."

She gave me a disappointed look but agreed. "Whatever helps you feel good and comfortable is the right choice. However, I'm sending you home with all these outfits. You must promise me to wear each one of them to whatever events are appropriate."

She went to the minibar and took out a small bottle of vodka and poured it into a cup with only ice. "This penthouse is fabulous," she said. "Breck knows how to show a girl a good time."

"We're not really dating," I said again. "Or, we are but I don't know. It's complicated."

She sank back into the chair and eyed me over the rim of her glass. "Why?"

"I don't have that much experience with men."

"But you like him?" Daphne didn't waste much time on small talk.

"Breck is nearly perfect," I said. "What's not to like?"

Recognition came to her eyes. "Oh, I see. You don't think you're good enough for him. I totally get that."

I exchanged the dress for the bathrobe. Was that right? Was my resistance because of feelings of inferiority? The voices in my head about my inadequacies were loud, this was true. How did people push those aside to make room for love?

"Why are you living in Denver?" I asked. "Wouldn't LA and all the movie stars be better? It has the beach and starlets who need styling."

She pursed her lips and unfolded her crossed leg. "Well, that's a good question. I suppose it's the same as you. Fear."

I decided not to address the fear quotient in regard to myself and stay focused on her. "What do you have to be afraid of?"

"Utter failure and dying alone in a gutter."

I laughed. "I like the extreme scenario. It keeps you nice and safe in Denver."

"Well said." Daphne stood and came to stand next to me in the mirror. "How will you wear your hair?"

"Down, I guess."

"Great then, I think you're ready."

"Not before shoes," Romero said. We turned to the doorway to see Romero carrying low-heeled silver sandals and ballerina flats in his hands.

"Sandals," Daphne said. "No question. If only every decision was that easy."

She could say that again.

16

BRECK

R omero and I were in the sitting room having a drink
when the ladies returned from the bedroom.
"A drink? I'd love one." Daphne shook her empty
glass. "Fill me up. Tiffany's found the perfect outfit for
tomorrow."

"I can't wait to see it." I'd been hoping she'd come out to
show us the different styles, but no such luck. Before heading to
the bar, I took a good look at Tiffany. She seemed much
improved in spirits than before dinner. Thank God for Daphne.
Tiffany had needed a distraction, and what better than new
clothes?

I poured Daphne a vodka with ice and a splash of soda and
handed it to her, mouthing a silent thank-you.

We all settled on the couch. Daphne and Romero entertained
us for a good hour with stories of their clients. When I saw
Tiffany yawn behind her hand, I knew it was time I got her to
bed. Tomorrow would be emotionally draining, and I wanted
her to have a good rest.

"It was great to see you guys," I said. "But it's getting late."

Daphne, bless her, got the hint and stood, motioning for

Romero to follow. There were hugs and promises of a visit to Emerson Pass. Daphne insisted on leaving all four of the style choices for Tiffany to take home. "You might need them for a night out or something," Daphne said.

"Thank you." Tiffany smiled shyly at her. "I did love them, but I can't afford all of them."

"Afford? No, dear girl, they're on the house. I get a lot of samples from various places. Doesn't cost me a thing, and I want you to have them."

Tiffany clapped her hands like a happy child on Christmas morning. "Thank you so much."

"My pleasure. Good luck tomorrow." Daphne and Romero headed toward the door with their portable clothes rack.

After they were gone, I turned to see Tiffany standing near the windows looking out at the Denver skyline.

"How are you doing?" I asked. "Can I get you anything?"

She slowly rotated to look at me. "No, I'm fine." She fluttered her fingers toward the bedroom. "It's not super late. Do you want to watch a movie or something before we go to bed? We could watch in there."

I swallowed my excitement. She wasn't inviting me to her bed. Most women I knew would use watching a movie as code for more, but I knew better than to believe that was the idea here.

"We could watch one out here if you'd prefer," I said.

"No, I think I'd like to watch from in there. I'd like you to be next to me."

I grinned. "Fine. I'd be honored."

"I'm going to brush my teeth." She hurried out of the room. I heard the bathroom door shut and then the sound of the shower running.

I wandered to the windows. The lights of the stadium were visible from here, as were various other restaurants and shops in the downtown area. As a kid, my dad had brought me to at least one baseball game a season. I smiled, remembering how much fun we'd had. In fact, they were some of my favorite memories of our time together. We'd stayed at a hotel and gone to the game and then out for steaks. The steakhouse we liked to go to had always been packed with drunk Denver fans. I loved every minute of it. We'd been to a game the weekend before his cancer diagnosis. Three months later, he was gone.

My mother often said she was glad he didn't have to suffer a long illness. She claims he would have hated to be bedridden and rely on others. It was better that he'd gone quickly. I knew she was right, but it had been so fast and so unbelievable to lose him that way. If only I'd known that it was our last Christmas or last game or final Father's Day maybe I could have prepared. But probably not. Losing him would have hurt as much.

My dad's death was my worst nightmare. I couldn't imagine a world without him in it. I still couldn't. There wasn't a day that passed that I didn't think about him. I felt him there with me during graduations and special occasions. I knew he was proud of me from where he watched from heaven. Still, I wished he were here in the flesh.

Dad, I said silently. Could you and God look out for Tiffany tomorrow? She's going to be scared and worried.

My father's voice came back loud and clear. *That's what you're for, son.*

AFTER MY SHOWER and a shave with one of the razors the hotel had sent up and a good brushing of my teeth, I put on one of the robes and went out to the bedroom. The scent of Tiffany's hair permeated the air. She was sitting on the bed with her legs spread out long and the remote in her hand. "They have movies, but they're twenty-one ninety-nine. Can you believe that?"

"Yeah, hotels overprice movies for sure."

"We could just watch something on television. There are quite a few channels. What kind of shows do you watch?"

"I don't really watch much other than sports," I said. "I never had the time when I was in school and got out of the habit. At night before bed, I mostly read."

"That's the same with me." She clicked the TV off. "Let's talk instead." She patted the spot next to her. "If you'd like, you can sleep here. This bed is gigantic."

My heart leaped at the idea. *Keep your pants on*, I told myself. This was simply a generous gesture. "Sure, that sounds a lot better than the couch." But I didn't have on anything under this robe. I'd washed out my boxers and hung them in the bathroom. What had Tiffany done with hers?

There I went again, thinking about things I should not be thinking about. I went over to my side of the bed and lay down on top of the covers. She was right about the bed. It was even bigger than my king at home. I turned on my side to watch her pull back the covers and slide into bed. I hadn't turned on my bedside lamp but hers was still on, casting a soft glow on her silky, shiny hair. Had there ever been a more beautiful woman?

"Your hair looks pretty in this light," I said. "Every light."

"I like your hair too." Her eyes stared at me from the other side of the bed. We were each as far to the edge as we could be without falling off. "Thanks for thinking of Daphne too. She's pretty funny."

"Yes, she is."

Tiffany lifted her head from her pillow and brushed her hair out of the way before returning to a relaxed position. "What should we talk about?"

"Politics?" I asked, joking.

"I quickly figured out when I joined the real world that the quickest way to start an argument was to ask about politics."

"Yes, religion, sex, and politics. None of those are supposed to be brought up at dinner parties. At least, that's what my dad always told me."

"What else did he tell you?" Tiffany rolled over to turn off her lamp. A draft of air hit me as she returned to her position.

My eyes slowly adjusted to the light as I thought about her question. What other words of wisdom had he shared with me? "So many things, none of which I can remember at the moment."

"Does it hurt to talk about him?" Tiffany's sweet voice reached to me from the darkness.

"No, it doesn't hurt. I like talking about him. You can ask me anything. If it's something I don't want to talk about, I'll tell you."

"What was he like? What kinds of things did you do together?"

I told her about our baseball games and the camping trips he would take Huck, Trapper, and me on when we were young. "He was a sportsman and outdoor enthusiast. We had some good times on those trips." I chuckled, remembering the time a bear had woken us in the middle of the night trying to break into our ice chest. We'd seen bears before, but not close enough to hear their breathing and smell the foulness of their oily fur.

"Garrett and my dad shared a love of fiction. Although Dad always said Garrett was the writer and he was the reader. They were the greatest of friends. My dad was super supportive of Garrett's writing career. He lent him money to take a year off from his real job to finish his novel. That novel turned into the mystery series that he's still writing to this day."

"I love his books."

"Me too," I said. "I'm proud about my dad's part in them."

"If not for him, they might not exist," Tiffany said.

"Exactly. Huck's family had run the newspaper since the twenties until Garrett sold it in the early nineties. He'd never enjoyed it as much as his grandparents and great-grandparents had. The legacy of books and writing is a long one in that family. I'm sure you've heard about Josephine Barnes and the library."

"Yes, of course," Tiffany said.

"In fact, legend has it that my great-great-grandmother Poppy and Josephine were the best of friends, even though they were drastically different. Josephine was quiet and bookish whereas Poppy was the first female vet in the state and used to run around in her Model T saving animals."

"It must be nice to know where you came from," Tiffany said, sounding wistful.

"You're about to find out a lot more about your family."

She was quiet for long enough I thought she might have fallen asleep. "I'm scared for tomorrow," she said finally. "What if he's disappointed once he meets me?"

"He won't be, but if so, it's nothing you can't handle. Not after what you've been through."

"Breck?"

"Yeah?"

"Could you get under the covers? I'm cold."

"Sure." She was cold? What did this mean? I swiveled my legs to the floor and pulled back the covers. By the time I returned to bed, she had moved to the middle. I brushed against her as I turned on my side.

"Hey there," I said.

"Hey."

"You still cold? If you are, just come closer. I'm a human heater."

The bed moved. Soon, I felt her very near me. "Breck?"

"Yeah?"

"I've never been with a man. I've only ever kissed Matthew."

"Oh, well, okay."

"So that's why it's taking a while for me to offer myself up to you."

I chuckled. "You make it sound so tawdry."

"You know what I mean."

"I do. And we've got plenty of time, so you take it at your own pace."

"Do you think we could spoon?"

I laughed again. "Spoon? Sure. Do you know what that is?"

"Yes, squished together like spoons in a drawer." I felt, rather than saw, her roll onto her other side. "Now you can put your arm around me."

I did so, adjusting myself to fit her body against mine. "Good night."

"Good night."

I listened to her breathing slow and then become steady. For at least an hour I lay there awake, wishing the night could last forever. Falling in love with her was the easiest thing I'd ever done. Falling out of love would not be. I prayed that at some point she would feel the same way about me. For now, I was content to be by her side.

17

TIFFANY

Breck and I sat in the back seat of a black sedan. My hands were locked in a death grip as we drove into the gated community where Mason Davies made his home. The morning had seemed like a movie, waking in the opulence of the hotel suite, dressing in my new clothes, and then sliding into a car that smelled of leather and newly printed bills.

I leaned close to the window, taking in palatial houses positioned on a golf course. Manicured gardens and lawns seemed almost fictitious in their perfection. Gardeners wearing straw hats pulled low over their foreheads pruned and mowed. Residents drove golf carts toward the country club.

Mason Davies was rich. I should have known, given the information provided by the agents, but seeing it now, I shivered with nervousness.

Breck whispered in my ear, "It's just money. Don't be intimidated."

"I'm glad for the dress." Whatever insecurities I had were hidden under the persona of glamour and taste. For now.

We turned up a long driveway, coming to a stop in front of a fountain. I pinched the inside of my arm. The house was a two-story Mediterranean style with a combination of stucco and white bricks.

"Here we are, Miss Birt." Our driver, Edward, wore a black suit. The fabric had a shiny gleam that came from many washings. He got out and opened the back door for us. I stepped into the warm morning. Bees buzzed, hopping between flowers. Birds chirped, as if welcoming us. Above the black roof, the sky was blue and cloudless.

Breck put his hand on the small of my back. We walked up a smooth cement path toward double doors with a decorative flower etched into the glass.

Breck rang the doorbell. Our town car remained in the driveway. Would Edward wait until we were done?

A figure appeared through the frosted glass of the double doors. I'd expected a maid in an old-fashioned uniform, but instead, it was a man in his mid-forties who opened the door.

"Hello, Tiffany." He held out his hand. "I'm Mason Davies."

I shook his hand without letting go of Breck's with the other. "Hi. I'm Tiffany, and this is Breck Stokes." My voice sounded wobbly.

"Welcome to my home."

My arms tingled with goosebumps. "Your eyes," I said under my breath. They were the exact color of my own.

"And yours." Mason took both of my hands. His gaze fixed upon my face as if he were trying to memorize every detail. "Look at you. Absolutely beautiful."

"Thank you. You look nice too." I flushed with heat. What was wrong with me?

In my defense, he did look nice, dressed casually, in jeans and a short-sleeved blue shirt that showed off muscular arms. His silver-and-blond hair was cut into precise disarray. Straight white teeth seemed to sparkle in the sunshine. This was a man who took care of himself.

My father. This was my father. My legs trembled under the camouflage of my skirt.

The men shook hands. Mason looked straight into Breck's eyes, as if assessing his character. I appreciated this. A teacher I'd had my first year at junior college had said you could tell a lot about a person by eye contact. He claimed men who looked you in the eye were usually honest. That or sociopaths. I really hoped Mason Davies wasn't a sociopath.

He asked us to come inside. "My wife's obsessing about the meal. She'll be out in a minute. We can sit outside by the pool or inside. Whichever you prefer."

"Is there an umbrella?" Breck asked. "Tiffany's fair, and she doesn't have sunscreen on."

Leave it to Breck to think of that right now.

Mason smiled. "We have an umbrella for that very reason. My wife's a pediatrician. There's never any juice for the kids or time in the sun without protection. The boys never get to have any fun."

We followed him across the formal living room through a set of double doors that opened to the patio. The little boys were playing in the pool, splashing and shouting and having the focused fun of youth.

"It's our first really warm day," Mason said. "Otherwise we would have had them wait to get in the pool until you got here. But then again, I wasn't sure what the protocol is for meeting a long-lost daughter." His mouth lifted in a lopsided grin.

"I'm glad you let them swim. This must be weird for them. Doing normal things will make it less so. Or, I would think anyway."

"That's very considerate of you," Mason said.

Joy and trepidation in equal measure swept over me. I had a whole family. Just yesterday, I had no idea they existed and yet here we were. I glanced over at Breck. "I have brothers and they're swimming in the pool."

"It's awesome." His eyes shone back at me.

"They'll join us for breakfast, but for now it's best for them to get all their wriggles out," Mason said. "They have a lot of energy. We waited until Lennox was through with medical school to have kids. Sometimes we feel old." He looked at his feet, sheepish. "Or, the boys anyway."

"It's okay," I said. "You didn't know about me. It's not the same."

He looked as if he wanted to say something further but instead, gestured toward the table, positioned just outside the outdoor kitchen. A rectangular awning covered the entire table. Several vases of tulips decorated the middle.

We sat in chairs with thick cushions while Mason fetched drinks. The outdoor kitchen was nice, with a cooktop, grill, and sink in addition to the refrigerator. This was probably where they spent a lot of their time during warm weather. It's what I'd wanted for so long. A family. Cookouts and swimming parties.

"Ah, here's Lennox." Mason's face lit up at the sight of her making her way across the pool deck. She wore a red sundress and wedge sandals. Thank goodness I'd chosen the dress.

Mason introduced us. Pretty, with big brown eyes and a dark complexion, she was similar in age to her husband. She wore her long dark hair teased into loose waves.

"I'm glad to meet you both," Lennox said. "Everything will be ready in just a few. I'm not much of a cook, unfortunately, so don't expect much."

I liked her immediately. We all gathered around the table. I'd expected there to be an awkward silence, but Mason and Lennox were gifted in the art of conversation. My stomach unclenched as we chatted. More details of my family unfolded. As we'd already learned, Lennox was a pediatrician. Mason was not only the CEO of a software company, recently purchased by a large conglomerate, but the founder. "I may be out of a job soon," Mason said, with humor in his voice. "But a less hectic schedule will be nice."

He went on to say that he and Lennox had lived in their house for ten years and were well-established in the community.

"We like it here. Quiet and a little boring," Lennox said. "I come from a tumultuous childhood, so my goal has been to create the opposite for the boys."

"You have a beautiful home," Breck said.

"Thank you." Lennox smiled graciously. *She's handling this so well*, I thought. I wasn't sure I would be as flexible.

Mason looked over at me, expression a mixture of apprehension and regret. "Do you want to talk about your mother?"

I nodded, too choked up at the thought of finally learning more about her to speak.

"I'll go check on the food," Lennox said, "and let you all talk."

The boys were taking turns going down the slide into the pool. As Lennox passed by, they called out to her. She stopped and returned to the edge of the pool. Two dark heads swam toward her. She knelt, saying something to them I couldn't hear. Would my sudden appearance hurt their idyllic childhood?

"Would either of you like a mimosa?" Mason asked. "I have a pitcher made up in the kitchen. I'd like one before we get into all this."

"I'd love one," Breck said.

"I'll just have the juice," I said.

"Back in a minute." Mason crossed around the table and headed toward the house. I had a feeling he needed a minute with his wife to steady his nerves.

When he was out of earshot, Breck leaned over to ask if I wanted him to stay or go.

"Please, stay," I whispered back. "I may black out and won't be able to remember what he said."

"I'll take mental notes." He tapped his head.

Mason returned minutes later with four empty flute glasses and two pitchers, one with mimosas and the other with pure juice. After he poured us each a glass, he sat back down. "All right, where do I begin?"

"Maybe tell me how you met my mother?" I suggested.

He took a sip from his glass first. "We dated in high school all through our senior year. From the beginning, we'd agreed to having fun with no strings attached. She knew I was leaving for college in the fall, and she'd planned on going to beauty school. We agreed to go our separate ways and ended it amicably. When I was away, I learned about her parents' deaths. I'm speculating here, but I think she started dating Lawrence Miller right after I left. As I told you, he was a neighbor. I'd never thought twice about him because he was so much older than us. He'd be out in his yard sometimes mowing the lawn or doing whatever old people did—at least that's how I thought of him."

"Did you ever talk to him?" I asked.

"Not much. One time he was over for a party Mona's mom threw for maybe the Super Bowl? I'm not sure. But I *do* remember he wanted to start a theater. Your mother was interested in acting. I'm assuming they got together to talk about all of that and started seeing each other. How he got involved in the cult, I don't know for certain. It wouldn't surprise me if he was looking for something to fill a void. I was a teenager—I wasn't very observant, but I had the feeling he was a lost soul."

"The type who would be attracted to Briar Rose," Breck said.

"That's right." Mason drank from his mimosa before turning back to me. "Do you know when your mother died?" His voice pinched with sadness. "Or did they keep all of that from you?"

"They told me she died trying to escape. The women told me bits and pieces, but always as a cautionary warning." I told him about the stigma I'd carried with me. "I was seen as a charity case. They didn't have to keep me or protect me since my mom had betrayed the flock. Those of us without a mother were given all the worst chores. I learned how to sew when I was very young, which gave me a job. One that was important to the community. At the time, I thought I needed that to secure my safety. However, when it was time for me to be promised to one of the elders..."

"At fourteen," Mason said.

"That's right. Elder Ryan, who was second-in-command, snatched me up in his first pick."

"Like it was football draft or something," Breck said.

Mason closed his eyes for a second, obviously pained by this information. When he opened them, he dotted his face with a napkin. "I'm sorry. I heard the rumors that she'd joined some weird religious group, but I never asked many questions. She was just a girl I dated in high school. I'm sorry. I wish I could tell you more."

"You don't have to be sorry," I said. "She didn't tell you about me. How could you do anything other than what you did?"

"I'd like to think I'd have tried to get you out of there."

"You wouldn't have been able to even if you'd wanted to. They kept us locked up behind an electric fence." I told him about Matthew and our attempt at escape. "If I'd done what they expected and drunk the poison, I'd be dead too." I stopped for a moment to get hold of my emotions. "Matthew told me to run, so I did. For years, I expected them to come for me. They never did. Eventually, I got on with my life. I tried to forget. Until everything came crashing back to the surface last week."

"It must have been hard for you to see all that on television," Mason said. "And then to learn about the man you thought was your father? I don't know what to say about that."

"He was a terrible man," I said, with conviction. "I'm still processing everything, but I can tell you that he didn't love me or protect me. I could never understand why, and now I do. I'm free."

"What do you mean by that?" Mason asked.

"I mean, I no longer have to think of myself as something to discard." I stared down at my lap.

"I would not have discarded you. If I'd known." Mason's face crumpled into intense emotion. "I wish I could change things."

"It's not your fault," I said. There were men to blame, but he was not one of them.

"Thank you for giving me a chance. For meeting with me." Mason reached over to touch me briefly on the shoulder. "It means a lot."

"I wasn't sure you'd want to meet *me*." I gestured toward the pool where the boys were now having a contest about who could make the biggest splash. "You have a family. A good life. Adding in an adult daughter with major issues doesn't exactly fit into your life."

"I don't care about that," Mason said. "You're my daughter. I want to get to know you. I'd love the chance to make up for lost time."

"Do I look like her?" I asked. "I don't even have a photograph of her."

"You have my eyes, which I got from my mother. Other than that, the shape of your face and your mouth are similar to hers. Although she had flaming red hair. Did you know that?"

"What, no? Really?" Red hair? I'd assumed she had brown hair like mine. I tried to imagine this redheaded mother of mine but drew a blank, as I always did. Had she worn that red hair long or short? "How did she wear her hair?"

"Kind of medium." Mason touched his shoulders, then smiled. "It was curly and thick. She often complained about how much work it was to keep it tamed."

"Red hair," I mumbled to myself. I hadn't seen that coming. Sadness enveloped me. "I'd have liked to see that." Although I was grateful for whatever Mason could tell me, it wasn't enough. I had so many questions. Ones that no one would know the answers to.

What had she thought when she found out about me? Was she truly in love with Lawrence Miller or was he only a way out of her circumstances? Had the cult seemed like a safe haven until she was there and realized how trapped she'd become?

Tears of frustration clouded my vision. Breck reached under the table and took my hand. I took in the strength from his warm touch.

"I'll look through some of my old photographs and year-books," Mason said, sounding stricken with grief of his own. "I'll find you pictures." He looked up at the roof of the awning. "I wish I had more details for you. I was a stupid kid focused on sports and getting into college and didn't think much about anything or anyone but myself. If I'd known about you, of course, things would have been different."

"Would you have asked her to marry you?" The question was from the part of me that remained six years old. Despite knowing the ending, I yearned for a happy story for my mother. However, I knew the truth. Even if she'd managed to stay out of Briar Rose, she and Mason Davies would not have married. I would not have the life my half-brothers enjoyed.

"I don't know. I'd have asked her, probably. My parents would have encouraged me to continue with the plans for my education. Either way, I would have been there for Mona. Whether she wanted to marry or not, I would have been a part of your life. If your mother and I had married, I don't believe we would have made it long. We were really different."

"How? Can you tell me?" I asked.

"We wanted different things. She was always searching for meaning in life, looking for something to cling to. I had my family, so it was different for me. I had that safety net, which meant I didn't have to look to other sources. That's not to say she wasn't a wonderful person. I want you to understand that. She was sweet and funny and very smart."

"Not smart enough to stay away from Lawrence Miller and Briar Rose," I said.

"It's hard to understand the motivations a person had to join a community like that," Mason said. "But she was young and vulnerable. They preyed on that."

I nodded, knowing the truth and wisdom of what he said. Still, I wished it were different. "Tell me more about your family," I said to Mason. He was here. He wanted a relationship with me. The least I could do was reciprocate. I had the opportunity, finally, to know partially, at least, where I came from. "Are your parents still alive?"

Sadness lifted from his eyes, replaced with joy and love. "Yes, they're definitely still alive. Right now, they're traveling in Europe. If you'd like to meet them, they'll be back next month. I haven't told them about you yet. If I did, they might cut their trip short. They'll be anxious to meet you."

"Really?" My spirits lifted at the idea of grandparents who would want to meet me. "They won't wish I'd stayed away?"

"Gosh no. My mother will be sad about how much time we missed with you, but she's the type who will move forward and focus on the present." He crossed one leg over the other placed his hands over one knee. "You won't believe what she did for a living before retirement. She was an event planner, mostly fundraisers."

"Really?" A thrill pulsed through me. I was like my grandmother. We were both party planners.

"That's amazing," Breck said.

"What about my grandfather?" I asked. "What did he do?"

"He owned a chain of drugstores. His father had owned the first one, and when Dad joined the family business, he grew it into a chain of twelve stores. A few years back, he sold it to one of the big chains and retired."

"You didn't want to carry on with the family business?" I asked.

"No, I was more interested in software than selling heating pads and cough medicine. My older sister joined Dad in the business. She's now a vice president at the company that bought Dad out."

An aunt. I hadn't even thought about an extended family. Were there cousins?

Mason went on to explain that his sister had twin sons who were around the same age as my half-brothers. "The four of them are thick as thieves," Mason said.

Lennox came out to the patio carrying a tray. Mason jumped up to assist her, bringing it to the table while his wife went back inside to fetch whatever was left.

"One moment, I'm going to get the boys out of the pool," Mason said.

We nodded. I watched as Mason knelt by the side of the pool and told the boys it was time to eat. My brothers. How strange. They swam to the end of the pool and, water dripping from their small bodies, darted up the stairs to grab beach towels.

"How are you holding up?" Breck asked me.

"Good. It's not as awkward as I feared."

"Mason's easy to be around."

"Like you," I said to Breck. "Easy to talk to and a great listener."

Before he could respond, the boys, still in swimming trunks but wearing T-shirts, took chairs at the table. Although their complexions were dark like their mother's, they resembled Mason. I could easily imagine the young men they would grow up to be.

Lennox and Mason returned with a platter of tiny quiches and a stack of pancakes with plump blueberries.

A flurry of activity followed as we all filled our plates. The boys ate hungrily between stealing curious glances at me while Mason and Lennox shared more details of the family. I learned that Mason's sister, Amy, also lived in Denver. Her husband,

Raymond, was an architect who worked with several builders in the area.

"He designed our house," Mason said.

"Neat," I said, unsure how to respond.

"We'll give you a tour later, if you'd like," Lennox said.

The younger of my brothers, Benji, having gotten his fill of waffles, now stared at me. I smiled at him, noting the adorable freckles scattered over his impish face.

"What grade are you in at school?" I asked him.

"I'm done with school until the leaves turn red," Benji said, followed by an exhausted sigh. "But I'll be in second grade next year. I don't know how many sleeps that is, but my mom does."

"I'm going to be in fourth grade," Josh said. "I *could* calculate how many sleeps until school starts, but not right now."

"Are you really our sister?" Benji asked.

"I am. Your dad is my dad too." I watched them carefully for clues about how they felt about this sudden development in their lives.

"But you had a different mother, right?" Josh asked.

"That's correct."

"Where is she?" Benji asked.

"Benji," Mason said, with a slight warning in his voice.

"It's okay," I said. "She's in heaven now."

Benji's big brown eyes blinked. "That's where our granny went. She died last year. We miss her a lot."

"My mother," Lennox said. "She had a heart attack. It was very sudden."

"Mom cried for a whole bunch of days," Benji said. "I cried, too, but not in front of anyone at school."

"I'm sorry to hear that," I said. "It's hard to lose someone you love."

"She was nice to us," Josh said. "And always had cookies in a jar on the counter. She gave us one anytime we went to visit her."

"Despite my instructions," Lennox said.

I turned toward her. "I'm sorry for your loss."

"Thank you. She was a great lady, despite her lack of following directions."

I wanted to ask after Lennox's father but didn't want to upset the boys with another question about a person they may have also lost recently.

Turns out, I didn't have to, because Josh offered up the information. "My mom never had a dad. She doesn't even know what happened to him."

I made eye contact with Lennox. Ah yes, I thought. Those of us who grew up without a parent understood the hole that could never be filled. She hadn't had a privileged upbringing either. Yet she'd gone to medical school and was now a doctor. Plus, she was in a happy marriage, from what I could see. And two beautiful boys. People made it out of their circumstances sometimes. With luck, faith, and hard work.

"So much for keeping any secrets around here," Lennox said softly.

This went over the boys' heads as they continued telling me more about their lives. By the time our meal was over, I knew the names of their best friends, twin cousins, and the previous school year's teachers.

"How do you do it all?" I asked Lennox as I helped clear the table. "Managing the boys and work?"

"By the skin of my teeth."

We laughed as we carried the last of the dishes into the kitchen. Breck and Mason were already there, chatting while they loaded the dishwasher. Were there more of these gatherings in my future? Would Breck be here for those too?

Later, Mason and Lennox lent us swimming suits, and we all enjoyed the pool for an hour or two. The hours slipped by until I realized it was nearly three.

I was sitting on the edge of the pool with my feet in the

water. Breck came to sit next to me, water pooling on his muscular arms and chest. I hadn't realized until I saw him without his shirt how fit he was. It was hard not to stare at him, as if he were a delicious meal made just for me.

"We should go soon," I said to him.

"Mason asked if we wanted to stay. I need to get back for work, but you can stay for a few days."

"I need to get back to work too," I said. "We don't want Scooter to fire me."

He shook his head before splaying both hands through his thick hair, making it stand up in wet peaks. "She can't fire you."

Mason was still in the pool, playing catch with his boys. My chest ached. If only I'd had him during my childhood. But that was a useless thing to want. None of this would have been here when I was a kid anyway. He was still building his business back then. Maybe if I'd been present he wouldn't have been able to finish school and find a job in the software industry.

That was the problem with what-ifs and wishes. Changing the past was impossible, but even if we could, would we? Change altered the course of our lives and perhaps even our characters. I didn't want to be different than I was, I realized. Everything I'd gone through had made me the person I was today. Did that erase the losses? Of course not. Still, the choice for joy was mine. I had the chance to embrace these new, unexpected blessings or remain bitter, wishing for a past that didn't happen.

I placed my hand on Breck's thigh. His muscle twitched under my touch. "Let's go home."

He covered my hand with his. "You got it."

18

BRECK

That evening, we pulled into a parking spot on the street in front of Tiffany's apartment building. We'd come home on Javier's plane, and I'd insisted on walking her inside even though it wasn't quite dark. The sun had set but left streaks of pink clouds on the deep blue horizon. She didn't argue, and we walked to the front door together without speaking. I didn't want to leave her. I never did.

At the doorway, she stopped and turned to me. Buzzers for the various apartments hung in a panel on one wall.

"I guess this is good night," Tiffany said.

"Yeah, I guess so. It's been an adventure."

"Thanks again for being here with me." Her eyes softened. She reached up to touch the side of my face. "I don't know if I could have done it without you."

"You could have. Still, I'm glad I was there."

"I'll miss you," she said.

"I'll miss you. However, I'll see you at work tomorrow."

"You could come up?"

"I should get home," I said. "And get ready for the week."

Out of the corner of my eye, I detected someone approaching. When I shifted my gaze, I realized it was Jamie and Stormi, each carrying a bag of groceries.

"Hey, guys," Stormi said.

"Hey, hey." Jamie's gaze went from one of us to the other. "Are you two just getting back from the trip?"

"Yes. How's Muffy?" Tiffany asked.

"Cute, snuggly, fluffy." Jamie grinned. "We had the best time."

"Are you two going up?" Stormi asked.

"In a minute," Tiffany said. "We're saying goodbye."

They seemed to get the hint and excused themselves, passing by us to enter the lobby.

"Anyway," Tiffany said.

"Anyway."

"I was wondering if you'd like to kiss me."

"Uh, yeah. Of course, I want to kiss you. Are you ready for that?"

She lifted her gaze over my shoulder. "Don't look now, but we have more company."

I turned to see Garth and Crystal walking toward us, holding hands and talking animatedly. Her stomach stretched large against her coat, and her long blond hair hung loose around her shoulders.

"Hey, guys," Garth said with the usual twang in his voice. "Are you waiting for someone?"

"No, I'm just dropping Tiff off," I said. "What are you two up to?"

"We just got done with our birthing class," Crystal said. "Garth said he needed a drink after the videos of the up-close-and-personal nature of the birthing process. We're headed to Puck's. Do you two want to join us?"

"We can't," Tiffany said, a little too quickly. "We have some other things we need to do."

Crystal gave me a curious look but was polite enough not to ask any further questions.

"Y'all have a good night," Garth said.

"You too," I said.

After they continued down the sidewalk, Tiffany said, "Maybe we should go inside before we get interrupted again." She had her hand on the door when Brandi and Trapper came out of the bakery. They must have spotted us from inside, because Trapper called out, "Hey there." He had baby Willow in a front pouch. Her legs kicked wildly as she babbled.

"What's up, man?" Trapper asked. "I've been trying to get in touch with you for days."

"I've been busy," I said, sheepish. I'd noticed his texts but had been too consumed with Tiffany to respond.

"He's been helping me with a few things," Tiffany said.

Brandi's pretty face was darting back and forth between us like she was watching a Ping-Pong match. I knew what she was thinking. Had I finally gotten the courage to ask Tiffany out? I'd only been talking about it for two years.

"What are you guys doing?" Brandi asked. "We're headed up to Puck's for dinner. Do you want to join us?"

"No, we're finishing a few things before calling it a night," Tiffany said.

"We've had a busy weekend," I said.

Willow beat her fists in the air and squealed.

"Willow wants you to come too," Brandi said.

"We're just back from Denver," I said.

Trapper narrowed his eyes, clearly getting for the first time that something might be going on between us. "Denver?"

"Tiffany had some business there, and I went with her," I said. Honestly, did everyone in town have to come by before I had the chance to kiss the girl?

"They're busy, honey." Brandi took hold of Trapper's arm. "We should go."

"Oh, got it. Well, we'll leave you to it then," Trapper said, after a pointed look at me.

Brandi brushed her fingers against my shoulder. "We should get together soon, though. And catch up. Clearly you've been busy."

"Yeah, sure. I'll call you," I said.

"Or just text me back," Trapper said. "So I don't think you're dead."

"Yeah, sure. Sorry about that." I would get so much grief for this later.

Finally, they continued down the street toward Puck's. "Could any more of my friends interrupt us?" I asked.

She giggled, somewhat manically. "Into the lobby. Now."

I couldn't get that door open fast enough.

When we were safely inside, I led her over to a spot hidden from the window and prying eyes.

I touched the side of her face with the back of my fingers. "You ready?"

"I'm ready." She lifted her chin and looked up at me.

I leaned close and placed my lips gently to hers. Her arms went around my neck, and she kissed me back.

She kissed me back!

My heart thudded hard. I drew her closer, holding her steady with one arm, and kissed her again, this time slow and exploratory. She sighed and pressed her chest against me. We kissed and kissed and kissed. An eternity and a second all at once. My destiny and my destination.

I would have gladly stayed and kissed her all night. However, I showed remarkable restraint by pulling away. "I'd say that was a darn good first kiss."

"I agree," she whispered. "My legs are all shaky."

I brushed a finger against the soft skin under her jawline. "You are exquisite. That's the best word I can think of. If I had my way, I'd make your legs tremble every day."

"Kissing is nice," she whispered.

"I agree."

"Thank you for waiting," she said.

"I'd wait a thousand years for you."

"I'm glad we don't have to test that theory." She raised up on her tiptoes and gave me a quick kiss. "And now I'm going to see Muffy and get ready for work tomorrow. Good night."

I bade her good-night and watched as she started up the stairs. Just as she was about to disappear, she ducked back for one last look into the lobby where I stood, dumbfounded and numb and so very happy.

"Of everything that's happened, you might be the very best thing," she said, before running the rest of the way up to the second floor. I listened until the sound of her footsteps was no longer. Only then did I turn away, practically skipping all the way to my truck.

THE MORNING after our trip to Denver, I made coffee before work. As the kitchen filled with the nutty scent, Huck came through the back door, sweaty from a run.

"Good morning," I said, trying not to act too cheery.

"Morning." Huck sat at the table and took his sneakers off and rubbed his sweaty feet. "How was your weekend?"

I told him the details of yesterday, including learning the truth about her father.

"Wait a minute—so you guys met her real dad?"

"Yes, and his wife and little boys. Great people. Tiffany was thrilled."

"That's a lot to deal with all at once," Huck said. "How did she handle it all? Is she okay?"

Huck might seem like a jerk half the time, but he was pure of heart. There was no one who cared more about his friends and family. He just did a great job hiding it from everyone.

"She's fine, actually," I said. "Happy to have found Mason and his family."

Huck helped himself to a cup of coffee. The pot hadn't finished brewing, and the stream fell onto the burner and sizzled.

"Can't you wait two minutes?" I asked, irritated.

"What does it matter?" He crossed over the refrigerator to get the half-and-half. "So, Trapper and Garth texted last night. They said you were standing in the doorway with Tiffany like you were about to kiss her."

I groaned. "They have the worst timing. I was about to kiss her for the first time and boom, there they were."

"She really held out on you," Huck said. "Two nights in the same bedroom and no kissing? That must be some kind of record."

"I have to treat her with extra care."

"She's been through a ton of crap," Huck said. "Good for you for taking it slow."

"She only has one speed."

Mom sailed into the kitchen, the ends of a silk scarf trailing behind her like a double tail. "What's this I hear about you and Tiffany? Trapper's mom said you two were kissing in front of her apartment building."

Huck threw his head back in laughter. "This town will never change. Who needs a newspaper when were have the gossip ring?"

"We weren't kissing," I said to Mom. "Not then, anyway."

"Interesting," Mom said.

"I think I'll ask her to dinner tonight," I said. "Maybe take her to the lodge."

"Perfect night for it," Mom said. "You should sit out on the patio. The stars will be visible."

"And it's a full moon," Huck said. "Maybe you'll get lucky."

"My mother's in the room." I would not be getting lucky, as Huck so delicately put it. Tiffany was not that kind of woman.

"I don't even know what lucky means in this context," Mom said, when she clearly knew exactly what it meant.

I sighed and went over to the coffee maker to pour myself and Mom a cup. "I have a good mind not to make either of you breakfast."

"C'mon, I'm starving," Huck said. "I'll shower if you make waffles and fried eggs."

"I'll make oatmeal and cut up some fruit. However, you still have to shower." I scooped some oatmeal into a pan and added water, then turned on the burner.

"Do we have bananas?" Huck asked.

I pointed toward the door. "Shower. You stink."

He shot me a look before limping out of the room.

I handed Mom her newspaper. Instead of opening it, she gave me a long hard stare.

"What?" The water on the stove started to boil. I turned down the heat and added a top to the pan.

"Is Tiffany another one of your injured animals? Are you sure there's any more to it than that?"

I waved a wooden spoon at her. "Don't. This is good, Mom. There's something special between us."

"Are you sure this is the kind of wife you want?"

"What kind is that?" I asked. Don't take the bait. She doesn't know what she's talking about.

"One with a whole lot of problems. Problems that will follow her all her life, which means if you marry her, all *your* life."

"Tiffany's stronger than she looks. She's a survivor. A warrior too. If you knew her, you'd get it."

"There's no need to get defensive." She looked at me over the rim of her cup. "I'm merely pointing out that you might want to be careful, given your history."

"Mom, Rachel was a million years ago." Rachel had been my

college girlfriend. My mother was under the impression that it didn't work out because there was something wrong with her. In fact, we were unsuited. Did she realize that before me? Well, yes. However, that was neither here nor there and had absolutely nothing to do with Tiffany and me.

"You haven't dated very many women. Maybe try out a few more?"

"Try out?"

"You know what I mean," Mom said.

"Not really." I'd dated a few other women since then, but not many. Veterinarian school had been exhausting and all-consuming. Since I'd come home, I'd taken a few women out but no one I clicked with. No one like Tiffany.

There was no one like her.

"Mom, she's special. I know you have an opinion—about everything—but in this case, you need to back off. I know what I'm doing."

"She works for us now. Do you really think it's wise to start an office romance?"

"Have you been talking to Scooter?" Annoyed, I splashed coffee as I set down my cup.

"She's worried, as am I." Mom set her cup aside and reached into the cabinet for three bowls.

"You know what? I don't care what Scooter thinks. She should watch herself or I'll fire her. She has no idea about what appropriate boundaries mean. You gave her too much power."

"That's ridiculous. The practice would fall apart without her."

"I disagree." I stirred the oatmeal before putting the lid on the pan. "In fact, I need you to butt out. The practice is mine now."

"I've stayed completely out of it." Mom huffed indignantly. "Am I not allowed to say something that's on my mind when it comes to you and your heart?"

There were times in every day I missed my dad. None were stronger than this moment. He would take my side and tell my mom I was smart enough to know my own mind.

"This isn't your business," I said. "Or anyone else's. This is between Tiffany and me. We're growing close, and there's nothing you can say that will dissuade me, so you can give it up." The words came out harsher than I'd intended, but she'd made me mad.

"I'm just trying to help you," Mom said, as if she'd heard my thoughts. "But I'll not say another word. You're right. It's your life." Her tone belied the words. I'd hurt her feelings. Right now I couldn't bring myself to care.

"When the timer goes off, that means the oatmeal's done," I said. "I'm going to work."

"What about breakfast?"

"You and Huck can figure it out for yourselves."

"I meant *your* breakfast," Mom said.

But I kept going, out of the kitchen and into the hallway and finally to my room. When I got there, I closed the door behind me and leaned against it. This room. The room I'd had when I was a little boy hadn't changed much. Diplomas and trophies had replaced toys. The bed was bigger. However, I felt the same when I came in here. Like a kid.

I'd moved in with my mother when I returned because I knew she was lonely. However, it wasn't good for me. I'd become the houseboy, taken for granted and ordered around. She and Huck needed to figure out how to take care of themselves. In addition, I fell into a subservient role to my mother's bossy personality. I needed to break free, from both this house and her control over the practice.

I needed to move out. That was the first thing. I should buy a place of my own. There was plenty of money in the trust my dad had set up for me. I'd left it alone, but buying a piece of land and building a house was a good use for it.

I flashed forward to a year from now. Would Tiffany and I be ready to marry by then? If so, I needed a house of my own. I couldn't exactly carry her across the threshold of my mother's home.

There had been several other times in my life when the solution to something had invaded my mind with no warning. This was exactly what happened. Right then, I thought of Crystal's property. Her house had burned to the ground, but the piece of land was nestled into the mountain with a good view and a pond. I'd always loved that spot. Should I make an offer before it went on the market?

I picked up my phone and punched in Crystal's number. When she picked up, I asked her if we could have lunch. "I want to talk to you about your property."

"As in, to buy it?"

"Yeah. It's still for sale, isn't it?"

"We were about to list it, but if you're interested, I'd much prefer to sell it to you."

We agreed to meet at the bakery for lunch to talk about price and other details. I hung up feeling better already.

THE MORNING SPED BY, leaving me no time to dwell on the disagreement with my mother. Scooter was busy with patients and seemed to be leaving Tiffany to do her job. By the time lunch came around, I was starting to think Scooter wasn't as big a problem as I'd been thinking. Perhaps I was exaggerating how much her attitude affected the rest of us. She *was* incredibly efficient. I had to give her that.

However, when I went into the lobby to leave for my lunch with Crystal, Scooter's voice stopped me cold. She stood behind Tiffany, instructing her in a loud voice on some detail of the scheduling software.

Tiffany was visibly shaking, clearly flustered by her superior standing behind her shouting orders.

"Not like that," Scooter said. "You're a complete idiot."

"I...I could you explain it again? I got lost on step three."

"For heaven's sake." Scooter grabbed the mouse out of Tiffany's hand and pushed her and the chair to one side. "I'll do it. If you weren't sleeping with the boss, I'd suggest he fire you."

"I'm not sleeping with him." I heard tears in her voice.

Rage consumed me. I stormed into the lobby. Empty of all patients, thank God. I shouted Scooter's name so loudly that both women jumped.

"Scooter, get out," I said. "You're fired. Done."

"Excuse me?" Scooter's voice dripped with contempt.

"You heard me. I don't want you anywhere near my staff or our patients. The way you spoke to Tiffany is so totally inappropriate that I don't even know what to say. This is my business — one that's been in my family for generations. It might have been fine when my mother was in charge, but this isn't the way I do things. You should be ashamed of yourself."

During my diatribe, Scooter's face had drained of color. "How dare you speak to me that way. I knew you when you were still pooping your pants. The way you're running this place, what with your naps and hiring imbeciles, you might as well still be in diapers. If you think you can operate without me, good luck. I'd love to be a fly on the wall when you and this dolt are trying to figure out how to bill people."

"We'll figure it out," I said. "Get your stuff and leave. I'll pay you through the week and whatever vacation pay I owe you, and then you're on your own."

"What about my severance?"

"There's no severance. Not when I'm firing you for cause."

By this time my other two employees, Miranda and Carrie, had come out from the back. They huddled together in the entryway to the hall.

"You should get her keys, Dr. Stokes," Michelle said.

I gaped at Michelle. She'd never said a word against Scooter. But she was right. One didn't give a disgruntled employee keys. "Scooter, get your keys out of your office and give them to me. Then leave."

She stormed out from behind the front desk, hitting Tiffany's shoulder with her own. I heard her marching down the hall and into her office. She came out seconds later carrying her purse. She hurled the set of keys at me. I was too quick, though, and caught them.

Scooter glared at me with fire in her eyes. "Wait until your mother hears about this. I'll be back, and you'll be gone."

"This is my business," I said, shouting again. "My family's business, which I now own. You're not family. You're not even an employee. Get your stuff and leave."

Scooter held her purse close to her chest. "You will pack up the rest of my stuff and send it to me. Between now and then I'll be preparing my lawsuit for wrongful termination."

Michelle spoke up again. "I don't think he'll have much trouble once I show him all the abusive emails you've sent Carrie and me over the years. He should have fired you the minute he took over from his mother. There's about a hundred reasons why it's the right thing to do."

Go, Michelle, I thought. She seemed taller suddenly. Had Scooter been bullying them all for years? I knew the answer. No wonder they all acted like scared kittens. Things were about to change.

Scooter huffed as she passed by me. I fully expected flames to come out of her mouth, but instead, it was only coffee breath. She kicked open the front door, and then she was gone. I breathed a sigh of relief.

Michelle and Carrie started clapping. Seconds later, Tiffany joined them.

"It's about time, Doctor," Carrie said. "Her reign of terror has gone on too long."

I raked a hand through my hair. "I'm going to an important lunch meeting. After work, however, I'm taking you all out for drinks. I want you to tell me everything you've been through and what I can do to make it better here. I'm open to your suggestions." I held up one finger. "However, I'm not giving up my napping cot."

All three ladies laughed. Had there ever been a lovelier sound?

"Come to lunch with us," Michelle said to Tiffany. "Mondays is half-price sandwiches at the Sugar Queen."

"Me? Really?" Tiffany's face lit up. "I'd love to."

"I'm off to buy some property, ladies. Enjoy your lunch." I left them all staring at me with questioning expressions. All would be clear soon.

19

TIFFANY

Without Scooter at work criticizing my every move, the rest of the week went by without turmoil. The news continued to follow the story of Briar Rose, but without the twenty-four-hour coverage. Thankfully, the news cycle had moved on to another salacious tale of broken hearts and lives.

Breck had asked if he could take me to dinner at the lodge on Friday night. As I got ready that evening, my stomach fluttered with excitement. I would have him to myself for a whole night. At work, he spent most of his time and attention on his furry patients, as it should be. Still, I was slightly jealous of our wet-nosed friends. I'd grown accustomed to having Breck's full attention. It hadn't taken long for me to grow fond of being someone's focus.

He arrived right on time dressed in slacks and a blue jacket and presented a box of chocolates and a bouquet of flowers. "I couldn't decide which you'd prefer," he said.

"Can I have both?" I asked.

"I'd give you the whole world if I could."

I laughed. "That would be hard to carry up the stairs."

"True enough."

I stood back to let him into the apartment.

"Good grief, you look beautiful," he said.

"Thank you." I'd decided on the sheath dress Daphne had chosen for me. Paired with high sandals that showed off my calves, the ensemble suited me. Honestly, I'd admired myself with a little too much enthusiasm in my full-length mirror. Say what you will about designer clothes being overpriced, I'd said to myself. This dress made me feel like a movie star.

"I didn't know what kind of candy you like," Breck said as he placed the box on the coffee table. "Nuts? No nuts? You can't imagine the list of questions still unanswered about my new favorite subject."

"Me?"

"Yes, you. What else could it be?" He had the bouquet cradled in one arm. With the other, he reached out and pulled me close for a quick kiss. The plain brown wrapper made a crinkling noise as I pressed against him.

"Please put those in a vase for me?" I asked when we drew away. "I'll run and get a sweater."

"I'd be happy to. But I'm not sure about a sweater. I'd hate for you to hide that beautiful figure of yours under a bulky bit of knitted yarn."

"You sound like Daphne." I tugged on the lapels of his jacket and resisted the urge to wrap my arms around his neck. If I did, we might not make our reservation. Kissing, as it turned out, was quite an enjoyable activity. We'd kissed in every room of the clinic so far this week. Clandestine moments that were the highlights of my days.

Breck traced a finger down the curve of my hip. "If she saw you in that dress, she'd agree."

That did it. I just had to kiss him. I threw my arms around him and pressed my mouth to his. I'd never initiated a kiss and at first, he stiffened, obviously shocked at the sudden move. But then his mouth softened against my stiff, awkward grip. His hands moved to gently touch the sides of my face, and he parted my lips with his and teased me with the tip of his tongue. This was not the apprehensive kiss of a boy but one from a man. A kiss that shook me from head to toe. I was lost to him. The feel of his lips moving against mine was so pleasurable I half expected to melt like the box of chocolates would on a hot day.

"You better get that sweater," he said gruffly.

I hurried off to the bedroom. What sweater could I pair with this that wouldn't ruin the fine drape of the dress? I stood looking into my closet for a moment before deciding on a simple black cardigan. I'd carry it and only put it on if needed. I smiled to myself, remembering Daphne's horror at my mention of a cardigan.

I took one last look at myself in the mirror. I'd decided to put my hair up and had spent extra time on my makeup. *You'll do just fine*, I thought.

When I returned, Breck had put the flowers in a vase and set it in the middle of the coffee table next to the chocolates. The bright flowers livened up the room. "Spring in a vase," I said. "Thank you for bringing them."

"Since we're on the subject, what are your favorite candies?" Breck asked as he put his hand on the small of my back and steered me toward the door.

"I like all chocolates. Are there people who don't?" I walked into the hallway.

He followed me out and shut the door firmly behind us. "My mother cuts them open to see what's inside before deciding if she wants it or not. She isn't one for nuts and despises nougat."

"Good. More for us," I said.

"Us. What a beautiful word." He grinned and took my hand, then brushed his mouth against my knuckles. The narrow hallway disappeared. I no longer smelled the new carpet or the scent of cookies coming from Jamie's apartment. It was the two of us wrapped in a moment as sweet as any candy.

"Thanks for taking me as I am," I said. "And not pressuring me about anything."

"I started out liking you and crushing big-time," he said. "But these last few weeks with you have been the best of my life. What started out as a crush has developed into something so much bigger. Nothing you could tell me at this point would change that."

"I know that's not exactly true," I said. "For example, what if I told you I was a serial killer?"

"Okay, that would change things. But you're not. Right?" Breck said the last part with mock fear. We'd reached the first floor by then. He held open the door for me. The sweet spring air, scented with flowers and grass, wrapped around me.

"No. But I am a virgin who was raised in a freakish cult where they auctioned girls off to old men. I have at least a dozen hang-ups and a business that doesn't pay the rent. Now it turns out I have a biological father who wants a relationship with me, which means more complications. I mean, Thanksgiving alone could be a nightmare."

We strolled down the sidewalk toward his truck. The setting sun swathed the sky with pink-cotton-candy swirls.

"You make life sweeter," I said. "Did you know that?"

"I know only how you make me feel." We stopped at his truck. He dug his key from his pocket and unlocked the doors, then opened the passenger side.

Before I took his offered hand, I looked up at him. The soft light reflected in his eyes made them more gray than blue. "Do you ever feel scared? About me? About us? Frightened this will lead us to heartbreak?"

He shook his head. "No, that's not how I think. After I lost my dad, I vowed never to take even the smallest of moments for granted. I'm here with you now. Do I hope tomorrow brings more of you? Yes. An emphatic yes. So, I operate on hope like that. What good would worrying about tomorrow do anyway, other than rob me of this moment?"

"I'll be around tomorrow," I said. "If you still want me."

"I will. There's not much I know for certain, but I know that." He brought my hand to his chest. "Do you feel that? Heart beating? Lungs pushing air in and out? Until my body ceases to do those things, I'll want you."

"EVERY TIME I'm in this room, I marvel at how many years the lodge has been here, hosting sweethearts," Breck said as he reached for a dinner roll. "How many people do you think have fallen in love here?"

I glanced around the busy dining room of the lodge. Photographs from earlier times were hung in various places around the dining room and lobby. Modern renovations had stayed true to the original rustic aesthetic with exposed beams and logs. Bay windows looked out to the ski mountain, as they always had. The interiors had been updated to include modern light fixtures and decor such as gas fireplaces and an impressive bar. Still, the ghosts of the past were there in the shadows. I could almost see the day Cymbeline Barnes won her first ski-jump competition and the entire town had celebrated her in this very room. It wasn't only the photographs I'd pored through from the archives when I'd first come to work for the Barnes family here at the lodge.

Downstairs, where the speakeasy had been during the twenties, was now a private banquet room where many of my brides had their receptions. Sometimes, as I supervised these events, I swear I could hear the sweet voice of Fiona Barnes singing accompaniment to Li Wu's violin. There were photos of them from the late twenties playing jazz music for the happy dancers and bootleg gin drinkers. It had been a simpler time. But there was something about Emerson Pass that seemed frozen in time. Even with the contemporary ski lifts and businesses and cars, on a morning after a snowfall it was as if no time had passed since those early days. Perhaps that's why I loved it here so much. I'd never lived in a simple time. Instead, I'd grown up in an environment of deception, greed, and lechery. Quinn Barnes, the town's first schoolteacher, would have been heartbroken to see me and the rest of the girls being raised for the sole purpose of the pleasure of an old man.

The server brought our first course, Caesar salads with garlicky croutons and large pieces of shaved parmesan. "I'm glad we're both having garlic."

"Why?"

"For kissing reasons," Breck said.

"Does garlic make a person a better kisser?"

He sucked in his lower lip as if to keep himself from laughing. "No, not that I know of. I was referring to garlic's strong taste and how it can make breathing a little horrendous if the other person hasn't also eaten it."

I flushed at my ignorance. "Oh, right. I'm sorry. I must seem like a child at times."

Breck's eyes widened before he shook his head rather vehemently. "Absolutely not. It makes you more interesting. Also, it helps me see the world with fresh eyes."

I didn't know if he was only saying that to make me feel better, but I guess I didn't really care. His words were like the feeling of fullness after a good meal.

There was nothing else I needed.

We talked about mundane subjects throughout the rest of our dinner. As tenderloin steaks melted in our mouths, we covered favorite colors, movies, and music. We both loved blue. He seemed to know every movie ever made, whereas I had a limited palette to share. Country music was our genre of choice,

He admitted to liking milk chocolate better than dark. "What is it with all this semisweet chocolate all of the sudden?" Breck asked. "I mean, I'm all for living healthy, but if you're going to eat something sinful, why not go all the way in?"

I laughed. "You go all the way in with most things, don't you?"

"How else would I live my best life?" He placed his knife and fork over his empty plate. "Now, how do you feel about naps?"

"I like them," I said. "Doesn't everyone?"

"My mother doesn't believe in naps or television. She thinks they make us soft. I like being soft. Plus, what's better than a nap after a movie?"

We were too full for dessert. Breck paid the bill, and we headed out the front door and down the steps to the parking lot. Above us, a cloud cover had moved in, making the night especially dark. I shivered, not from a chill but from a feeling of dread.

"You cold?" Breck asked. "Do you want my jacket?"

"No, I have my sweater in the car. I just felt weird for a second. Like something bad was going to happen. But then I remembered I'm here with you, and we're having a normal night like couples do."

"Couples. I like the sound of that," Breck said as he held the passenger-side car door open for me.

"I like the word well enough too."

"Me too." He leaned down and gave me a kiss. This was a new variety; not a peck or the lengthy, exploratory one of earlier but somewhere in the middle. Just enough to send warmth throughout my body and the wish for more.

20

BRECK

The next few weeks passed without conflict or tension. My mother was away visiting a friend. Huck was busy at his new house. Work was pleasant without Scooter. Best of all, there was Tiffany. Most evenings we spent together making dinner or going out to eat. During this time, we talked and talked and talked. And kissed.

On a Saturday morning in late May, I puttered away in the kitchen making a batch of homemade granola. I was in great spirits. The kitchen smelled of cinnamon and dried apple, two smells that made everything particularly homey. I'd just heard from Crystal that the official title to the property was now mine. Next week, I would meet with the architect to begin plans for my new house.

Unfortunately, I hadn't had a chance to tell Mom about the new house. I'd wanted to tell her in the right way and at the right time. Thus far that opportunity had not presented itself. She'd returned last night from her trip, but I hadn't seen her yet.

I was just taking the last batch of granola from the oven when Mom appeared. "Hi, Mom. How are you? Did you have a good trip?"

"The trip was fine. But I've been better." She peered at the pan of granola. "Is this for the horses?"

"Very funny. It's delicious. Give it a try."

"No thank you."

I studied her for a moment. She wore saggy leggings and an old sweatshirt. Her hair hadn't been combed. A pink flush spotted her cheeks and neck. Her red-rimmed eyes glittered angrily. Had something agitated her? Kept her up all night? I had a feeling it was me.

"Everything all right?" I braced myself.

"It's one thing that you do the opposite of what I want in nearly every realm of life. However, I'd appreciate it if I didn't have to hear about your latest escapades from Trapper's mother." She sniffed. "Apparently, you tell everyone's mother about your life. Everyone's mother but me."

"Are you referring to my trip to Denver?"

"What, no. You went to Denver?"

"With Tiffany," I said.

"For heaven's sake. I don't even want to know. I was referring to your uncalled firing of Scooter. What were you thinking?"

"It amazes me that you have to ask. She's a terrible person, and I no longer want her poisoning my place of business with her spite."

"She gave this family thirty years of loyal service. I can't believe you would do this without asking me."

"My name's on the business now," I said. "I own it and can do as I please with it. And Scooter does not please me."

"Your father would be ashamed of you."

My mouth dropped open, shocked that she'd gone there. As much as I knew my father would not be ashamed of me, hearing the words stung. "Dad was kind to everyone he ever met. He would have encouraged me to run my business with compassion. If he'd heard how Scooter spoke to the others, he would have fired her too."

"Your father let me run the business as I wanted. He knew it was my choice. The practice was left to me by *my* mother."

"It was sold to me by *my* mother," I said, not backing down. "If you're so worried about Scooter, you can hire her to work for you in another capacity."

She looked as if she wanted to say something else but didn't. Instead, she went to the coffee maker, which I'd left on in case Huck or Mom wanted a late-morning cup.

I got the cream out of the refrigerator for her and set it on the counter. She furiously scooped three teaspoons of sugar into her coffee.

I'd made her really mad. How would I tell her about my offer on Crystal's property? Maybe another day, I decided.

Mom's shoulders rose and fell before she whipped around to look at me. "Then, in the same conversation, I had to learn about your offer on Crystal's property. Why didn't you tell me?"

"Like I said, you haven't been around." I sounded glib, but I was truly remorseful. As irritating as Mom could be, I didn't like to hurt her feelings. "But yes, I made an offer and she accepted it. I'm meeting with an architect next week."

"Your father didn't leave you that money for you to waste it."

"How is buying a piece of real estate wasting it? I mean, a Vegas gambling trip, yes, but investing in land has always been a wise thing to do with money. Dad always told me that."

"He wouldn't want you to buy another piece of land when you have a perfectly good home right here. This house and property are part of our family's legacy."

"As much as I appreciate all you and Dad did to set me up for the future, this is not my home. This is your home. I'm a grown man who should not be living with his mother. You, on the other hand, should be enjoying your time while you're still young."

"I'm hardly young."

"You're young enough to be living better than you are now. Why haven't you ever dated since dad died?"

"I was married to the best man on earth," Mom said. "A man who could have had anyone but chose cantankerous me. He had everything—intelligence, looks, and money. Why he chose me, I could never figure out. I'm sure the rest of the town couldn't fathom it either."

"I know Dad was the best. He was to me too. However, he's gone. He's been gone for more than ten years. You're healthy and vibrant. Why not spend this next season with someone? The best years of life are still to come. You're free to travel and do whatever you want. Wouldn't that be better with a partner?"

She bored a hole into me with her sharp eyes. "You don't understand."

"I guess I don't. Actually, Mom, you baffle me."

"My best years already happened. When your dad and I were young and you were little and the practice was thriving under my leadership—those were the best days."

I couldn't argue with her, obviously. She knew her own mind. Still, it frustrated me that she was so closed off to the idea of another chapter. One that could be her best yet. She wouldn't know if she didn't try.

"And as far as bafflement goes, you baffle me," Mom said.

"I know I do." I turned back to my granola, moving it about with a spatula to make sure it didn't stick while it cooled.

"For example, why would you spend your Saturday morning making food fit for horses instead of people? I mean, what are you doing here? It's a beautiful day and you're in here. If you want to do chores so badly you can go into the clinic and do work that actually matters."

That was just it, I thought. She'd never understood that it didn't matter what you did for a living, even if it was your soul's calling. Family and home were the most important elements of a life. After Dad died, we'd felt lost because he'd been the one who had made this place a home. He cooked. He was there when I got home from school. He attended all my games and activities. Mom did her best, but work always came first. Granted, Dad's job had been done from his study. It was easier for him to be around for me. I'd never minded my mother's devotion to the practice. Not really. But now, with her sharp tongue attacking who I was, resentment pierced me with a sharp hook.

"We've been lost," I said. "Since Dad died. We have nothing to anchor us except for work. You said you wanted to retire, but you didn't really. Did you?"

Her face seemed to fall. "I did though. I'd given this town all my best years. It was time to focus on myself."

"I agree," I said. "But you haven't done that. Instead, you've continued to look over my shoulder and question every decision I make. If you wanted to keep the practice, you should have."

"I'm keeping you from making mistakes." She said this without the conviction of earlier. Had a fissure of doubt entered her mind? Could she see from my point of view that her interference wasn't assisting me but undermining me?

"It feels like criticism."

She didn't say anything, going back to her cup of coffee and dumping another teaspoon of sugar into it as if it were a weapon. "You're too soft. That's all. I've coddled you."

I had to take in a deep breath to keep from tearing into her before I turned the oven off and put the oven mitts away.

"I want my own home where I can do what I want without being condemned."

With her back to me, she took a sip of her coffee, then set it aside. "You do whatever you want. You always have. I've always been second place to your father, even more so after he died.

But I am who I am. You say you want acceptance? Well, it goes both ways. I don't want to eat oats and sour yogurt. I like my scotch and buttery popcorn. You can't mold me into Trapper's mom by sheer will."

For the second time that morning, my mouth dropped open in astonishment. "I'm not trying to mold you into Trapper's mom. Whatever gave you that idea?"

"Huck's mother then? Both of them would have been the type of nurturing, bread-baking, flower arranging mother you wanted. Instead, you got me."

"And you got me instead of Huck. So I guess we're even."

"I guess we are." She turned on her heel and stormed out of the room.

I stood there, staring at the spot in the kitchen where she'd just stood. We'd never argued. Not like this. Apparently, there were a lot of resentments that had gone unmentioned by both of us.

I sank onto one of the stools at the island. What did I do now? Conflict was not my expertise, and the aftermath of an argument had made me physically ill.

I did what I'd done since I lost my dad: I reached out to my best friends.

Meet me at the grill at 3?

Answers came back almost immediately.

Trapper: *Yeppers.*

Huck: Yes, but you're buying.

For a Saturday afternoon, Puck's wasn't as busy as it was during summer months or school holidays. Between ski season and summer, locals had a reprieve for a few months. We loved April and May not only for the spring flowers but for a return to no traffic and our seats on the patio being uncluttered with tourists. The doors to the inside were open, making the patio seem like a part of the bar. I spotted Stormi bartending. They must have needed someone. I'd never seen her back there before. That girl worked harder than anyone I knew.

DURING THE LULL between lunch and dinner, we were the only ones on the patio sipping our first beers while Huck and Trapper waited for a plate of nachos. I'd ordered a salad with beets and goat cheese, a new item on the menu. One that Huck found suspicious.

"Who eats beets on a salad?" he said after our waitress walked away.

"A lot of people do," I said.

"What's going on?" Trapper asked.

"It's my mom. We're having some conflict."

"Conflict is a war," Huck said. "Not a tiff with one's mother."

"Hey, we're here to listen and be supportive," Trapper said, admonishing Huck. As far as I could tell there were only a handful of people who were not scared of Huck and didn't care if they poked this grumpiest of bears.

"Listen, if you want my opinion," Huck said. "You—"

"He probably doesn't," Trapper said, cutting him off.

"No, it's okay. What were you going to say?" I asked.

"Your mom's having trouble transitioning into the retirement."

"I realize that," I said carefully when I wanted to unleash my fury onto him.

"Regardless, she can't be telling Breck what to do all the time." Trapper twisted his wedding ring around his finger while he talked. "I mean, she wanted this. Basically, she pressured you into this by talking about it since you were like ten. And now she's having issues. Ones that are hers to work out, not yours."

I nodded, grimacing at the memory of Mom's chart she had on the wall during my school years. She'd had it projected from kindergarten through vet school. I'd done what she wanted, but it didn't seem like it was enough. "She didn't take the news of my imminent departure well. That made everything worse."

"Right, she's losing both of us," Huck said. "She would never admit it, but I think she's afraid of being alone again."

I dropped my gaze toward my beer mug. "It's not good for our relationship to be living together."

"You and me?" Huck asked. "What's your beef with me?"

"Not you, idiot. Breck and his mom," Trapper said.

"Oh, right." Huck took a swig from his mug of beer and then wiped the foam from his upper lip. "Well, at least there's one person in my life who isn't mad at me."

"My mother's mad at me, not you," I said.

"I was referring to Stormi. We had a disagreement this morning."

"About what?" Trapper asked.

"I didn't like the photos she took for the festival story," Huck said. "They looked too much like art shots. This is the news, not Vogue."

"They sound great," I said. "All the cute kids in their gunnysacks. The pie-eating contest. People dancing in the park."

"Like you, I own a business, and it's my prerogative to run it as I wish. If Stormi doesn't like it, she can take photos for someone else."

I decided, as I often did, to let that one go. The last thing I needed was Huck mad at me. I'd have to sleep at Trapper's.

"Anyway," I said, changing the subject. "I'm going to start building as soon as I can. In the meantime, I need to find a place to rent."

"You can move in with me," Huck said. "Unless you think it'll get me in trouble with your mom too."

"You can do no wrong," I said. "You know what she needs? A boyfriend. Someone to do things with."

"She has her book club," Huck said. "Those ladies are a hoot. I sat in last month. They'd read some romance book about a woman who meets a man on a cruise after she gets dumped at the altar. It was actually pretty good."

"You read a romance book?" Trapper asked. "You mock romance books."

"I do. But that's just to irritate my dad. Genre books and all that."

"You can be such a jerk," Trapper said, shaking his head. Huck sighed. "I know."

"Well, thanks for the offer to move in with you," I said. "It would only be temporary. But I do think it would be best if I gave Mom some space."

"It's great you got rid of Scooter," Trapper said. "She's legacy wicked witch."

"I'd had enough. I don't know how someone as smart as my mom thought she was a model employee."

"Different management style," Trapper said. "There was bound to be collateral damage. It's unrealistic to think otherwise."

Everything out of Trapper's mouth always sounded so reasonable.

"My mom and I said some pretty bad things to each other." I finished the rest of my beer and set it down on the table harder than I meant to. "She admitted she'd rather have you for a son." I gestured toward Huck.

"No way. No one would want me over you." Huck poured more beer into my glass.

"She said it, not me." I pulled my glass closer. Suds spilled over the sides and onto the table.

"She doesn't mean that," Huck said. "She was probably just

mad. You know how it is when you're mad—you say stuff you don't mean."

I didn't know if that was true. Whatever her intention, she'd hurt me. I'd never been enough for her. It was time to give up the idea and move on with things. I was almost thirty years old, after all.

"It'll blow over," Huck said. "You'll both cool off and all will be forgotten."

Trapper punched me lightly in the shoulder. "Cheer up, man. Tell us what's happening with Tiffany."

My mood lifted at the mere mention of her name. I filled them in on all that had transpired over the last few weeks. "To make a long story short, I'm crazy about her, and I think she likes me too."

"Here we go again." Huck groaned and dropped his head into his hands. "Another one bites the dust. You'll be married by this time next year and then it'll be like this guy here—we'll never see you after a baby comes."

"Maybe you should consider looking for a wife of your own." Trapper topped off his beer glass. "Although it would take a complete overhaul of your personality."

"I can't change," Huck said. "I'm a donkey's ass and always will be. No woman's ever going to put up with me, even though I desperately need someone to help redeem me."

Was he serious? Did he actually want someone? I exchanged a quick glance with Trapper. He'd heard it too.

"Jamie's single," I said. "And super pretty."

"No, not my type," Huck said. "Way too perky."

"Perky's not bad," Trapper said.

"There's always Stormi," I said. "She's feisty and opinionated. Just your type."

"Other than the fact that I loathe her, sure." Huck gestured toward the pitcher and slid his glass over to me.

I tilted his glass to decrease the foam. "You know, I'm not

going to wait on you hand and foot when I'm your roommate. Not if I pay rent. The bed-and-breakfast is closed."

"Fine. I can return to my stop at the bakery for a doughnut." Huck sipped from his beer.

"Now you're just being mean," I said, laughing.

"Doughnuts are not mean," Huck said. "Doughnuts are your friend."

21

TIFFANY

"Then what happened?" Jamie's eyes were the size of walnuts as she lifted a potato chip to her mouth and washed it down with a sip of white wine.

"This is a wild story, only it's not a story." Stormi gathered her knees to her chest.

The three of us were sitting on the floor in Jamie's apartment, sharing a bowl of chips. They'd called earlier to see if I wanted to come over and catch up on the events of the last few weeks.

"I told them everything I could remember," I said, referring to the FBI agents. "And then they dropped a bomb. The man I thought was my father isn't." I shared the rest of the story, including visiting Mason, Lennox, and my half brothers.

"Unbelievable," Jamie said.

"The whole thing feels surreal." I dotted the top of a piece of pizza with a napkin to get rid of some of the grease before taking a bite. "My head's swimming. Mason has been very welcoming. Still, it's nearly impossible for me to think of him as my father. Not yet anyway."

"Give it some time," Stormi said.

TESS THOMPSON

A knock on the door made all three of us jump. "I wonder who that could be?" Jamie leaped up to answer it.

Muffy, who was curled up next to me, raised her head lazily to see if it was anyone of interest.

I craned my neck to see around Stormi. Darby was at the door. "I wanted to let you ladies know that I'm having a party tonight. You're all invited."

Jamie backed up to let him inside.

"What kind of party?" Stormi asked, still on the floor.

"Just some of the guys and a few of my teacher friends." He looked down at his feet, encased in those sports sandals that the locals favored during warm months. "It's my birthday."

Stormi scrambled upright. "What? It's your birthday? How come you didn't tell us? We could've gotten a cake."

"It's kind of a last-minute thing. I was over at the grill earlier and ran into Huck and Breck. When Breck found out it was my birthday and I was planning on spending it eating a burger and drinking alone, he suggested a get-together. It has to be at my apartment, because Breck lives with his mom and Huck's house isn't quite ready."

Stormi picked up an abandoned crust from her plate and waved it around like a flag. "What kind of mood is Huck in?"

"He seems good," Darby said. "Why do you ask?"

"I'm not going if he's in one of his dark moods," she said flatly. "I put up with him enough at work. I'm not spending my weekend evenings with him too."

"I know what you mean," Darby said. "But he and the guys seemed in good spirits. They're on their way over now. Breck said he wanted to grab beer and snacks first."

"I hope no one's driving," I said.

"No, they walked over to the store," Darby said. "And I anticipate they'll stay over at my place tonight."

Maybe Breck would stay with me. I liked that idea a lot.

248

"Are any of your teacher friends cute?" Stormi asked.

"They're all women," Darby said. "And one guy who swings for the other team."

Stormi deflated but said she'd be there as long as Jamie and I were in.

"If Breck's there, I'm in." I grinned as they all turned to look at me.

"Look at this—she's talking about him in public," Stormi said. "Is this getting serious?"

"I shouldn't kiss and tell." I made a zipper pantomime over my mouth.

"Kissing?" Stormi asked, squealing. "You've been kissing him?"

"Maybe a little." I flushed with heat, embarrassed but also delighted. I was the girl Breck chose to kiss. Little old me. He'd texted earlier to say he was hanging out with his friends. I'd been disappointed not to see him, but I understood how important friends were to him.

Darby grinned. "You could do worse."

"What about you, Darby? Is one of the teachers your girlfriend?" Jamie asked, casually.

"Me? No, they're just friends. Although, just between us, I'm hoping Huck and one of my colleagues will hit it off. She's the other English teacher at the high school, and I think they might like each other. She's all sunshine to his grumpy."

"Don't tell him, whatever you do," Stormi said. "He'll run the other direction just to be obstinate."

"Totally," Darby said. "If he ever finds someone, it'll be despite his resistance to anything good happening to him."

"That's the truth," Stormi said. "But I'm all for it. Maybe a girlfriend would help his foul disposition."

"We'll see you in a few," Jamie said. "We're not dressed for a party."

I looked down at my leggings and tank top. We'd planned for a girls' night.

Muffy had gone back to sleep. I patted the top of her head absently, thinking about Breck. Would he want to see me at the party? What if he'd wanted a night without me?

As if in answer to my question, my phone buzzed with a text from the object of my affection.

Headed to Darby's. It's his birthday. Care to join us? No pressure if you have other plans.

I typed back: Darby stopped by. Jamie, Stormi, and I are all three coming over after we get cleaned up.

Breck: I've been thinking about you all day.

I smiled down at the phone before typing: *Same.*

"That was Breck," I said, as if anyone had asked. "Inviting me to the party."

"Awesome. I guess this will be a good birthday after all." Darby gave a quick wave before heading back across the hall to his apartment.

"Are you girls sure you don't mind breaking up our night?" Jamie asked. "Just because boys called doesn't mean we have to drop everything and head over there."

"I wanted an excuse to see Breck anyway." I smiled. "I'm one of those types of girls now."

"Good for you." Stormi thumped my foot with hers. "Let's get dolled up and head over. I want to see who this woman is that Darby thinks would be good for Huck."

For a woman who claimed to dislike Huck immensely, she was certainly interested to know more about his love life.

"But wait," Jamie said. "Tell us about all this kissing first."

BY THE TIME WE ARRIVED, Darby's party was in full swing. More than a dozen people milled about the front room. Country music played in the background. A few sad bowls of chips peppered the coffee table, and a growler dripped beer onto newspapers in one corner. Red plastic cups were stacked on a side table.

I scanned the room but couldn't find Breck. "I'm going to look for Breck," I said to the girls.

"Your boyfriend?" Stormi teased.

"Maybe he is," I said.

"He is. He definitely is," Jamie said.

Darby's apartment was laid out exactly as mine, only in reverse. The kitchen was just off the living room, but unlike the modern great room spaces, it was through a doorway. Which at this moment was occupied by Huck and someone I assumed was the English teacher Darby had wanted to introduce him to. They were in a discussion about a political book that was currently on the best-seller lists. I hadn't read it and didn't intend to.

Breck was indeed in the kitchen, putting together a tray of charcuterie. "There you are." The expression of joy on his face when he saw me warmed every inch of me. Would that ever get old? I doubted it. "I thought you'd never get here." He moved from the counter and held out his arms with his hands raised in the air. "My fingers are greasy, so be careful. I'd hate to wreck that outfit."

The mere mention of his fingers on me sent a bolt of electricity through me. I let him wrap me in his arms, without his hands obviously, and lifted my mouth for him to kiss. He did so, tasting slightly of beer. Even beer smelled good on his lips.

"You look amazing." He stepped back to get a better look at me. "Those jeans are just, um, delightful?"

I laughed, shy. "They're kind of form-fitting."

"No, they hug everything just right." He went to the sink to wash his hands. "I put some food together since Huck insisted we get a growler." A container of layered bean dip and some tortilla chips were next to the charcuterie platter. All of it looked like a photo in a magazine.

"You always make everything look so nice," I said.

"Thanks, babe."

Babe? I liked the sound of that. I was someone's baby. Who would have thought it possible? With Breck, though, elements of my life that I thought were off-limits or without possibilities had been easily awakened. He was not only a pet doctor but a doctor of broken hearts. He'd fixed mine.

Goodness me. I was in love with him. *Slow down*, I warned myself. *Keep your defenses up so he doesn't hurt you.*

For once, I ignored the annoying voice in my head. "What have you been up to today?"

His expression saddened. "It's not been the greatest day, actually. Or, at least the morning was bad. Let me grab a beer and I'll tell you about it. Do you want anything?"

Various spirits and bottles of wine, as well as large plastic bottles of soda, took up one portion of the counter. "Root beer for me, please."

"You got it." He twisted the lid off the soda bottle, causing a small explosion. "I need an ice bucket to keep stuff cold."

He started rummaging around the cabinets until he found a large bowl. I went to the freezer to see about ice and found several bags. "Do you want one of these?"

"Yeah, great. I brought those just in case we needed them."

"You're quite the party planner." I lugged the heavy bag onto the table.

He ripped open the plastic bag and dumped the ice into the bowl. "Maybe I can come work for you?"

"That would be a turnaround, wouldn't it?"

Breck wrapped his arms around me and kissed me. "I want you all to myself and I'd suggest we go to your apartment, but I promised Darby I'd keep drinks circulating and food coming." He abruptly let go of me. "Oh shoot. The quiches." He yanked open the oven door. Rows of mini quiches had baked to a golden brown on a cookie sheet. "I almost burned these. You're distracting." He put an oven mitt on and took them out, placing them onto the stovetop.

I found a spatula from one of the drawers and scooped the quiches onto a platter. This was fun, hanging out in the kitchen with Breck. "Do you want to mingle?" I asked. "I can take over in here."

"I want to be wherever you are." He pulled me close and kissed me again. My insides went all gooey, as did my mind. I couldn't think straight with this man in my proximity. Maybe that was a good thing. I spent altogether too much time thinking.

We took the trays of food out to the other room, leaving them on the coffee table before returning to the kitchen together. As he bustled around the kitchen, he told me about the argument with his mother.

He didn't say it, but I had a feeling Camille didn't approve of me. I couldn't blame her. If my son were involved with a former cult member, I might be nervous too.

Breck took a box of baklava out of the freezer and started to arrange it on the empty baking sheet. "We don't normally argue. It upset me all day."

"Firing Scooter might have been the tipping point," I said, thinking out loud.

He nodded. "Yeah, that really set her off."

"But you have to run the practice how you see fit."

"But in the end, it's good. I made an offer on Crystal's property. I'm going to build a house."

I stared at him. "Just like that? How much money do you have?"

He sat next to me and took my hands. "I haven't really told you this, but I have a lot. My dad left me more than I could ever need." Tilting his head, he seemed to be waiting for me to say something. When I didn't, he asked, "Please tell me that doesn't change your opinion of me."

"Why would it?"

"I don't know. Rich people are always the villains in movies."

"You're not a villain." More like my hero, brave and strong. "Anyway, it's none of my business."

"If things go as I hope they will, someday it might be very much your business."

A fire swept through me as the meaning behind his words became clear to me. "I guess we'll see about that, won't we?" I lifted my chin and let my eyes sparkle back at him.

"I guess we will." He leaned over and kissed me, lingering as the sounds of the party continued on the other side of the door. "I've kissed away all your lip gloss."

"I can reapply."

He laughed and kissed me again.

I looked at the clock that hung on the wall above the doorway. "I should take Muffy out for a bathroom break. She always goes out right at eight."

"You want me to help?"

"No, stay here and keep an eye on the baklava. I'll just be a few minutes."

I HEADED across the hall to my place. Muffy greeted me at the door in her usual enthusiastic manner, as if it had been much longer than thirty minutes since I'd last seen her. I gathered her up for a quick snuggle before latching her leash to her collar. We were halfway down the stairs when I realized I'd left my keys upstairs. Should I go back and get them? No, I'd just leave the door ajar while Muffy did her business.

The night air chilled my warm cheeks as she headed toward her usual tree. This time of evening, even on a Saturday, was fairly quiet on Barnes Avenue. The bakery and cooking shop were closed, as was the ski and sporting goods store. Our gourmet grocery store remained open, although the flowers that spilled onto the sidewalk during the day had been brought in for the night.

I wrapped my sweater closer as a breeze lifted my hair and rustled the newly budded leaves on the trees that lined the street. A sweet scent of lilacs tickled my nose. The sounds of the party drifted out of an open window, the bass notes a faint backdrop to the chattering of voices. I shifted my gaze to look up at Darby's windows, seeing the outline of people. Breck would be taking out the baklava about now. I'd go upstairs, and there would be more kissing. Maybe later he would come over to my place and we'd talk most of the night away. Soon, not tonight, but very soon, I would be ready to invite him to stay for more than just sleeping.

A sense of rightness washed over me. This was my life. Friends, parties, work that paid the bills. Muffy, of course. And Breck. Sweet, sensitive Breck who spent most of his time at parties looking after everyone. How was it that he'd fallen for me? *Thank you, God,* I prayed silently. *For all of it.*

When Muffy was done, I scooped up her latest gift with one of the plastic bags in my pocket and stuffed it into the public doggy poo container the city had put in for Emerson Pass's many pooches. As I turned to head back up the steps, a man emerged from the alleyway between my building and the bank next door. He wore black, including a cap pulled low over his forehead. Glittering eyes caught the light. I knew those eyes. Beady and calculating. A beak of a nose. That thin mouth that curled into an evil grin at any moment.

Elder Ryan. The man I'd been promised to all those years ago. Fear prickled my skin. Shouldn't he be in jail? Had they let him out? The others too? I hadn't been watching the news the last few days, needing a break from it all. I'd done my part, and now it was time to move on with my life.

Elder Ryan might not agree.

I backed away as he approached. Muffy, by my feet, growled and then barked as ferociously as her little body allowed.

Something shiny glinted in the light cast from the building. A knife. Silver. Sharp. My thoughts swirled. The faint remnants of root beer soured in my mouth.

"Look at you," Ryan said. "You haven't changed much, other than the makeup and this outfit that makes you look like a whore."

"How did you get out? Aren't you supposed to be in custody?" I was surprised I managed to get anything out of my dry mouth.

"Even religious leaders are allowed bail."

Muffy growled and lunged at his ankles. I lifted her into my arms, afraid of what she might do if I didn't. She might think she could fight against this man, but I knew better. My precious furry baby was no good against a knife.

"What do you want?"

"What do I want?" His voice sounded like sandpaper against rough wood, like a smoker. I didn't remember him smoking. But maybe he did? I hadn't been privy to any of the luxuries afforded the elders. The girls who had to sacrifice their bodies to these men were only playthings to them, kept in the dark as if they were only dolls in a toy box.

"You're coming with me." He pulled the knife all the way out of his pants pocket. "Come around the side of the building nice and easy."

My stomach had hollowed out. Muffy wriggled in my arms and before I could stop her, leaped down to the steps and through the open door. *Go, Muffy. Go find Breck and tell him what happened.*

Ryan grabbed me around the neck and hauled me into the

alley. He pushed me against the rough brick. His fingers pressed into my neck, choking me.

"Do you know what you've done?" Ryan asked, snarling. "You've ruined everything. We should never have assumed you'd wandered off somewhere to die." He pushed harder into my windpipe, pinning me to the wall. I struggled to get away, but it was no use. He was too strong. Then he plunged the knife into my middle. I screamed in pain. He stabbed me again. I cried out in agony.

I was going to die. I knew it with everything in me. This was how it would all end. After all this time, I would die the same way as my mother. Executed like a stray, rabid animal.

That was when I heard footsteps and shouting. My eyes skirted to the left. Agents. The FBI. They'd come. Too late for me. But they'd get him.

He let go of me and took off running down the alley. But it didn't matter. He would be caught. They were here. They would get him. I would not be taken out to some remote location and left for the birds. Breck would know what happened to me. There would be consequences this time.

I slumped to the ground. Oh God, the knife was still in me. I was too weak to lift it out. It was time to rest. A deep sense of calm came over me. I would die here on this street where I'd made a new life. A happy life. No one could take that away from me. I'd won.

Breck. If only I'd told him I loved him. An image floated across my mind from earlier. Breck in the kitchen, his face glowing with happiness at the sight of me. The loving look in his eyes. Oh yes, the way he looked at me. That was enough. I'd had love. The kiss. Baklava. More kissing. I smiled to myself. Breck Stokes had loved me. I would rest now.

22

BRECK

My dad had once told me that when he was a kid he'd been out hiking in the woods with his dog when a heaviness had overtaken him. A premonition of something bad. He'd thought it was the devil for a moment, trying to take over his soul. But then his limbs had gone numb. Something was wrong. Something terrible was happening to someone he loved. He couldn't explain it, but he'd started to run toward home, sure it was his sister or mother who was in trouble. As he approached the house, he saw smoke coming from one end of the house. His father had been away for work, but it was still the winter holiday at school. His sister and mother had planned on spending the morning making cookies for his dad's return.

It was a fire in the kitchen, he'd realized. Without thinking, he ran in through the front door. Smoke made it hard to see, but he heard screams coming from upstairs. He'd run back outside to see the faces of his mom and sister in one of the upstairs windows. They were trapped.

He'd gotten the ladder from his dad's shed and gotten them

out only minutes before the fire took over the entire second floor.

"Intuition, son. Never dismiss it if something that strong comes over you."

As I took the baklava from the oven Muffy rushed into the kitchen, barking furiously. At the sight of her trembling little body, the feeling my dad had described came over me. My limbs became cement. A pounding in my ears thumped in time to my racing heart. The baking sheet slipped from my hands and crashed onto the floor. Baklava scattered about my feet.

Muffy barked and barked, convulsing now.

Huck barged into the kitchen, his face tensed and contorted. The clanking sound of the metal sheet pan had frightened him, I realized in some compartment of my brain that remained detached from the unexplainable dread that coursed through me. Reminded him of terrors he never spoke about but that lived near the surface ready to explode from him.

"What's the matter?" Huck took hold of my shoulders.

"Something's wrong. Tiffany." An image of her came to me. A man had his hands around her tender neck. "She took Muffy out and didn't come back with her."

"I'm sure she's on the way back up." Huck sounded so reasonable, so sure.

"No, she's in trouble. I have that feeling. The one my dad had when the house was on fire."

Huck understood my shorthand. He picked up Muffy and held her close. She quieted in his arms but continued to shake. "It's okay, girl. Show us where Tiffany is." He sounded calm and collected, but the glittering in his dark eyes told a different story. He believed me. He knew I was right.

The music in the other room quieted for a second between songs. A scream from below barreled through the open windows. Tiffany. My feet were superglued to the floor. "Tiffany."

Huck's mouth moved, forming words, as if he were a poorly made puppet. A ringing in my ears made it impossible to hear him. He broke away from my near-death grip and ran toward the living room. I stumbled after him, nearly blind with fright.

Stormi stood at the window. Flashing red lights illuminated her face. She pointed toward the street. "It's...it's..."

What I saw on Barnes Avenue made my blood run cold. FBI agents dressed in dark uniforms had swarmed the street like ants. A man had been wrestled to the ground. Frantic, I looked from one end of the street to the other. Flashing lights from the FBI units pulsed, mimicking the fires of hell. Where was Tiffany?

Huck handed Muffy to Stormi. "Keep her up here."

She nodded and held Muffy tight against her chest.

I tore down the stairs and out into the warm spring night, vaguely aware that Huck followed closely behind. An agent grabbed me before the door had even closed behind us. "Where is she?" I asked.

"Follow me. She got away from him, but he got her first."

"Got her?" What did that mean? "Is she hurt badly?" *Is she alive?*

But my questions were not answered. Instead, he took hold of my arm and led me around the corner of the building. Tiffany. There, surrounded by several agents. One seemed to be doing some kind of first aid.

I rushed to her. "Tiffany, it's me." I dropped to my knees beside her. A knife stuck out from her chest. She whimpered like an animal caught between the unforgiving blades of a trap.

Through pain-glazed eyes, she stared up at me. Her soft moaning ceased. A slight smile lifted her mouth. "There you are."

Blood had soaked through her blouse. The knife's steel handle mocked me. I looked up at the agent. "Can't you get this out of her?"

"It's better to leave it in. The paramedics will know what to do."

Tiffany clutched my shirt between her fingers and spoke in a raspy voice. "It was Elder Ryan. He had a knife. I'm sorry." The muscles in her face contorted with pain. Her hair fanned out around her in perfect waves, as if it didn't get the signal that something was terribly wrong.

"Don't be sorry. You've done nothing. You fought them. You've won. Don't ever think you didn't." My words became sobs. Tears blurred her fac. I'd never lied to her before now. They would win if they took her from me. Robbed her of the life she fought so hard to live.

"Will you take Muffy?" Tiffany asked.

"Yes. Just until you get home. She'll be so happy to see you. Keep imagining that, okay?" I couldn't see her. Fear had blinded me, red and hot like blood. *No, no, I must keep her in focus.* If I kept her in my vision, she would be fine. This bastard wouldn't rob us of happiness. Not after everything she'd lived through.

"The agents were there," she whispered. "They got him, but not before he stabbed me. It hurt so much. I'm dying. Don't leave me. Please? Just until I'm gone."

"I'll never leave you." I dried my eyes with the back of my arm and drew in a shaky breath. "Listen to me. You're going to hold on. The ambulance is going to take you to the hospital. They'll fix you. They have to fix you."

"It doesn't hurt any longer. Nothing hurts. Only the good remains. I hadn't expected that. Your face. That's what appeared when it occurred to me that I might be dying." Her beautiful mouth twitched into a thin smile. "I love you. More than I thought I could. I hadn't known I could feel this way. I thought they'd killed that part of me a long time ago. But they didn't. My heart survived. Do you know what's weird?"

"What's that?"

"Telling you how much I loved you became the most important thing in the end. The only thing I wanted to do before I left. You always show up for me. You're the only one that's ever done that, and I haven't thanked you properly."

"Don't speak. Save your strength." The finality in her tone paralyzed me into a trembling terror. I could no longer cry. Fear had iced me into a tearless holding pattern.

"I've been quiet my whole life," she whispered. "I can't be quiet anymore. Not now."

I stopped myself from shushing her. If she were leaving me, I didn't want our last words to be contentious. "Say whatever you want, baby. Keep talking. As loud and furious as you want."

"He wanted me to pay for talking. Isn't that funny? After I kept their secrets all this time? But I'm not sorry I told the truth. I'm not sorry for anything the last few months. You gave me a whole lifetime."

"No, I didn't. We're going to have so many good years together. But you have to hang on, all right? Help is coming. I love you. Please, you have to fight."

The look in her eyes went terrifyingly blank before her lids shuttered closed. Her lips seemed to have changed to a shade between purple and blue. *God, please, let her be okay.*

I looked up at the agents, nearly demented with panic. "Do something." *Please God, please, please, please.*

The sound of an ambulance's siren was an answer to those prayers. If it wasn't too late. My darling. My sweetheart. *Please fight. One last fight. For us.*

MY FINGERS GRIPPED the wooden arms of the stiff hospital waiting room chair. I hated hospitals. The antiseptic smell. Nurses with stoic expressions. The click of shoes on tile floor.

The knife had done internal damage. They wouldn't know how much until they got in there and looked around.

For a second, I was fifteen again, waiting in this same room for news about my father. I couldn't remember any of the details of those visits, only a blur of uncertainty and fear. Always the same question perched on my lips. How many months? Then, how many weeks? Finally, when they sent us home and told us to begin hospice, how many days?

I remained grateful to this day that I'd had the chance to say goodbye to him. I'd met others in a grief support group who had lost loved ones without warning. Most wished they'd had a chance to say things they'd thought they had plenty of time to say. Still, it made no difference. Not really. He was gone.

If I lost Tiffany before we even had a chance to begin—no, I wouldn't allow myself to go there. She would pull through the surgery. After everything she'd endured and escaped from, dying on an operating table could not be the end.

Our friends gathered around me. Trap and Huck, of course, just as they'd been when I'd lost my father. Stormi and Jamie huddled together in a love seat, trying to look brave but failing. Brandi had a sleeping baby Willow in a sling. Garth and Crystal had come even though they'd been asleep when Trapper called them. Darby had packed up the food from the party and brought it with him in case anyone was hungry. No one was.

I love you. I held those words close to me as I clung to hope.

It was nearing one in the morning when the surgeon came in to tell us that they'd repaired damage to one of her lungs and sewn her back up. "There's no reason she won't have a full recovery. She was lucky."

My vision went black and my legs almost buckled with relief. Huck and Trap had to put their hands on my arms to steady me.

After that, I convinced everyone to go home and get some rest, promising to text with any updates. "I want to be there when she wakes up," I said when Stormi suggested going home to sleep and coming back in the morning. "If she wakes tonight,

I don't want her to think she's alone." I'd promised her never to leave.

"All right." Stormi went up on her tiptoes to give me a kiss on the cheek. "You're one of the good ones, Breck Stokes. She's a lucky girl."

They all trailed out, leaving me alone with Huck. He sat across from me, his black leather jacket zipped up to his chin. Cold, most likely. It was cold. I hadn't noticed until now.

"I appreciate you staying," I said to him. "But it's really not necessary." I rubbed my eyes, weary but happy. My Tiffany was going to make a full recovery.

"Nope, I'm good," he said.

"You really should go home," I said.

"Nah. My place is here with you."

"Thanks, man."

Huck dug into the bag of mini quiches and handed me one. "We should eat a little something. Keep our strength up. Isn't that what you always tell me?"

I wasn't hungry, but I took one anyway. My blood-soaked shirt had dried and now clung to my skin. "I wish I had a change of clothes."

"I could run home and get you some."

"Later, maybe." I rested my head on his wide shoulder. "I hate hospitals."

"Who doesn't?"

"I dropped all those baklava on the floor."

Huck started laughing. "What does that have to do with anything?"

"I don't know."

"Your dad dying young—is that why you're such a freak about food?" Huck asked, as if it were the first time the idea had occurred to him.

"Have you really never thought about that before?" He offered me another quiche, but I shook my head no.

"I was too busy being annoyed," Huck said.

"When you lose a parent young, you inevitably obsess with death. Your own. Others'. I didn't want you to go to Afghanistan. "

"I almost died a few times over there." He said this so quietly I almost thought I heard him wrong.

"You never talk about it."

"I know. I probably won't. So don't take this as an invitation to push." He reached into the bag for another quiche and bit into it with his perfect teeth.

"You know I'm here if you ever want to talk," I said.

"Everyone knows that. You're a nice person. It makes me feel meaner when I'm around you. My guess is your mom feels that too."

I had to think about this for a moment. "I annoy you because I'm nice?"

"No, it's not annoyance. We feel bad about ourselves. Because we're not very nice people."

"You're here when the chips are down. That's good enough for me."

"I don't deserve you," he said.

"I guess that's up to me to decide, isn't it?" I nudged him with my elbow.

The nurses were speaking quietly to each other behind the front desk. The coffee maker, on hiatus from spurting out terrible lattes, purred. My eyes grew heavy from lack of sleep.

Huck moved over to sit next to me. "Come on. Put it here." He tapped his upper arm.

"Just for a minute." My head, without much prompting from my brain, tilted to rest on Huck's shoulder.

When I woke, Huck was gone. It was a little before six. I rubbed the crick in my neck, contemplating coffee.

My mother appeared, as if she'd teleported. She carried a bag

265

in one hand and a coffee from the Sugar Queen in the other. I'd recognize that pink-and-white cup anywhere.

"Mom, what are you doing here?"

"Huck told me what happened." She handed me the latte. "Nonfat milk, just like you like it."

"Thanks." I drew in the smell of coffee before taking a tentative sip. Perfect temperature. "You didn't have to come."

She set the bag on the chair next to me. "I brought you some clothes and your toothbrush."

"Appreciate it." I wasn't sure what to say to her, so I sipped my latte and pretended everything was fine between us.

She settled in the chair across from me. Wearing a long skirt and denim shirt, she looked as if she were headed to an appointment. "Do you want something to eat? The cafeteria's probably open."

"No, I'll wait until I head home later."

"How is she?"

"She's sleeping but doing well. I wanted to be here when she wakes."

"Right." She smoothed her skirt with both hands. "Have you decided on house plans?"

"I'm looking at a few options."

"It'll be nice for you to have your own home. I shouldn't have let you move in with me. It was too easy. For me, not you."

"It's time, that's all."

"It'll be quiet without you boys," she said. "Huck's moving the rest of his things today."

"I'm sure you'll miss him."

She clicked her tongue. "I'll miss *you*, honey. You're my son. My family. I'm sorry I'm so hard to get along with."

I wanted to dismiss her apology, but it was true. She was difficult. Still, she was my mom and I loved her. "We're different. Very different."

"I know. And I shouldn't always assume that my way's the

best." Her brows came together as she seemed to contemplate what to say next. "It's just that I want everything to be perfect for you. Losing your dad like that—was such a blow. I'd have done anything to have taken his place. You'd have been better off."

"Not true. You've been a truly great mother. I'd have given everything to have kept both of you."

"Everyone said what a good man he was, you know, after he passed. As if I didn't know. I'd loved him all my adult life. I knew him better than anyone. I could have spent the rest of my life listing all his wonderful attributes. When he was gone, I couldn't reconcile how it could be that I was the one left. He shouldn't have had to go like that. So much pain in the end." Her eyes glassed over with tears. She reached into a pocket in her skirt and brought out a tissue. "I didn't think I could keep going. I'm not sure I would have had it not been for you. And your friends, too. Not that I loved them more than you. It's not that. It was the way you all brought so much life to the house. Your father had filled up such a big space in my heart and my house, and when he was gone, it was too quiet, too empty. I've been holding on to you too tightly, scared of what it will be like when you're gone for good. Anyway, I'm trying to apologize for interfering with your life. Whoever you love and however you want to run the practice is your choice."

"Thanks, Mom."

A nurse arrived, one I didn't recognize from earlier. Perhaps the shifts had changed. "Miss Birt's awake and asking for you."

I stood so quickly that I spilled some of the latte on my jeans. "I should change," I said. "I don't want her to see this shirt."

"Good idea."

My mom said she'd wait for me and to take my time before I hurried to the bathroom to clean up and change. As I brushed my teeth, I glanced out of the bathroom windows to the horizon. The sunrise painted the sky pink. I'd made it through the longest night of my life to once again see the sun. Even the darkest of hours eventually ended.

TIFFANY WAS PROPPED up on pillows when I entered her room. Her hair was in a braid and although she looked considerably better than she had when I last saw her, she was still pale and weak.

"Hey," I said softly. "How are you feeling?"

"I think I'm high, because I'm feeling happy and kind of floaty."

With great care, I perched on the side of her hospital bed. "Is there anything you need from home?"

"Not yet. Wouldn't Daphne be appalled at my hospital gown?"

"She'd think you looked beautiful."

"The nurse told me you've been here all night. You should've gone home."

"I wanted to be here when you woke up. I promised I wouldn't leave you."

"The last thing I remember is your face over me. Did I tell you I loved you or was that only in my head?"

"You told me." I smiled and picked up her hand to bring it to my mouth for a kiss. "But I won't hold you to it."

"I do love you. How could I not?" Her eyes were glassy and unfocused. She gave me a lopsided smile. Definitely high.

"Huck says I'm annoyingly nice," I said.

She shook her head. "You're nice, but it's not annoying. Not to me."

"Do you remember what happened?" I asked.

"Yes, the nurses told me." Tears glistened in her eyes.

"I hope you don't mind but I called your dad," I said. "So that he didn't see it on the news."

"Was he upset?" Her eyes grew wider. "My dad. You just called him my dad."

"Or Mason. Whichever you prefer. Yes, he was upset but grateful when I told him what the agents did. He wants all this to be over for you. We all do." I told her about everyone gathering in the waiting room while she was in surgery. "You're loved. I hope you know that."

"They were all there?"

"Until the doctor came out to tell us how well you came through the surgery," I said.

"I ruined Darby's party."

"We can have a do-over. Don't worry about that. You need to heal so you can come home. To me."

"I'll do my best." Tears leaked from her eyes. "I thought I was going to die. It made everything very clear. You. You're everything."

"That's all I can ask." I brushed her hair from wet cheeks. "Don't cry. Everything's going to be fine now."

"As long as you're here, then yes."

"I'm not going anywhere."

23

TIFFANY

My recovery took longer than I liked even though my doctor assured me I was making faster progress than he'd expected. For several weeks, I had to stay home from work. Breck practically moved in with me, caring for me during the evenings and early mornings. Jamie and Stormi divided up the daytime duties between them. After my wounds healed enough that daily changing of the bandages was no longer necessary, I convinced the girls I no longer needed them taking time off from their busy work schedules to check on me.

Jamie's inn had finally opened for business. She was delighted to have half the rooms rented for most of May. By Memorial Day weekend, she was sold out of rooms.

Stormi had taken on yet another shift at the bar even though her photography bookings were almost back to normal. Our summer calendar was full. Right after I came home from the hospital, I was surprised the phone started ringing, asking about last-minute bookings for weddings at the lodge. By the time I was back on my feet, I had weddings scheduled for every weekend until after Labor Day. Wc had another half dozen couples scheduled for weddings around the holidays.

Meanwhile, Breck had hired Scooter's replacement, a woman who had run a similar-sized practice in Denver but recently moved to Emerson Pass. Not only was she pleasant and fair to the rest of the staff, she'd revamped several outdated systems and convinced Breck to buy a new scheduling and billing software the staff loved. All in all, things were going well. She'd hired a receptionist to take my place who seemed suited for the work.

One night, Breck and I were sitting in my living room on the couch discussing all the changes at the clinic. Surprisingly, I missed my work there. I'd liked the administrative work more than I thought I would. Organizing chaos gave me a sense of accomplishment and purpose. However, weddings still called to me.

Working with couples over the phone and email while I recovered on my couch reminded me that the world continued, no matter what. I was alive and ready for this next season in my life.

"I've been thinking," I said. "About the future."

"Yeah?" Breck brought my feet onto his lap and rubbed them with the pad of his thumb.

"I think the next wedding I plan should be ours."

His fingers wrapped around both my feet and grinned. "Is that right?"

"What do you think about a Christmas wedding? The reason I ask is that the lodge is booking up, and it would be nice to reserve a space."

"Is that the only reason?"

I smiled shyly. "Not the only one. You have something to do with it as well."

"Interestingly enough, the contractor told me today my house will be done before the first snowfall. I could carry you over the threshold." He paused, resuming the massage to my feet. "But I did kind of want to ask you the right way. In a less business contract kind of situation."

I laughed. "I'm a wedding planner. I can't stop."

He sobered. "Are you sure? We haven't been dating that long, and part of that you've been recovering."

"I'm sure. You?" I held my breath. What if he'd changed his mind? Perhaps seeing me at my worst had dissuaded him.

"I've been sure since the first night I slept in your bed."

Since I'd been home from the hospital, Breck had stayed over to make sure I was all right. With my injuries, however, our relationship had continued to be chaste by modern measures. "About that—the doctor told me this morning that I'm healed. He took my stitches out today." I felt under my shirt to the scar that would permanently mark that terrible night. When I thought about how much worse it could have been, I shivered but then immediately filled with gratitude. "I don't want to put anything else off. I'm ready to start living." I spread my hands in the air. "All in, savoring every moment. Starting tonight."

"I see what you're saying." His eyes were soft as he moved his hands up to my ankles and then my calves. I tensed with pleasure and anticipation when they traveled up to my thigh. "I'm not going to turn you down. The last few weeks have been a test of my willpower."

He leaned closer and then pulled me under him, kissing me until I'd forgotten any thoughts of weddings, mine or otherwise.

24

TIFFANY

On July Fourth, we went down to the river spot to watch the fireworks. A floating device was erected in the middle of the river where they lit them, worried as we were about fire danger. Trapper's father, who was the head of the fireworks committee, had promised a long program to celebrate the rebuilding of our town. I found it ironic that we were celebrating recovering from a fire with fireworks, but I kept that to myself.

We were seated on a blanket near the water. Breck had packed us a picnic of fried chicken, potato salad, and brownies from the Sugar Queen. It was a holiday, he'd said, when I'd raised my eyes about the fried nature of the chicken.

We'd invited Huck and Stormi to join us on our blanket. I'd conveniently left out that the other would be there. I'd had to stifle a laugh when they sat as far away from each other as was possible. Breck and I had a theory. One that we grew more confident of as the long days of summer rolled along. Their animosity masked a primal attraction. Neither would admit to such a thing, of course. Not that I would have suggested it to them. These two bullheaded people would balk at the idea and probably delay the inevitable for longer.

Breck opened a bottle of wine to share with our friends as we dug into the picnic food. I scanned the grass for other people I knew and spotted Camille sitting with Huck's parents. There was another man with them too. "Who is that with your mother?" I asked Breck.

"That's Henry Wu. I'm surprised to see her with him. She claims to despise him. They went head-to-head on some city council issue."

"I don't think they came here together," Stormi said. "Perhaps they were tricked into sitting on the same blanket."

Camille and Henry were sitting as far apart as Huck and Stormi.

"I don't know what you're talking about," I said.

Jamie was there with her brother, who had come out to meet with Breck about the interior design for his new house. Trey Wattson was there with his pretty wife and their toddler, a little redhead who seemed as sweet as her mother. Jamie was in auntie heaven, currently holding her niece on her lap as she fed her slices of strawberries.

"How's it going with the book?" Stormi asked, referring to the project I'd finally agreed to collaborate on with Huck.

Huck wiped his mouth with the corner of a napkin. "We're making progress."

"How does it work?" Stormi asked. "Do you just write down what she tells you?"

Huck frowned, clearly irked by the question. "Yeah, that's all there is to it. She tells me stories and I transcribe them like a typist."

"You don't have to be a jerk," Stormi snapped. "I'm not a writer, so how would I know?"

I jumped in, hoping to avoid more bickering. "I *do* tell him everything I can remember about a certain time frame and then he writes it up and sends it to me to see if he got all the facts right. His writing is stupendous. He makes it much more interesting than it really was." I had an image of endless drudgery. "He left all the boring parts out, but there's so many details and descriptions that it's like watching a movie. I don't know how he does it. He's turning my story into a work of art."

"Jeez, thanks, Tiff," Huck said, giving me a fond smile. "You make it easy." He turned to Breck. "She remembers a lot. More than I thought she would."

"It's cathartic to tell my story," I said.

"I'm glad," Huck said. "I'm just hoping to do it justice."

After dinner, we put the remnants of our picnic back in the basket. Twilight had transformed the sky into a purple backdrop. As we continued to chat and laugh, even Huck seemed to relax and enjoy himself. Before we knew it, the sky had darkened and it was time for the fireworks display. Even the children returned to their spots to watch.

They'd created a playlist to go with the display, including patriotic songs from country and pop singers. As I sat there watching the sky with Breck's hand in mine, I thought about what it meant to be an American. Even after an experience like mine, we had the opportunity to break free and reinvent ourselves. Perhaps it was my early imprisonment that made me see it through that lens? I hoped the rest of the spectators felt that swell of pride as the true meaning of the holiday played out in the sky above us.

Now Breck let go of my hand. I glanced over at him to see him take a small box out of his pocket. As another display cascaded around us, he shifted so that he was partially facing me. In our low chairs, his legs seemed even longer than usual. He kissed the side of my face near my ear, then whispered, "I thought it was time to make it official. Will you marry me?"

From the box came a shiny solitaire diamond ring. It caught the last of the light thrown from the cascading sparks.

TESS THOMPSON

"Yes, I'll marry you." I held out my left hand, and he slipped it over the knuckle of my ring finger. We kissed as another batch of fireworks exploded into the sky.

The crowd continued to *ooh* and *aah* as another explosion lit up the sky.

"You're my dream come true," he said. "You've made me the happiest man in Emerson Pass."

"Only Emerson Pass?" I asked, teasing.

"I didn't want to overstate. "

I laughed and then leaned in for another kiss.

By the time the show ended, we'd returned to watching so that the final display of red, white, and blue sparks followed by a rainbow of pinks, purples, and orange seemed to be just for us. A celebration of the miracle of true love.

All those years ago when all had seemed lost and I'd been afraid and alone, I'd never have imagined arriving to such a place in my life. Friends, a career, and the mundane joys of an ordinary life were all mine. Best of all, Breck Stokes had come to me. My best friend. Soon to be my husband. Perhaps even the father of my children, if we were so blessed.

We remained sitting while the rest of the park's spectators packed up to go. I'd almost forgotten Stormi and Huck until I noticed that they'd disappeared, leaving only their chairs and Stormi's sweater. Where had they gone? I turned to Breck. "Our companions have vanished."

"They're there." Breck pointed to the swing set across the park. I blinked, uncertain if my eyes were playing tricks on me. But no, it was real. Stormi was in a swing with her legs stretched out in front of her. Huck stood behind her, pushing her with both hands as she swung back and forth. She looked like the silhouette of a beautiful doll under the light of the moon and stars.

"I didn't even see them leave," I said.

"Huck knew I had the ring. I think they were making themselves scarce."

"Why the swings, I wonder?"

"A good place to fall in love?" Breck's mouth twitched into a smile. "Or at the very least, call a truce."

We returned to each other and watched as the moon rose higher in the sky and reflected in the river water. I sighed with contentment. "What a spring and summer it's been."

"Just the beginning to our joyful life together."

I smiled back at him and for a moment, everything but his eyes faded from view. My anchor. My love.

My future.

ALSO BY TESS THOMPSON

CLIFFSIDE BAY

Traded: Brody and Kara

Deleted: Jackson and Maggie

Jaded: Zane and Honor

Marred: Kyle and Violet

Tainted: Lance and Mary

Cliffside Bay Christmas, The Season of Cats and Babies (Cliffside Bay Novella to be read after Tainted)

Missed: Rafael and Lisa

Cliffside Bay Christmas Wedding (Cliffside Bay Novella to be read after Missed)

Healed: Stone and Pepper

Chateau Wedding (Cliffside Bay Novella to be read after Healed)

Scarred: Trey and Autumn

Jilted: Nico and Sophie

Kissed (Cliffside Bay Novella to be read after Jilted)

Departed: David and Sara

Cliffside Bay Bundle, Books 1,2,3

BLUE MOUNTAIN SERIES

Blue Midnight

Blue Moon

Blue Ink

Blue String

Blue Mountain Bundle, Books 1,2,3

EMERSON PASS

The School Mistress, Book One of Emerson Pass Historical Series

The Sugar Queen, Book One of Emerson Pass Contemporaries Series

The Spinster, Book Two of Emerson Pass Historical Series

RIVER VALLEY

Riversong

Riverbend

Riverstar

Riversnow

Riverstorm

Tommy's Wish

River Valley Bundle, Books 1-4

CASTAWAY CHRISTMAS

Come Tomorrow, Castaway Christmas, Book 1

LEGLEY BAY

Caramel and Magnolias

Tea and Primroses

STANDALONES

The Santa Trial

Duet for Three Hands

Miller's Secret

ABOUT THE AUTHOR

Tess Thompson is the USA Today Bestselling and award-winning author of contemporary and historical Romantic Women's Fiction with over 40 published titles. When asked to describe her books, she could never figure out what to say that would perfectly sum them up until she landed on...Hometowns and Heartstrings.

She's married to her prince, Best Husband Ever, and is the mother of their blended family of four kids and five cats. Best Husband Ever is seventeen months younger, which qualifies Tess as a Cougar, a title she wears proudly. Her Bonus Sons are young adults with pretty hair and big brains like their dad. Daughters, better known as Princess One and Two, are teenagers who make their mama proud because they're kind. They're also smart, but a mother shouldn't brag.

Tess loves lazy afternoons watching football, hanging out on the back patio with Best Husband Ever, reading in bed, binge-watching television series, red wine, strong coffee and walks on crisp autumn days. She laughs a little too loudly, never knows what to make for dinner, looks ridiculous kickboxing in an attempt to combat her muffin top, and always complains about the rain even though she *chose* to live in Seattle.

She's proud to have grown up in a small town like the ones in her novels. After graduating from the University of Southern

California Drama School, she had hopes of becoming an actress but was called instead to writing fiction. She's grateful to spend most days in her office matchmaking her characters while her favorite cat Mittens (shhh...don't tell the others) sleeps on the desk.

She adores hearing from readers, so don't hesitate to say hello or sign up for her newsletter: http://tesswrites.com/. You'll receive an ebook copy of her novella, The Santa Trial, for your efforts.

Made in the USA
Middletown, DE
12 February 2023